I0534261

Afterglow

Other Books By Annie Hoff

Georgette Alden Starts Over
The P-Town Queen

Written As Ute Carbone

Dancing In The White Room

Deslisle Publications

Afterglow

By

Annie Hoff

CLIMAX, SK
CANADA

This is a work of fiction. The characters, incidents and dialogues in this book are of the author's imagination and are not to be construed as real. Any resemblance to actual events or persons, living or dead, is completely coincidental.

No part of this book may be reproduced or transmitted in any form or by any means, electronic or mechanical, including photocopying, recording, or by any information storage and retrieval system, without permission in writing from the publisher.

Dedication

For Jim.

Acknowledgements

It might not take a village to write a book, but it surely does take a whole town to get that book up and ready for publication.

Thanks to Deborah Jelley, Sherry Steffensmeyer, Carolyn Saari, Suzanne Ahmad, Kathy Pile, Alex Hayes, Fran LeMoine, Tammy McCracken, Teresa Jones, Kate Johnson, Harriet Reindeaux, Kim Brady, and Suzanne Shriver, who listened and read as I struggled through early drafts.

And a special shout out to J. Ellen Smith, who gave this book a chance and to my partner in crime, Diane Badzinsky, whose diligent edits polished all my words.

Chapter One

The Rocky Road

My first affair with Cherry Garcia lasted nearly three weeks. It ended when my best friend, Eva, threw a shoe at my head. My Reebok sneaker to be exact. "Enough," said Eva from the bedroom door. "You cannot wallow forever. Besides which, I am getting very tired of walking alone. I've started talking to myself, for God's sake. I've started talking to the dogs along the way." She raised her arms like a conductor ready to strike up the band. "Get your hiney downstairs in five minutes or I will dress you myself." She turned with runway model flourish and sauntered away. I do mean sauntered. Eva was nothing if not dramatic.

I should never have given Eva a key to my house. But I had, and she repaid my trust by yelling up the stairs, "Five minutes, India," as though it were a curtain call. Knowing that there was not the slightest chance that she'd give up and go away, I got up, dug my oldest sweats from the bottom of the hamper, and put on both sneakers.

"You look like misery's leftovers," Eva said when I came down the stairs. I gave her what I thought was a smoldering look, though in truth I don't smolder well.

"Let's just get on with it," I said.

We walked the same route we'd walked nearly every day for twenty-five years, discounting my cha cha with Cherry Garcia. It was about two miles long, this walk, down Queen's Boulevard, along Park Street to Third Avenue, down McKinley past the elementary school, and back around to Easterly Street, where Eva and I resided in side by side Dutch colonials, mine with a maple in front, hers with a willow to the side, at numbers 140 and 142.

"You know what you need?" Eva said as we rounded the

corner on McKinley. "You need a night out."

"I don't need a night out. I can barely handle in."

We'd just passed the gold brick of McKinley Elementary where I had taught kindergarten for twenty years, ever since my daughter, Allie, had started school. We'd trekked out together, Allie and I, all those years ago. Up until my unfortunate fall-in with Ben and Jerry's, I'd kept trekking along, as trusting as those kids in my class.

"Mrs. Othmar!" Jenny cute-as-a-bunny Mantillo came bounding down off her porch as we walked by. "You're feeling better! Mrs. Langtree said you'd feel better and then you'd come back to school." Jenny started walking with us, backward, "Guess what? We got a new puppy. His name is Delmar and maybe, can I bring him in for show and tell?"

"Of course, Jenny. As long as someone's there to take him home."

"Oh, Mommy will. I know she will. And Mrs. Othmar? We made you a big card that says welcome back when you come back."

"Are you going back?" Eva asked after Jenny bounded back up to her porch.

"Yes. Probably. I think so."

"You know, I don't envy you your job. God only knows how you deal with a roomful of snot-nosed carpet rats all day long. But you love that job." We walked past the tennis courts, where the Saturday morning enthusiasts were out enjoying the first of the warm weather. Where my husband, Tom, had played tennis on Saturday mornings with our son, Patch. My soon-to-be ex-husband, Tom. And my dear, soon-to-be-if-not-already devastated son, Patch. I walked a little faster, trying to outrace these last thoughts. Eva kept pace. I was glad she wasn't a mind reader. In fact, she was on a different wavelength all together. "What exactly did you tell Lila Stroud as far as your little absence is concerned?" She marked absence with imaginary quotation marks.

"I told her I had tuberculosis."

"You didn't, not that old Lila couldn't use a little shaking up. But India. Well, it's brilliant, I'll give you that."

Actually, I'd told Lila, the principal at McKinley, that I wasn't well and needed some time. Since Tamsett is a small town, where gossip travels faster than electricity, it's not much of stretch to imagine she knew exactly why I needed time.

"Looking at you, though, I might think tuberculosis myself," Eva said

"I'm just taking some time. I'm allowed to take some time."

"So? What? You're going to lie in bed scarfing saturated fat until you die? You have got to get yourself out of this funk. I can't be dragging you out of bed every day."

"I came, didn't I?" I pointed to my feet. "See? Sneakers. I'm walking." I did a couple of exaggerated marching steps to illustrate my point.

"It's a start," Eva said.

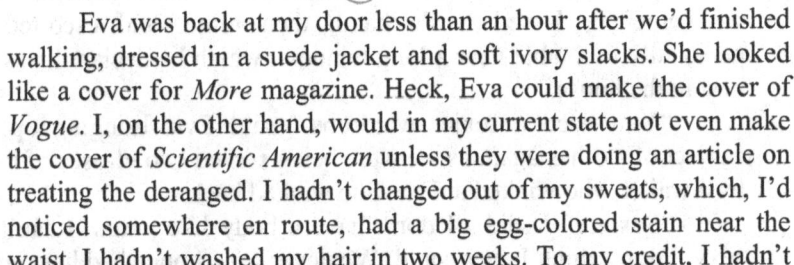

Eva was back at my door less than an hour after we'd finished walking, dressed in a suede jacket and soft ivory slacks. She looked like a cover for *More* magazine. Heck, Eva could make the cover of *Vogue*. I, on the other hand, would in my current state not even make the cover of *Scientific American* unless they were doing an article on treating the deranged. I hadn't changed out of my sweats, which, I'd noticed somewhere en route, had a big egg-colored stain near the waist. I hadn't washed my hair in two weeks. To my credit, I hadn't slunk back into bed. I'd found some orange juice, stuff that must have an amazingly long shelf life because I surely hadn't bought it recently, and I'd managed to pour myself a glass. And drink it.

"Date this early in the day?" I asked Eva. Eva had been divorced since I'd known her. And since I'd known her, she practiced the art of being single. She was a master at being single. The world's best date, she never went out with any man for longer than a few months. As a result, she had a phonebook-sized list of men who would do anything from fix her muffler to fix her a martini. They adored her. They were at her beck and call. It didn't hurt that she looked like Sophia Loren.

"I do have a date," Eva said. "So get dressed."

"Since when do you need a chaperone?"

"You are my date. I'm taking you to lunch at Franco's."

"That's what you're wearing?" she asked when I came downstairs, having showered and pulled my hair back into a chignon so the oil wouldn't be as obvious, and wearing a pink blouse and white chinos.

I tugged on a matching blazer. The whole outfit had grown a little tight. Such are the perils of bedding Ben and Jerry. "What's

13

wrong with it?"

"You look like a kindergarten teacher."

"I am a kindergarten teacher," I said. "I have school clothes and workout clothes. Oh, and those old jeans I wear for gardening."

"Hopeless," Eva said

Franco's was tucked away in a brick building on Main Street, a tiny bistro with five tables and a reservation list that stretched to next January. Getting seated for Saturday lunch on a whim was impossible unless you were a celebrity. Or you were Eva, who had dated Franco, the owner-chef. He came out from his kitchen when we came in, kissed Eva's hand, then mine, and escorted us personally to a table near a long window, which he declared was the best in the house.

"You need a sexier wardrobe," said Eva, bringing up the subject of clothes again as we were being served two glasses of Pinot by a waiter who winked at Eva. She winked back.

"Sexier?" I said. "I don't have a body like yours. I can't do sexy. I don't think I ever could. Whatever sexy I once had has retired south."

Eva tsked as only Eva could. "Nonsense. Complete and utter nonsense. You are a good-looking woman, India. You need to get out. Date. Get back on the horse, so to speak."

"I've ridden the horse. I'm still married to the horse. I can't just pick up and pretend thirty-one years of my life didn't happen."

"You're still married to the horse's ass. You deserve something better than rump roast. Putting him out to pasture is the wisest thing you've ever done." Eva picked up her glass and toasted the window. "There are men out there, India, lots of men, who would like nothing more than the opportunity to spend time with you."

I glanced out at the street, half-expecting a parade of bachelors holding single red roses. It was ridiculous, of course, to even imagine other men. I'd met Tom in college, when I had a better figure and sexier clothes. There had been a pretty parade of boys then. And, Tom, fairest of them all, had stolen my blithe little heart. But that was long, long ago, before children and wrinkles and mid-life crises.

Eva was nothing if not relentless. Over herb-encrusted salmon on a bed of wilted arugula, she pulled a business card from her purse and pushed it towards my plate. "J. Hank Sorenson," she said. "He's

14

a developer. I sold some of his condos in Wuthering Heights. He's divorced, well, all but the signing. Fifty-five, but I swear to you he does not look a day over forty. I'd date him myself if it weren't for rule number one."

"Rule number one?"

"The cardinal rule, darling. Never mix business with pleasure. God knows, I love men. Love them to pieces. But it's taken me years to build up my real estate business and no man is going to muck around in it." She took the card, folded it in half lengthwise and stuck it into my purse. "You, on the other hand, have nothing to lose."

Nothing to lose? I didn't say it out loud, but I thought it. Slightly miffed, I took a bite of salmon. Nothing to lose, indeed. I had my whole life to lose. Then again, I already lost Tom Othmar, the man I'd been married to for most of that life.

"The next thing we need do," Eva said as we finished lunch, "is go shopping. A new wardrobe is just what you need."

"A new wardrobe? I can't afford a new wardrobe."

"There's where you're wrong, darling. Have you never heard of American Express?"

"Yes, but…"

"But you pay off the bill every month like the good, boring little citizen that you are."

"Oh course we do. That's not boring. That's prudent. Tom…" I was going to say, 'has always been careful with financial planning'. We'd planned ahead, for the kids' school. For retirement. We'd planned for the future when there was a future. What kind of plan could you have for a future you no longer owned?

"About time Tom woke up to the reality of credit card debt, don't you think?" asked Eva, tossing back the last of her wine.

I wasn't so sure. It had been a very long time since I'd used plastic without thinking it out first. It was fun, though, shopping with Eva. We tried on clothes and shoes and admired each other's choices as though we were teenagers. We did it all, leather skirts, crop tops, a pair of red stilettos with six-inch spikes. When I tried on a black cocktail dress cut low enough to show cleavage with a pair of black patent leather sling backs, Eva clapped her hands. "That is it. That is it. That is so you."

I glanced at the woman in the mirror. Decent enough legs, though they needed shaving, some drifting around the midriff.

Breasts were a little saggy. Though not too bad, really. "It's not me. I'm way too dumpy for this get-up."

"Size twelve is hardly dumpy. It's curvaceous. Curvaceous is good."

"Maybe. But I'm pasty. I look pasty."

Eva tsk-tsked. "Being a green-eyed blonde with alabaster skin is such a burden. Tragic, really. Don't they have a telethon for that?"

I smiled at her. "Point taken. But really, do you think?"

Eva took me by the shoulders and pointed me towards the mirror so that we were both looking at my reflection. "Repeat after me," she said. "India, you look fabulous."

"India," I said with mock seriousness to my mirror image. "You look fabulous. You look maah-velous, darling. Youse look friggin' terrific. Hubba hubba." I did a little hula dance in front of the mirror. Eva joined me, the two of us looking like crazed women at a luau. We both burst into gales of laughter.

"Not half bad, huh?" I asked when the giggling subsided.

"Honey, that dress needs you to look good. Buy it. Buy it now."

I had not dared to look at the price tags attached to any of the clothes we'd been trying. It was just dress up, after all. Just a game. I glanced now, and it nearly made me topple off the heels. "Five hundred dollars? My God, Eva. My wedding dress cost less than that."

"This isn't a sweet little bridal dress, honey. This is a knock-em-dead dress. This is your super woman outfit. Which, as they say in the commercials, is priceless."

"I can't," I said, peeling myself out of the dress. Carefully now that I knew how much it cost. "I just can't"

"Of course you can. Sasha Peterson would buy this dress. She has an entire closet full of dresses like this."

Naming Sasha was a dirty trick. I'd spent three weeks in a chocolate-and-fat induced haze trying to forget her. Sasha was the black hole that my marriage had fallen into. That Tom had fallen into. The very thought of Sasha Peterson in a little black dress, in my little black dress, made me hyperventilate. Especially considering that she would look a lot better in the little black dress. She was twenty-four years younger and twenty-four years thinner than I was. "I'll take it. With the shoes," I said.

"Martinis would be just the thing," Eva said. We were back at my house with the packages. She scrounged around my kitchen and uncovered a dusty bottle of gin and another of vermouth. The phone rang as she stirred.

"India, sweet India, it's terrible." My soon to be ex-mother-in-law was on the other end of the line. "Why did you not tell me?"

Because I knew you'd make a huge fuss, was what I wanted to say. But I didn't. "I didn't want to worry you."

"Not worry? Of course I worry. Why, you're my children, India. Tom is broken all to pieces. It is as though he swallowed glass."

I couldn't help myself. I liked the idea of internal bleeding. He ought to be bleeding. He ought to be gushing blood.

"You need to come to Providence. You and Tom could have dinner. Talk it through." Marissa lived in Rhode Island at a place called Paradise Point, billed as a retirement center for active seniors. They had a dining room. It had a chandelier, which was just the kind of thing Marissa adored. I could picture her, planning a dinner for two with crystal and china and linen. In Marissa's world, crystal and china and linen could solve any problem.

"I can't do that, Marissa. It's not that simple."

"But of course it's that simple. A nice meal. Candlelight. I fear the two of you haven't had much candlelight. What with Tom working day and night at that PR firm of his."

Working day and night on Sasha, more likely. "What, exactly, did Tom say to you?"

"That he's moved out. He didn't want to talk about it, of course. He's a man. I had to pull the information. He told me to call him at his Boston condo if I needed to get in touch. I couldn't imagine why I'd need to call him there. Of course I grilled him, but you know how he hates to talk about anything personal. And he hates to confide in his mother."

I could understand why he wouldn't want to confide in his mother. Her talking to me was exactly why he wouldn't want to confide in his mother.

"I'm still going to pass on dinner," I said.

"Think about it. At least tell me you'll think about it." So I told her I would think about it, because it was the only way that

17

Marissa would let me hang up.

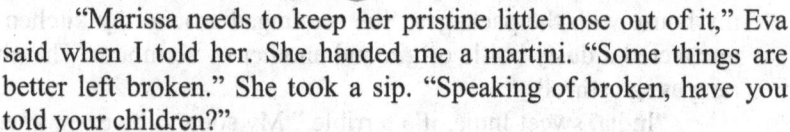

"Marissa needs to keep her pristine little nose out of it," Eva said when I told her. She handed me a martini. "Some things are better left broken." She took a sip. "Speaking of broken, have you told your children?"

"No." My daughter, Allie, was in Africa, far from a phone. My son, Patch, was on an extended business stay in Washington. "God, should I call Patch? I can't tell him over the phone."

"It would be better if he heard it from you."

"I don't know what to say to him." I really didn't know what to say. Because there was more to the story than Tom's leaving me for a younger woman. It happened that the younger woman had been Patch's girlfriend. It happened that they'd lived together for three years. The fact that they'd broken up last fall didn't ease the burden of telling one little bit.

"Tom ought to be castrated," Eva said. "And as a woman who loves men, that's no easy thing for me to say."

"That's a little harsh. He made a mistake. Okay, a huge mistake."

"Mistake? Mistake is when you bring home the wrong brand of shampoo. Mistake is not cheating on your wife with a flock of women including your son's girlfriend."

"No flock," I said weakly. I didn't want to believe there was or had ever been a flock.

"The evidence shows…" Eva looked over at me. Even she had the good sense to know when to quit.

Chapter Two

Out To Lunch

"I'm going to talk to Vaughn White," I said. It was Sunday morning. Eva managed to get me walking a second day.

"There are thirty million divorce attorneys in greater Boston. You're choosing Vaughn White? Is that wise?"

"He's a friend, Eva. I need a friend who is also a lawyer."

"You need a lawyer who is also a lawyer. Not a man who still hasn't forgiven you for breaking his tiny wooden heart thirty-odd years ago."

True, I'd broken off a romance with Vaughn to be with Tom. "Back in the dark ages. It's ancient history. We've been friends for a very long time. And he gave Patch a job."

"He gave Patch a job because Patch graduated first in his class at Brown. Vaughn would have been stupid not to give Patch a job."

Eva knew the ins and outs of my heart pretty well. She knew how proud I'd been of Patch when he graduated law school. Tom and I had celebrated our twenty-sixth anniversary the week after that graduation. Tom had given me a diamond pendant, meant to represent forever. A forever that ended when I confronted Tom with his infidelity. I had proof. And he had no way out.

He'd taken the bags I'd packed for him and gone to the condo he kept in Boston. Without hearing me out. Though I would have told him to leave. Despite the pain and heartache and fat intake that followed, I would have said go. Had it been anyone, anyone except Sasha, I might have found a way to make it to thirty-two years and beyond. But Sasha Peterson— of all people. Sasha Peterson, with whom our son, of whom we were so very proud, had been serious enough to propose marriage. Sasha said no. Then Tom…Some things were just too much to move past. Some things were plain unforgivable.

I called Vaughn the next morning and got through to his secretary, who told me that he was exceptionally busy. I told her I was an old friend, which had no effect at all. Then I told her that I was Patch Othmar's mother. The mention of Patch was the key to unlocking her boss's time.

"Patch is such a doll," said the secretary. She sounded very young suddenly, as though she had a crush on my sweet baby boy. Sweet baby boy who would be thirty next Christmas.

"India! So good to hear from you," said Vaughn when the secretary let me through. It didn't sound as though he meant it. Despite what I'd told Eva, I hadn't seen Vaughn or his wife, Danielle, in nearly ten years.

Tom and I lived in tiny Tamsett, thirty-five miles from Boston, and several light years away from the Boston social circles in which Vaughn and Danielle White traveled. But that wasn't the real reason, either. The real reason was that the animosity between Tom and Vaughn ran as deep and wide as the Mississippi River. They'd tried to be friends, but they'd never really succeeded. And although I'd advocated for keeping Vaughn and Danielle in our lives, those feelings and the fact that I wasn't all-told crazy about Danielle made the effort less than worthwhile. The other thing I hadn't mentioned to Eva was that animosity was what made me think to choose Vaughn as my divorce lawyer. Because Vaughn had a soft spot for Patch and he liked me well enough. It was Tom he couldn't stand.

I told Vaughn that I'd like to see him. There was a pause on the other end of the line as Vaughn calculated my sudden boldness. "Why don't Danielle and I have you and Tom to dinner?" he said. Always smooth, was Vaughn.

"I meant professionally. I need an attorney," I said.

"An attorney?" Another pause. As though he were trying to figure out whom to tell me to call.

"Could we have lunch?" I asked.

"Lunch? Sure. How about— I'm useless with schedules. I'll have to ask my secretary…"

"I thought that we might meet today."

That calculation again. Vaughn wondering. "Today?" he nearly stuttered.

Pause again. My bravado left me. Vaughn was a busy man. A very successful man. I couldn't ask him to just pack up everything and have lunch on the basis of a worn-out friendship and the memory of a once-upon-a-time short romance.

"Maybe I could help you now," Vaughn said. "Answer your question while I have you here on the phone."

"I want a divorce," I blurted.

I might have told Vaughn I'd wanted to divorce *him*. "A divorce?" he asked. I could hear incredulousness in his voice. Also, just a hint of glee. "You and Tom? Divorce? Really?" Then he gave me the address of a little café where he usually ate lunch and asked if I could be there in an hour.

"A divorce?" he asked as we sat down at a wobbly little table near a window overlooking a parking lot.

"Tom had an affair." I took a deep sip of the iced tea I'd ordered so Vaughn wouldn't see my upper lip quiver.

He sipped at his own iced tea, though his lip wasn't trembling. It was turned up. Smirking. He was smirking.

"With Sasha Peterson. He had. Is having. With Sasha. Peterson." I could not look at him now.

"Sasha?" I could feel the calculation again. Vaughn trying to figure out who the heck Sasha Peterson was. Then he coughed and spit iced tea all over the table. I handed him a napkin, several actually. They were those thin paper ones in the black dispenser. He dabbed it over his shirt. "Patch's girlfriend?" he asked.

I nodded. "Ex-girlfriend."

The smirk broke into a grin. "I guess she would be, wouldn't she?" he said.

I started to think that lunch had been a terrible idea. Eva was right, asking Vaughn to be my lawyer was a terrible, awful, horrid idea. I was an idiot. Then Vaughn surprised me. A little, anyway. "Good God, she's a child," he said.

"Twenty-seven," I said. "Old enough to know better."

"How's Patch taking all this?"

"Patch doesn't know. You've kindly kept Patch tied up in Washington for weeks."

"You're welcome," said Vaughn. "Fair warning though, that Washington business ends this week. He'll be home Friday." Vaughn waited as the waitress refilled our iced teas. "Though I'm sure you already knew that."

I had known that. I talked to Patch at least once a week. Though in the last few weeks I'd spent our phone conversations trying to act upbeat. As though everything were just hunky-dory. Hunky-dory took a lot of energy. Patch could have told me he'd been abducted and taken to a planet far, far away and it probably wouldn't have registered.

"Don't worry, India," Vaughn said. " He's a fine lawyer. He won't let his personal life get in the way of his career." Leave it to Vaughn to worry about career. If Vaughn hadn't been so focused on getting into Yale Law, I might have stuck with him and not succumbed to Tom's charms. Ancient history again. Water under the proverbial bridge. I wouldn't let my personal life interfere, either. Vaughn agreed to represent me in the divorce. Then we went about setting up a legal separation.

On Friday, I went back into to Boston to have lunch with Marissa. Having lunch with a soon-to-be-ex-mother-in-law was, according to Eva, the second dumbest idea I'd had all week. But Marissa always treated me like a daughter. And like any good daughter, when Marissa got on the phone and said we hadn't done lunch in ages and she was going into Boston and it would be her pleasure and her treat, I said yes. She named Millegro's, a pricey bistro on Beacon Street that had long been a favorite of hers.

The traffic was snarled and by the time I got to Beacon Street I was five minutes late. Then a car pulled into the last available spot and I had to circle the block, all to no avail. I ended up parking by Vaughn's building, in the small lot reserved for clients, and running the five blocks back to Millegro's in heels that clomped along the sidewalk as though I were a racehorse.

By the time I got to the restaurant, I was winded, fifteen minutes late, and my face was red with exertion. Millegro's was a very popular eatery and, as a result, very crowded, which made it very hot, which put my antiperspirant into over drive and, given my age and current condition, caused a hot flash. I stopped just inside the door, trying to catch my breath and regain the sense of composure that everyone else in the place seemed to come by naturally.

Marissa was hard to miss. She is a tall and stately woman, and she streamed towards me like the *Queen Mary* parting the waters of the Atlantic. She kissed both my cheeks, French style, told me I looked fabulous (which was an outright lie) and took me by the elbow. We parted the waters together, cruise ship and tug boat. It wasn't until we were very nearly on top of the table we were cruising towards that I caught on. There was Tom, studying the menu.

Tom looked up from the menu and smiled brightly at his mother. Then he caught sight of me and the smile became a grimace. He put down the menu, clearly as anxious to escape as I was.

"Please, India." Marissa indicated an empty seat. I considered wading back to the door. I really, really wanted to wade back to the door, run the five blocks back to the car, get in, break the sound barrier driving back to Tamsett, and lock myself in the house with Ben and Jerry. But the look on Tom's face stopped me. I wouldn't give him the satisfaction of easy escape. I sat. Then I noticed that there were but two chairs at the table.

"Marissa," I said or, more to the point, growled. I rose slightly. Marissa's hand on my shoulder pushed me back into the seat.

"Now," she said. "I'll be back in twenty minutes. You two need to talk. You've been married for over thirty years, for goodness sake. You can fix this." And off she went, parting the water back to the door and leaving me stranded on Tom Island.

I stood and stared after my audacious soon-to-be-ex-mother-in-law and considered my options. I stood there for so long that when I heard the sound of Tom's chair scraping over the floor, it felt like a jolt of electricity. "I'll go," he said, quietly to my back. "You sit. She'll be back soon."

"Oh, no, you don't. You are not leaving me here to explain to your mother why we can't make it all better."

Tom sighed and sat back down. "You are bound and determined to make this difficult, aren't you?"

"Difficult?" I rounded on him now. "You're sleeping with your son's ex-girlfriend, and you think I'm being difficult?"

"India, please. Sit down."

"Goodbye, Tom." I waded back to the door, looking half as elegant as my mother-in-law had been. I wished I'd said more. I wished I'd made a scene. But it wasn't like me to make a scene. I wasn't a boat rocker. I marched back to my car. My cell rang halfway back to Tamsett. "India, why are you being so stubborn?" asked Marissa.

"Ask your son," I said. And, for the first time in my life, I hung up on Marissa Othmar. It occurred to me that I should have done it a long time ago.

Chapter Three

I Shaved My Legs For This?

"It's just one date." Eva held out the package.

"Spanx?" I asked, reading the label.

"Don't you watch the *View*? *Oprah*? All of Hollywood's leading ladies are wearing it. It's like a gym in a box. Tone without the trouble."

I unwrapped the girdle-like contraption and held it up, doubtful it could do much besides make me uncomfortable. "And this man. This card you gave me. You called him?"

"On your behalf, yes." I frowned at her as I'd been frowning at the girdle contraption. "Well, someone had to."

"Explain to me again why you won't date him."

"Rule one," Eva said as though lecturing a child.

"Never date a man you do business with," I recited.

"Correct. Also, rule two applies here. He's a friend of Carl Phillips, who I dated, when was that? Anyway, rule two. Never date the good friend of a man you've slept with."

"I didn't realize that dating was so complicated."

"Very complex. You're a bright woman. You'll catch on. And J. Hank is the perfect primer date. He's a nice man, once you get past the whole prison thing."

I dropped the Spanx. "Come again?"

"Strictly white collar. A few months for a little tax mix up."

. "Shouldn't there be a rule about dating an ex-con?"

"Oh, for God sakes, India. Martha Stewart went to prison." Eva held up both hands as though she were the scales of justice. "Insider trading, a little tax problem. Hardly the same as rape and murder. And you don't have to marry him. In fact, more than one date is inadvisable. He's just for practice."

25

"Practice?"

"Darling India, you haven't dated in thirty years. J. Hank is good practice."

"Practice dating. Great."

"All you need do is put on the killer dress. Spanx underneath, you'll knock our Mr. Sorenson off his Gucci loafers. Which will be an enormous confidence booster for you. Also, you're both getting divorced, which should give you a lot to talk about."

Saturday night's date with J. Hank did not serve as a confidence booster. It served as a reminder of why blind dates were at the bottom of the date feeding chain. This, I found out, was as true today as it had been thirty-odd years ago.

The evening started off well enough. A sharply dressed man with a not-too-awful toupee came to pick me up in a Mercedes coupe. He brought with him a dozen red roses. Eva and I had spent the afternoon at the salon getting our hair and nails done. The Spanx wasn't too bad, if you didn't mind feeling like a sausage in casement. And the effect of all this pampering wasn't lost on J. Hank. He handed me the flowers and looked me over. Five hundred dollars of damn good, was how Eva had evaluated the dress. Judging by the look he gave me, J. Hank would have agreed.

J. Hank wouldn't win any awards as the world's handsomest man, but he wasn't bad. Toupee aside, he had a nice straight smile and dark brown eyes. He was tall, the kind of man you might call lanky, sporting the near perfect body for his suit, which, by the looks of it, was probably hand sewn by a little bald tailor somewhere near Torino.

The hello part was, I'm sorry to say, the highlight of our enchanted evening. J. Hank and I went to a charity function, being held at the DeCordova, an art museum just outside of Boston. As I've mentioned, Tom and I never traveled in the sort of social circles that included five-hundred-dollar-a-plate dinners. J. Hank, apparently, did travel in them. He, in fact, gave away the five-hundred-dollar-a-plate cost as we drove down. In fact, he mentioned the cost twice. Money was, in fact, all we, or rather, he, talked about on the way down. And yes, the suit was Italian. And it cost him two thousand dollars to have made.

I could have written off the money talk as a need to impress a

26

first date if not for the rest of the evening. When we got to the museum, J. Hank handed me a glass of champagne, said he had to say hello to someone, and left me standing in the middle of a room full of strangers in Italian suits and designer dresses. None of whom I knew. And none with the slightest inclination of saying howdy to me. I sipped the champagne and wandered aimlessly among the exhibits. J. Hank did collect me for dinner, where we sat at a table of well-heeled philanthropists, all of whom had known each other since their days at Alpha Phi Kappa Beta and none of whom J. Hank bothered to introduce. He laughed and joked and drank. And drank. And drank. I sat. And sat, and picked at apple-glazed seared yellow-fin tuna and wondered how long I'd have to endure.

A while longer, it turned out. After dinner, when everyone began wandering off again, J. Hank spotted an emaciated blonde woman in a low-cut white gown. He caught me by the elbow, whispered that the white witch was his ex-wife, steered me in her direction, and introduced us.

"Kat Sorenson," he said, pushing me forward as though I were show and tell. "This is India. My girlfriend, India."

"Really?" True to her name, Kat looked at me as though I were a goldfish and she'd like nothing better than to spear me with a claw. "How nice for you, J."

"Yes, it is, isn't it? Nice. Very nice." J. Hank put his arm over my shoulder and began exploring my tonsils with his alcohol-tipped tongue. "We were just about to go home, weren't we, darling?" The words were slurred. But the word 'home" came at me loud and clear. There was nothing in this world dearer to me than that little word at this moment.

"Yes, home," I said. At which J. Hank gathered my wrap, pulled it over my shoulders, and staggered me towards the door. The valet drove up in the car. J. Hank started to get into the driver's seat. "How about I drive?" I asked.

J. Hank looked at me as though I'd asked for his liver. "Drive?" he said. "My car?"

"I've always wanted to drive a Mercedes," I said, grabbing the key. "Indulge me. Please?" I batted my eyelashes in a way that would have made Eva proud.

The car was standard. I hadn't driven a standard since high school. And, even then, I hadn't done it well. J. Hank might have been a drunken lout with a prison record, but he was nobody's fool.

"Do you know how to drive?" he asked after several bucks and stalls.

"Of course," A few more bucks and stalls and we were on our way, me trying to remember to shift while J. Hank's mouth lulled dangerously close to my right ear.

Thankfully, J. Hank passed out about halfway home. He woke up when the car reared up and stopped cold in my driveway. "Not my house," he said, after sitting up, wiping the thin strand of drool that connected us from his chin, and assessing the situation.

While he assessed, I fried my brain trying to remember where he lived. Eva had told me, but the lights in Eva's house were off and nobody was home. I didn't want to spend the night joggling through the countryside while being drooled upon.

"It's my house," I said.

J. Hank skewed in a way I know he must have thought was rakish and said, "Are you asking me in?"

"Long enough to call you a cab," I said. J. Hank was already out the door. He made a grab for me as we climbed the steps and clung to me like seaweed. I fumbled through my tiny sequined handbag for keys. He put his hand down the front of my dress as I struggled to unlock the front door, his fingers finding their way into the cup of my push-up bra.

I managed to free myself of the hand and open the door at the same time. And then he turned and disgorged the five hundred dollar dinner over the floor of the front foyer.

"Embarrassing," he said. He didn't seem the least bit chagrinned.

I helped him to the downstairs bath, where he knelt, hugging the porcelain. I left him to heave in private, thinking I ought to call Eva and tell her to come clean the mess. Of course, I did no such thing. I cleaned the mess myself, went upstairs, and changed into sweats. It was past midnight. Unlike Cinderella, I liked the idea of turning into a pumpkin. When I came back down, J. Hank was rinsing his mouth out in the sink. "I owe you an apology," he said to my reflection behind him in the mirror.

"It's fine," I said. It wasn't fine at all, but at least he'd the decency to apologize.

"I'm going on home now." J. Hank staggered towards the front door, slipped in the wet spot left from the mopped up vomit, and fell on his keister. "Where are my keys?" he said.

I called the only cab company in town and got a recording. I

28

called Eva, got voice mail, and hung up before I said something I'd regret in the morning. "I have a spare bedroom," I said to J. Hank, who had gotten to his hands and knees and was making his way back to a standing position. The idea of J. Hank sleeping under my roof bothered me considerably. But the thought of him swerving off a dark road, leaving me forever responsible for his untimely demise, bothered me considerably more. I led the way up the stairs to the room that used to be Allie's.

"You could stay here with me," said J. Hank when I switched on the light. He began nuzzling at my neck.

"I don't think so," I said. I gritted my teeth and gave him a hard shove. Somehow, I managed to push him onto the bed.

"Meow," he said, holding up a hand claw-fashion and scratching the air.

"Sleep well," I said, backing out of the room. He didn't get up and I shut the door firmly, wishing to God it had a padlock.

Another thing I'd learned that evening was that five hundred dollars a plate does not necessarily guarantee decent food. The tuna had been dried out. The rice under it was mushy. The dinner companions were loud and loaded. So, once I heard J. Hank's snores rising from the other side of Allie's door, I tiptoed downstairs and headed for the freezer. A little Phish Food to celebrate the end of my first date in thirty years would be just the thing.

I turned on the kitchen light and there was Patch, sitting on the island stool in the dark, with a jelly glass half full of an amber liquid. The bottle stood on the counter.

"Mommy—" Patch raised his glass and swayed on the stool. By the look of things, it wouldn't be long before I helped him kneel in front of the porcelain receptacle.

I took the glass from him, the smell an unfortunate reminder of my night with J. Hank. "How much of this stuff have you consumed?" I asked.

"A *lot*," Patch said. "A whole big frigging lot."

"I'm going to make a salad," I lied. Though I had bought a head of lettuce and a few cucumbers in an attempt to get the Chunky Monkey off my back. "Have you eaten anything?"

"You are such a mom, Mommy. Always feeding me." He took the jelly glass from me and took another swig.

"You're going to get sick," I said.

"I'm already sick." He put his hand to his chest. "I got a

broken heart, Mommy. Terrible, terrible thing."

I took the salad fixings from the crisper and laid them on the counter. Patch picked up the head of lettuce. "Alas, poor Yorick," he said. He pulled himself off the stool and began shredding it leaf by leaf, throwing the leaves on the floor. "Why doth she protecteth him, Yorick?" he asked the half-head he had left. He raised the head high. "He doth be slime. He doth be the slimiest of slime."

"Patchie," I said, gently taking the head from him.

Patch sat down among the discarded leaves. I slid down next to him. "I went down there to Boston, to that little place he keeps, and who should answer the door in her nightie? They were having a sleepover and they didn't even invite me." Patch took back the lettuce and began shredding again. The kitchen floor was starting to look like the bottom of a hamster cage.

"This is such bullshit," Patch said. " All these years we play happy crappy family and for all that time there's Mommy and Daddy and the happy dumb kids and I'm really wasted and nothing makes sense."

"I'm so, so sorry, sweetie. I didn't want to tell you over the phone."

"Is he here?"

"No. He's living there. In Boston."

"They deserve each other," Patch said. He took the heart of lettuce and flung it across the room.

Chapter Four

There's Got To Be A Morning After

I slept uneasily, my bedroom door firmly shut, with J. Hank passed out on Allie's old bed and Patch passed out on the couch downstairs. It felt as though an entire army of drunken men had invaded and were snoring away in my house.

I woke to talking in the front hall, thought about Patch and J. Hank meeting under these unfortunate circumstances, stuffed myself into my sweats, and virtually flew down the stairs. But it was Eva, chatting amiably with Patch in the front foyer.

"How are you feeling, sweetie?" I asked my son, casting a wary gaze the way of my best friend.

"Like I've been thrown off scaffolding," he said. He offered to make coffee and ventured down the hall, Eva's eyes planted squarely on his tush.

"Good God, he's pretty," Eva said.

"You leave my baby boy alone," I said, only half kidding.

"Your baby boy done growed up, Indie."

"He knows about Tom and Sasha."

"All the more reason to take care of him. Men love being cared for."

"Don't you dare. He already has a mother."

"Don't get all huffy, India. I was just kidding." We probably would have argued there in the hall if the sound of shattered glass hadn't interrupted us. The sound was followed by Patch's cursing. We found him leaning over the sink, blood spurting from his right hand.

"I broke the carafe," Patch said. "Happens when strange men walk into your mother's kitchen wearing your sister's bathrobe."

Sure enough, there was J. Hank, arms sticking out of the too-

31

short-for-him sleeves of Allie's scruffy old pink robe, head left in its natural un-toupeed state, looking pale as the refrigerator. I grabbed a dishtowel and wrapped it around Patch's hand.

"What's he doing here?" asked Eva.

"Who the hell is he?" asked Patch.

"He was going to get some aspirin, but he thinks it would be better to get dressed and go home," said J. Hank. I handed J. Hank two Tylenol and he slunk back up the stairs.

"You weren't supposed to keep him," Eva said once he'd gone. "Rule number three, never sleep with a man on the first date."

"You *slept* with him?" Patch asked. He held tight to his tea-toweled hand, a cranberry stain growing on the sunflower pattern.

"I think you might need stitches," I said, taking Patch's hand and re-wrapping it in a fresh towel. "I would never sleep with him. I wouldn't even date him again."

"You're *dating*?" Patch asked.

"Surely you exaggerate," Eva said. "He comes highly recommended."

"By whom, the Massachusetts Department of Corrections?"

"You had to bring that up. It was a commuted sentence. Did I mention that?"

"He was in *jail*?"

"If you want to sleep with him, be my guest," I said. I grabbed Patch by the arm and guided him towards the kitchen door. The Mercedes blocked me and I thought about moving it by ramming my Camry into its grill and nudging it out of the driveway. But one accident a day was my limit.

"You're *dating* him?" Patch asked as we climbed into his Civic.

"Dated. Past Tense. Once and never again."

Patch cradled his hand and slumped into the seat. "That's his car?" he asked of the Mercedes.

"Yup."

"I hate guys with expensive little sports cars. It's so damned pretentious." Tom drove a Corvette. A little blue number that he polished once a week with Turtle Wax. I thought that was a midlife crisis. I hadn't considered where sports cars could lead.

"You're right," I said. "Very pretentious."

The ER at Tamsett Memorial was quiet, as though it were taking a break after the chaos of Saturday night. Patch and I were the only people in the waiting room, but even so the triage nurse told us to have a seat. So we sat. And we waited.

"What are they doing back there, saying Mass?" Patch asked.

"That only happens at St. Mary's," I told him. "This is a non-sectarian hospital."

"Everyone gets to bleed to death while waiting, regardless of race, creed, or sexual orientation," Patch added. The seepage had stopped, the cranberry stains in the towel drying to a sullen maroon. I understood Patch's impatience. My poor boy was bloodied and it was hard to just sit.

"I'll find someone," I said. I checked the triage station. Empty. So I went down the corridor. There were a set of double doors that said 'Do Not Enter Without an Escort.' I considered that and thought that maybe I should go and sit back down and wait for authorized personnel. But then I thought about the tea towel and all the hurt that my poor son had endured in the past twenty-four hours. I dove on through the door. The ER was as empty as the waiting room. What looked like the main desk was deserted.

I was about to turn around and tell Patch that maybe we'd better drive to the next available hospital, when a tall man in scrubs came out of one of the closed examining rooms. "Get someone from the psych unit," he said into the room. "And stay with him until they get here. Make sure he doesn't eat the thermometer."

When he turned, he nearly walked into me. He had a thick shock of auburn hair. He was young, though old enough to support a few laugh lines around the most beautiful pair of light brown eyes. Full mouth. The word kissable skirted over my brain. I took note of all this as we stood there staring at one another.

"Mrs. Othmar? India?" A wide smile broke over his face. Like the sun coming out from a mass of clouds. He knew me. How did he know me? If I'd met him before I was pretty sure I would have remembered it.

"Mitch," he said when it became clear I didn't recognize him.

"Mitch Tinker?" Mitch and Patch had been friends when they were kids. In fact, Mitch had spent so much time at our house that Tom and I had joked about adopting him. Then, when Mitch was ten, his parents divorced and he'd moved with his mother to Michigan. On closer inspection, I could still see a hint of that ten-year-old. But

33

it was abundantly clear that the man in front of me had spent the last twenty years growing up.

"Are you okay?" Mitch asked.

"What?" My heart had done a little flip, but, really, I was fine. Then I remembered that we were in the emergency room. I remembered my poor bloodied son.

"Patch," I said.

"He's here?" Mitch was still staring at me.

"He's waiting. In the waiting room. His hand." I raised my hand in illustration.

Mitch nodded as though he understood perfectly. "We should go get him."

"Yes. Yes, we should." I walked back out the double doors with Mitch behind me. "Look who I found," I said to my son. "Mitch."

"Tinker?" He examined Mitch twice over. "It's really you. Holy shit. Tinker." He stood up and gave Mitch an awkward hug. "What are you doing here?"

"Saving human kind," said Mitch. Then he told us that he'd been back in Tamsett for six months. He'd taken a job as an ER doctor after finishing a residency at Brigham-Women's in Boston.

"So how is it, being back?" asked Patch as Mitch led us to an examining room.

"It's getting better all the time," Mitch said, looking at me in a way that made me flush again. "Let's have a look at that hand," he said to Patch.

Mitch put in two stitches and bandaged the hand. "You've improved your technique since you pulled that splinter from my thumb," Patch said.

Mitch smiled and nodded at the almost compliment. "It was terrific seeing you again." This I think, was addressed to both Patch and me, though Mitch looked directly at me. "You still over on Easterly?"

"Easterly. Yes." Those eyes. I got lost there for a minute.

Until I heard Patch say, "That would be okay with you, right Mom?"

"Sorry, honey?"

"I asked if Mitch and I could watch the game on your plasma TV. At your house."

"On Easterly," I said, still looking at Mitch. I tore myself free.

"Yes, sure. That would be terrific."

"Mitch Tinker," Patch said as we were driving home. "Who would've thought? Weird, huh? Five minutes, and it's like he never left."

I nodded and mumbled something about old friends.

"Mom, are you okay?"

"What? Sure, honey. I'm fine. It's just been a long day. Long night."

"Tough times," said Patch. "I'm sorry."

"For what?"

"Last night. I was so caught up in, you know. I didn't think about how awful this must be for you."

"I'll live through it. We both will," I said.

Eva had gone to Dunkin Donuts and come back with a Box o' Joe and fifty munchkins. "I cooked," she said, "just for you and that gorgeous blue-eyed boy of yours." Patch smiled. I grimaced. The toilet flushed. "He's still here," Eva said.

"Why is he still here?" I asked.

"He's locked out of his car. Says it's your fault."

"My fault?" I relived the drunken pawing. The saliva on the shoulder. The vomit. Oh, God, the vomit. Had I locked the keys into the car? It was entirely possible that I could have missed the beeping in light of 'ooh baby, I'm going to be sick'. I fished out my triple A card just as J. Hank came into the kitchen, his suit wrinkled and stained with yesterday's dinner. He glared at me. I handed him the card. Another card fluttered to the floor.

Patch picked it up. "Wuthering Heights? There's a place called Wuthering Heights?"

"That's right," said J. Hank, grabbing the card. "I built that place. I live in that place now, since my wife got the house."

"Your wife?" said Patch. "You have a wife and you're dating my mother?"

"Dated," I said. "With all due respect, please don't call me."

"With all due respect, I wouldn't call if you were the last..."

"Munchkin?" Eva asked.

"Easy Peasy," said the triple A guy, prying a wedge into J.

Hank's window. "Happens all the time. Though I'd be careful, what with a nice ride like this here." J. Hank scowled at him and blanched when he pounded on the wedge with a mallet.

"You'd think the car was his girlfriend," Patch said as we watched J. Hank pull onto Easterly and speed away.

"It's easy to get jealous of a nice car," Eva said. "Some men adore their cars."

Patch poked his head into the refrigerator. "Red peppers, lettuce, and Diet Coke," he said. "your stash is worse than mine. What are you living on?"

"Lean Cuisine, chocolate, and Karamel Sutra," I said.

"Karamel Sutra?"

"Ben and Jerry. And why are you taking inventory?"

"I was hoping for beer."

"No beer," I told Patch.

"There's always beer. Got to be a six-pack hiding somewhere."

"There was beer. I don't drink beer." Tom liked to have a bottle after mowing the lawn. The grass was getting tall, I'd have to mow it myself. Last time I did, it had taken a half an hour of pulling the cord to realize that the mower was out of gas. Live and learn. This week, the lawn. Maybe next week, I'd change the oil in the car. As though Tom ever changed his own oil.

Chapter Five

Seems Like Old Times

He's early, I thought, when I heard a car pull into the drive a few minutes after Patch left. I glanced out the window. Mitch had taken a taxi. Who in Tamsett takes a taxi? Who can even get a taxi in Tamsett?

But it wasn't Mitch who got out of the back. It was Allie, short blonde hair flying in the breeze. We'd called Allie Pixie when she was little, and it was a name that suited her even now. She could have played Peter Pan, my Allie. She'd been almost as far as Never Never Land. She'd been in Africa, in Chad, studying the migration patterns of elephants. Allie had left in January and wasn't due back until August, when she was supposed to visit for a week before I drove her to New York City, to Columbia, to work on a graduate degree in zoology. I'd been relieved at her choice. It had taken Allie six years to get a bachelor's degree. She's majored in chemistry, anthropology, forest management, and marine biology before settling, hopefully for good, on elephants.

Only, here she was, paying a taxi driver who'd pulled into my drive. It was April, not August. Chad was a long ways to come for a weekend visit. And considering the heavy suitcase she dragged from the taxi's trunk, it looked as though she were planning a very long weekend.

"Mom!" she said, cheerful as the pixie she still was.

"Allie?" I gave her a big squeeze and a questioning look.

"I know. I know. What am I doing here? Long story." Allie the pixie turned into Allie the waif on the front porch steps. "Do I still have a room here?"

"Honey, you'll always have a room here." Together we humped the heavy suitcase up the stairs.

"Somebody's been sleeping in my bed," said Allie. A mop of hair sat on the dresser. Allie poked at it cautiously. "I think they left something behind."

"Oh God. Toupee." Now it was Allie's turn to give me a questioning look. "Long boring story," I said, throwing the toupee in the wastebasket and grabbing a new set of sheets from the linen closet. I wondered idly if I should burn the used ones.

"Do tell," Allie tucked the flat sheet in on one side as I tucked in the other.

"Overnight guest," I said.

"Boring, yes. Long, no. I had an existential crisis."

"Really?"

Allie sat on the bed and shrugged. "I'm only twenty-five, so I don't think it's a mid-life crisis. I have to call it something." She looked so forlorn sitting there that I began to wonder if she, too, had a broken heart. Turns out she did, but she didn't tell me about it then. Then she said, "I've discovered that I hate Africa. We lived in a tent with no running water. It's dusty and it gives new meaning to the words 'fly-infested'. Dust and flies. You can't eat without grit in your teeth."

Allie took the pillow and held it like a teddy bear. "The thing is, I thought I was better than that. Grandma Marissa always thought I was such a princess. And it turns out I'm a worse comfort slut than even she could imagine. I hate being hot. I hate being dirty. And when it comes down to it, I'm not so crazy about those big nasty beasties, either. I don't want to spend my life examining excrement. And I'm not all that nuts about hyenas or gazelles or lions. Or those big termites. Or storks. What am I going to do?"

"It's not the end of the world, honey."

"Oh, but it is. I know that I've had a little trouble finding myself. Turns out I'm still not found. Turns out I'd rather go to Burger King than cook over an open flame. I like the idea of elephants, but the real thing sucks. Life sucks."

It was hard seeing Allie like that. Though she was right, she was taking her time in finding herself. "I was going to study Russian Literature," I offered up. There was something I hadn't thought about in years. The pre-Tom me, all full of hope and ambition. "I'd fallen in love with these long, sad fairy tales my Granny Smirtoff used to tell. Little did I know that the language came with a whole other alphabet. And *War and Peace* goes on and on. I found Tolstoy a little long-winded." I smiled at Allie, at the thought of my granny, who'd lived with me and my father to take care of me after my mother died.

"And you gave it all up?"

"I found a liking for Dr. Seuss, what can I say?"

"So you switched to Elementary Education, met Dad, moved to Tamsett, and lived happily ever after."

I worked hard at keeping the smile on my face. Allie didn't know about Tom's leaving. She'd been in Africa, after all, and Africa wasn't exactly known for its stellar communication network.

"Someday my Seuss will come," Allie said.

"Everybody has a Seuss. You just need to find yours. Think about what you love."

"Shoes," Allie said. "I've always loved shoes."

She said this with such conviction. I couldn't imagine. Allie was an L.L. Bean kind of girl. Hiking boots and sneakers all the way. "Shoes?"

Allie laughed. "I'm kidding, Mom. I'm kidding. Though there is something to be said for a nice pair of espadrilles."

"I suppose that's true." I thought about the sling backs I'd bought to go with the little black dress. They'd cost more on sale than I normally paid for two pairs.

"Who's the guy?" Allie pointed out her bedroom window. There, getting out of a shiny blue sedan, was Mitch Tinker. "He looks like he stepped off the cover of a romance novel." It was true: the dark red hair, the six foot and a lot of change frame, the chinos and chambray shirt with rolled sleeves, carrying flowers no less, did make for quite a picture. Mitch probably could have a future as a model at Chippendale's. "The hair looks familiar," Allie said.

"Tinker, I don't believe it." Allie flew into Mitch's arms once we'd answered the door.

"Pixie." Mitch held Allie out at arm's length. "You haven't changed. Still about the same size."

Allie popped him in the shoulder. "Did you come by to insult me?"

"Certainly not. You look fabulous." He handed me the bouquet of daisies he'd been carrying. "For you. They're your favorite, right?"

"I'm shocked you remember."

"Some things you never forget." And there I was. Zapped again.

We settled into the kitchen. I uncovered a dusty box of brownie mix in the back of the cupboard and set to. I was just pulling them from the oven when Patch walked in and sniffed.

"Brownies," he said. "Perfect companion for Molson Ale." He held up a twelve-pack and nearly dropped it when he saw his sister. "Allie. You're not in Africa."

Mitch took the beer from him and put it in the fridge while Allie gave her brother a long-time-no-see hug. "You're not in Boston," she said.

"Boston's an hour down the road. Chad, on the other hand, is a tough day trip."

"I came home," Allie said.

"Just like old times, isn't it?" I said, beaming at both my children and a bemused Mitch.

"It is like old times," Allie said a few hours later. We were having a pizza and beer party in the living room, camped out in front of the ball game, which had just finished. "Only thing missing is Monopoly. You guys remember how we always used to do family game night?"

"I could probably dig the board out of the attic," I offered.

"Remember how we had our own rules? You didn't have to have a monopoly to buy houses. And Patch always had to be the dog and Daddy got the sports car." Allie stopped. "Where is Dad, anyway? I figured he's probably out playing marathon golf with Mr. Hessler, but shouldn't they be done by now?"

Patch found a sudden need to look out the window. "He's not here," I said.

"No kidding, Mom." Allie glanced over at Patch. "So, what's going on?"

"Nothing," Patch said, affecting a smile.

"You're lying," Allie said to her brother. "You were always bad at lying." She looked to Mitch, who studied the label on his beer bottle with an intensity usually reserved for research papers. "Tell

40

him, Mitch. Tell him why he always lost at poker."

"You played poker?" I had a sudden image of my kids, Patch age ten, Allie age five, in a smoke-filled room with cigars and cognac. The things you don't know about your children.

"We would play for pennies," Mitch said. "Out in the tree house. Patch usually gave up his allowance. He always bit his lower lip when he was bluffing."

"Like he's doing now," Allie said.

"I do not bite my lip when I bluff," Patch said. "Tell them, Mom."

"Your father and I are separated," I told Allie. Patch groaned. "And you do bite your lip when you bluff. Everyone knows that," I added. Allie and Mitch were both staring at me.

"Separated?" Allie looked around the room as though Tom were going to jump out from behind the drapery and yell 'gotcha'. "As in we're going to break up this family and get divorced?"

"Your father moved out. About a month ago." I said it with more calm than I'd imagined possible.

"And you were going to tell me when?" Allie pointed an accusatory finger at her brother. "You knew about this and we've been sitting here having a grand old time while our whole family is dissolved?"

Patch's neck and arms were mottled with red splotches. He was as awful at hiding his feelings as he was at bluffing. He got up and walked to the kitchen without a word.

I took Allie's hand. "I'm sorry, honey. I should have told you sooner. It's just that you were in Africa, for goodness sake. And then today, you came home unexpectedly and you had that existential crisis and well, I just hadn't found the right time."

Allie pulled her hand away and turned her back to me. Mitch got up and collected the empties. "I'm going to go get another beer," he said. "And Allie? You can tell me this is none of my business and you'd be right, but I know a little something about divorce and I don't think it's fair for you to lay this at your mom's feet. It takes two to separate. I'll go get that beer now."

As he walked from the room, I assessed the new, grown- up version of Mitch Tinker again. There were the romance-cover looks and the expertise he'd shown in stitching up Patch's hand. But there was more. I saw it in the way he walked. With assurance. As though he'd been dealing with gravity for a long time and he knew just how to measure each step.

My pixie of a daughter was a grown up, too, though right now she looked much like a little girl. And my little girl was crying. I put my arms around her and drew her in, the lump in my throat swelling yet again. I thought I'd cried enough during the last few weeks to dry out the reservoir. I'd been wrong.

We had a good long cry together, then we walked arm in arm to the kitchen, where we found Mitch and Patch with their heads together. You would have thought that they'd seen each other every day for the last twenty years. Mitch jumped up when we came in.

"Just for the record," Patch said. "It's not going to get all better. And we all know it sucks." He stopped biting his lip and made a fist with his good hand instead, folding and unfolding his fingers. He turned to me. "Did you tell her?"

"Patch," I said. It seemed that the only thing I could do was say my son's name.

"I've got to be in early tomorrow. Monday is a zoo in the ER," Mitch said. He turned to Patch. "The offer stands. Think about it."

Things grew quiet after Mitch left. Somehow, it had seemed easier when he was there.

"So what else was it that you didn't tell me?" Allie asked.

"What was Mitch talking about, an offer?" I asked Patch, hoping to skirt Allie's question.

"Mitch bought a house over on Robinson Drive, near the hospital. He's got this basement apartment, used to be an in-law apartment, and he said he'd rent it to me. It would be a lot cheaper than my place in the city and twice as big."

Patch lived in a studio near Copley Square. I never asked about rent. He made a decent wage at Vaughn's firm and he'd never once asked for money. I could give him money, if he needed it. I told him as much.

"It's not the money."

"You don't have to worry about me, Patch," I said. "Allie's back and she's going to stay for a while so I won't be rattling around here all alone."

"That's the thing, isn't it?" Allie asked. "Living alone?" Leave it to Allie to state what should have been obvious. Patch had rented that apartment with Sasha. They'd picked out the furniture together. Then Sasha left him with the apartment and the furniture.

"You could always come live here," I offered. The irony

42

wasn't lost on me. This was the house Tom and I had bought together all those years ago. He, too, had left me with the house and the furniture. Not to mention the shrubbery we'd planted along the front walk and the lawn and the maple tree. But I never considered leaving. The memories would keep me here, because they included Patch and Allie. They included Eva. They even included Mitch. Those memories were about a lot more than a marriage.

"Thanks, Mom. But I think I'd be better off on my own."

"You'll be happy at Mitch's," I said, though it didn't come out as a question, I was asking.

"A good time will be had by all," Patch said.

"I'll help you move," Allie said. The query into my own life had been forgotten and I was more than glad to let it lie.

Chapter Six

Goody Two Shoes

"What you need is a good man," Eva said as we walked past the school. It was Saturday again. A month of Saturdays had passed since the date with J. Hank. I'd gone back to school, had a banner and cupcakes to welcome me back, and received way too much sympathy from the rest of the staff. A few of the teachers were divorced and they took it upon themselves to comfort me with their war stories. It took a week or two, but the stories had faded and things had gotten nearly back to normal.

Allie was living with me, looking for herself, and not finding anything just yet. Patch moved into Mitch's apartment, which, it turned out, faced a green back lawn and was twice as big as Patch's old place at half the price.

Eva, in usual Eva fashion, was relentless in her efforts to initiate me into single-woman date-hood. I told her that one blind date had been plenty, thank you very much. If that was the dating life, I'd just as soon get myself a cat. To which she said I was hopeless and asked what I was doing that evening.

"Cooking a big batch of chili," I said. "Patch and Mitch are coming over to eat with us. You can come too."

"You're incurable," Eva said. "You need a date."

"I like cooking for them," I said. They lived on fast-food and frozen dinners most of the time. And they both appreciated a real meal. It was nice having them around. Mitch came around often, sometimes with Patch and sometimes by himself. Allie and I fed him and in exchange he mowed the lawn and re-caulked the bathroom tiles. I got zapped in the solar plexus every time Mitch Tinker looked at me, though I was careful not to let it interfere with what was fast becoming a friendship. Still there was no denying I had a crush on

him. I think Allie did, too

"Hopeless," Eva said as we rounded up the hill for home.

"Have you figured out what you want to be when you grow up?" Patch asked Allie over chili that evening.

"She told me she wanted to go into the shoe business," I said.

"There's no business like shoe business," Patch said.

Allie hit him with her spoon. "Very funny. Mom was kidding about the shoes."

"I have a lot of shoes," Mitch said. "Five thousand pairs." He took a sip of beer and raised his eyebrows.

"Enough," Allie said.

"No, seriously. Five thousand pairs," Mitch said.

"The only way he knows to get women is to buy them shoes," Patch said, taking another slice of cornbread. "But seriously, he really does have five thousand pairs."

"Shoe fetish?" Allie asked.

"That's right, Pixie. I get off on shoes," Mitch said.

"Why do you have five thousand pairs of shoes?" I asked, curious now.

"Long story," Mitch took a second bowl of chili.

"But that has never stopped him from telling it," Patch said.

"Do tell," I said.

To which Allie said, "Yes, Mitchell, I'd love to hear the tale."

Mitch put down his spoon and leaned back in his chair. "Man came into the ER about six months back. He was having a coronary. It was touch and go for a while, but we pulled him through. He went in for bypass surgery and after he was discharged, he came back to the ER. Just to visit. He told me that he had had a vision, a kind of out-of-body experience. It had a talking frog in it."

"Really?" I said.

"Oh yes. Talking frog. He was very clear on that point. And the frog told him that he needed to thank me. A week later, a truck pulls up to the ER loaded with shoe boxes. Turns out that the guy owned this little shoe factory, Klein's shoes, down on Mill Street. They'd gone out of business a few years back."

"I remember that place!" Allie said. "You remember, Mom? They had that little outlet store. You had to go up these stairs."

"Klein's shoes," I said. "I haven't thought about them in

45

years."

"Mr. Klein, as you might have gathered from the whole talking frog thing, was what you might call a tad eccentric," Mitch said.

"That store was in a terrible location," I said. "Back behind the factory, off a vacant lot. And the shoes were, even back in the day, a little outdated."

"I haven't checked them out," Mitch said. "They've been in my basement for three months and they're probably a fire hazard." Mitch looked at Allie and raised his eyebrows again. "So if you want to go into the shoe business, I'm your guy."

Eva was intrigued when I told her about Mitch's shoes. "Horace is doing a fund-raiser for the lost boys," she said. Horace Galloway was Eva's latest paramour, a large man with a hooked nose who taught history at Tamsett Community College. I'd met him once and, quite honestly, I thought he was a bit of a bore. He seemed to have two channels, twentieth century military history and what great stuff I do to benefit others. Eva had been dating him for a month and the enchantment still hadn't worn off. So despite myself, I asked who the lost boys were.

"These kids from Sudan or Ethiopia or some awful place in Africa. They're refugees. Terrible stories, Horace says they break your heart."

"And they need shoes?"

"No, silly. It's a fundraiser. We'll sell Mitch's shoes and donate the money."

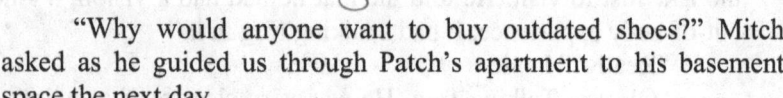

"Why would anyone want to buy outdated shoes?" Mitch asked as he guided us through Patch's apartment to his basement space the next day.

"You'd be surprised," Eva said. "You can get people to buy anything if you've got the right angle."

Mitch pulled the light cord. There were shoes boxes piled into every nook and cranny. "It's a shoe infestation. If they were alive, I'd have to call an exterminator."

"Still in the original boxes," Eva said. "That's a great selling point." She pulled a pink box off a tall pile, sneezed as she dusted it

46

off, and pulled out a purple platform shoe, size eleven and a half.

"Nice," I said. "They could use it as a prop in the remake of *Saturday Night Fever*."

"Oh my God. Look at this." Eva pointed to the platform under the toe. "A place for goldfish."

"Goldfish?" Mitch questioned, taking the shoe from her and examining it.

"You're too young, darling," Eva said. "Goldfish shoes. Popular during the disco era, long before you were born. You have no point of reference."

"I'm not that young," Mitch said. "And, by the by, I've seen *Saturday Night Fever*. Disco was awful."

"Disco was awful," I agreed. "Almost as bad as those shoes."

"Are you kidding?" Eva said. "I know a transvestite who would die for shoes like these." She pulled the tissue paper from the pink box. "Where's the match?"

Mitch took the box from her. "I guess there is no match," he said.

"There's got to be a match." I pulled down another box. One child's black patent leather Mary Jane. I held it up. "Another singleton"

"Let me see that," Mitch took the box from me as Eva pulled down a third. One penny loafer; size six.

"You have got to be kidding," she said, dangling the single shoe by the heel.

Mitch pulled out another box, and held up a red Ked's high-top sneaker. "Just the one," he said.

"You mean to tell me you have a basement full of single shoes?" Eva asked.

"It looks that way," Mitch said, a big smirk pasted on his face.

"What do you mean, it looks that way? They're your shoes." Eva slammed the top back down on a single brown wing-tip.

"I never actually looked in the boxes," Mitch said.

"You never actually looked in the boxes?" Eva turned to me. "Boy Wonder never actually looked in the boxes. How are we supposed to sell five thousand single shoes?"

"Maybe there are some pairs," I said. "Maybe over there." I went over to a pile by the water heater. "Or not." I held up the single pink fuzzy slipper I found.

"Oh, this is just ducky," Eva said. "How can you sell us single shoes?"

"I'm not selling you anything," Mitch's eyes danced over the pile. "Mr. Klein is a tad eccentric."

"What am I going to tell Horace? He's counting on five thousand *pairs* of shoes," Eva said.

"It is kind of funny," I said. "I'm sure Horace will understand."

"Humor is not Horace's strong suit. I'm going to have to endure a long lecture on how much I've disappointed not only Horace, but a whole tribe of lost boys. God, I hate it when he lectures."

"We could sell the shoes to amputees," Mitch said.

"Planters," I said. "We can sell them as planters."

The idea was just crazy enough to work. The three of us discussed it over coffee and I went home with a head full of thoughts on logistics: potting soil and flats. Could we buy the stuff in gross? Could we do, say, five hundred shoes and see how it went? Would Horace be okay with a promise of five hundred planters?

I called to Allie from the hallway. "You'll never guess," I said, breezing into the living room, where I stopped short. There, with Allie, was Tom. Sitting on the couch as though he'd never left.

Chapter Seven

Would You Like A Little Gin With That New York Super Fudge Chunk?

Tom got up when I walked in, the picture-perfect corners of his mouth pasted into a smile. "India."

"Mom." Allie, unlike her father, looked as though she'd just gotten her hand stuck in the cookie jar. "You're back."

"Mitch's shoes," I said. Which didn't make any sense, given the circumstance. My own shoes felt as though they were on too tight, and the whole story of singletons and planters didn't seem nearly as funny or bright as it had when I'd walked in the door. The whole idea seemed a little dumb, in retrospect.

"I've come by to see Allie," Tom said.

"Dad thinks he might have a job for me." They were both talking at the same time.

"A job?" I asked Allie, not wanting to look at Tom. Tom ran his own PR firm and made a good living at it. Allie had majored in a lot of things, most of them science oriented. What did she know about PR?

"She knows colleges," Tom said, answering my unasked question. "Sawyer wants to start a new science program. She knows science programs." He sounded defensive, as though he were trying to convince himself.

"I'll go change," Allie said. "Dad's taking me out to dinner." And off she went.

"I'll be in the kitchen," I said. "Make yourself at home." It came out with a little more vehemence than I intended. Or maybe vehemence was just what I had in mind.

I thought that would be the end of it. I'd retire to one corner, Tom would wait in another. Allie was still his daughter, after all. He had every right to take her to dinner. And give her a job. Like he had given Sasha a job when she was still Patch's girlfriend. Sasha had majored in communications and business at Brown. And good God, I'd thought how considerate that he would give the girl her first job.

I poured myself a glass of water, sat at the kitchen island, and waited for everyone to leave. And then there was Tom, standing in the doorway. He was still a good looking man. He still had the same soft blue eyes and the same blond hair. "We should talk, I guess," he said.

"Been there. Done that."

"I didn't mean to hurt you, Indie. If I did, I'm very sorry."

I knew he was trying to make amends. Coming here alone meant that. Following me into the kitchen was a big step. I knew that, too. But I wasn't having any of it. "That's not enough, Tom. It's not enough."

"We can do this amicably, Indie. We can make it all work."

I took a deep swallow of water. "Work? Yes, fabulous. You and me and Sasha Peterson. Maybe you could find a third woman and we could all live on a compound like fundamentalist Mormons. Gosh, we could all share the same bed."

Tom's face went tight. I turned to see our daughter standing in the doorway. "Oh, my God," she said. And she ran back up the stairs and slammed the door to her room.

Tom and I stood looking at each other, united by the distress of our younger child. Without a word Tom went up after her and I followed. He knocked on her door and asked if he could come in. I stood there for a few uncomfortable minutes, then, feeling unneeded and unwanted, retreated back to the kitchen.

A car door slammed, and Mitch ambled up the walk with three shoe boxes.

"You've got company," he said, noting the blue Corvette parked in the drive. I'd missed it entirely. I'd pulled in next to it without thinking twice. My head had been full of musings about shoes. Or maybe it just seemed that Tom's car should be parked in the drive. I still thought of it as our driveway. Our house. Old habits die hard.

"My husband."

Mitch's smile fell. "I'm barging in."

"No. No. He came to see Allie." The concern on Mitch's face nearly did me in. I changed the subject. "What have you got there?"

Mitch opened the boxes and lined three shoes on the counter: a gold-toned pump with a spiked heel, a man's disco shoe in fluorescent green, and a plum-colored high-top. "I thought you might want them for inspiration."

"Wow." I picked up the florescent green. "They're interesting."

"Interesting, that's one way of putting it." Mitch scratched his chin as the two of us stood there admiring the shoes.

I could imagine them, in my mind's eye, a sprig of pansies or violets in place of a leg. There was optimism in this, the thought of making something whimsical to bring a smile to someone's face. It nearly made me forget my own troubles. "This might just work," I said.

"If anyone can get these shoes to look good, it's you."

Then there were footsteps on the stairs, a call back to trouble. The front door shut and then Allie was in the kitchen. Allie, who even on a good day looked as though she could be carried away by dust mites, looked so much like a spent dandelion that I felt her hurt in my own spine.

And there was Tom, sitting in his damn sports car ready to pull out of the drive and go back to Boston, back to Sasha, leaving poor Allie as surely as he'd left me. I marched out the kitchen door, leaving Allie and Mitch in my wake. I took hold of the passenger door and got in.

I banged the door shut. Tom hit the brake hard at the end of the drive. And then we were flying off, down the familiar street, turning at the familiar corner.

He pulled over at the curb next to McKinley school. I got the odd feeling he was driving me to work. As though nothing had changed between us. I looked out the passenger window, but through the corner of my eye, I could see his Adam's apple bob up and down. It always did that when he was upset. The way his hands folded and unfolded on the wheel. The bob. Upset. Thirty-two years and I figured I'd learned how to read Thomas Othmar. I knew the signs. But not all of them. Not the ones that said, "I'm seeing someone else." Not the ones that said, "I don't want you anymore."

"I understand why you're angry, Indie, I do."

"I'm not looking for an apology."

"Allie won't talk to me. I tried to explain, but she won't listen to me."

"Then you keep trying."

"I am trying."

"No, Tom. You're not. You waltz in after a couple of months and suddenly it's supposed to be all better? That's not trying. Then you waltz out again without fixing it with Allie. That's not trying, either."

"I can't do anything else. Damn it, India. What do you want? Just tell me what you want from me."

What did I want? Wasn't it obvious? I wanted my life back, the life I had lost to him. And having lost it to him, I was unwilling to forgive him anything. I opened the car door again and climbed out and walked the five blocks back to my house. I realized, after half a block, that I was in my stocking feet. Realizing this, I almost turned back and demanded that Tom drive me home, because the car was still parked near the curb, three doors down from the school.

I didn't go back. And Tom didn't try to follow me home. I walked home in my socks. Mitch and Allie were still in the kitchen when I got there. "Look," I said pointing to my feet.

Mitch got up and handed me the high top. "Wish I had the match," he said.

"The planter idea is great," Allie said after Mitch left. "I think I've figured out how to keep the soil in." She picked up the pump. "Plastic inserts. Dr. Scholl's for planters."

"Inserts." I took the shoe from Allie. "That's brilliant."

"Two heads are better than one. Actually, three heads. Mitch helped." She picked up the high top.

"He's good to have around."

Allie put the shoe down and went to the freezer. "Got any Cherry Garcia?" She was my daughter, after all.

They had eight pints of Ben and Jerry's in the freezer case at the corner Seven-Eleven. We bought them all, along with a stash of Oreos.

"The shoes might make good ice cream bowls, too," said Allie on the ride home. "Shoe Sundaes."

"Great idea," I said.

"So, you're going to divorce Daddy."

"It looks that way."

52

"This party needs Oreos," Eva said. She'd pulled into her drive, dressed in red with heels to match, just after we returned from our Ben and Jerry's run. We lined the pints up on the counter like ducks in a shooting gallery.

"Got those," I told her, pulling the cookies from the bottom of the bag.

"Also martinis," Eva said.

"Can you have martinis with ice cream?" Allie asked.

"Of course, darling, martinis go with anything."

I pulled Oreos from the sleeve and passed one to Eva. "You're back early."

"It's over," she said. "You've timed your pity party perfectly."

Eva made martinis and I got spoons, one for each flavor. "Tell the truth," Eva asked, handing me a drink, "Has he always been a bore or did he get zapped by the quotidian fairy while I wasn't watching?"

"Honest truth?" I asked, sipping the near-overflow from the wide-rimmed glass. I glanced at Allie, who looked up from sampling Cherry Garcia and shrugged. I didn't want to say anything I'd regret.

"Boring, right?" Eva said into the silence. "I knew it. I knew it when he said he hated the shoe idea."

"He said that he hated it?" Allie asked.

"He didn't say hated, exactly. I outlined it for him, all the stuff your mother and Mitch and I talked about. Five thousand shoes, five thousand flowers. Which, by the by, is a great slogan. He pursed his lips and said it was an interesting idea."

"Interesting idea, hah!" Allie said.

"It's a really dumb idea," I said

"It's a brilliant idea, Mom."

"She's right, India. The man can't tell a brilliant idea from a lost boy. All he ever talks about is the Battle of the Bulge. And the Spanish-American War. And the invasion of Granada."

"He was pretty awful," I said, burying my spoon into New York Super Fudge Chunk. "The quotidian fairy conked him on the head long before you came along."

"Why did you go out with him?" Allie asked.

"I don't know," Eva said. "He was available. He owned his own car. He knows how to read."

"You need to up your standards," Allie said.

"Yes, well. I'm not the one hosting this ice cream social."

"How's Allie?" Mitch asked the next day when I went to pick up more shoes.

"Hurt. Angry."

"I told her it was hard. I was pretty upset when my parents split."

"That was a long time ago."

"And you get over it. I was totally annihilated when my marriage split, but I got past it. It's been two years now."

"You were married? And divorced?"

Mitch nodded as he opened the door to his storage room. "Yup. You're in good company. I know what it's like to be the walking wounded."

"What other secrets are you keeping from us, Dr. Tinker?"

Mitch turned on the light and stood holding the pull string. "Not that many," he said softly. "No more than your average guy. If you stick around, I'll share a few with you." He smiled, but there was a hint of something else in his eyes, concern maybe, or longing. It matched my feelings and that made me a little uncomfortable.

"Like what, for instance?" I said, wanting to melt the discomfort away.

It worked. The smile rose into his eyes . "I'll tell one if you will," he said.

"I like gravy on my French fries," I said.

"Yummy. I sing along with my iPod when I'm alone."

"What kind of music?"

"Springsteen, mostly. No fair, that's two. You owe me one."

"*The River* is one of my favorite albums."

"And?" he raised his eyebrows, waiting.

"Okay. I really like to finger paint. And sometimes after school I paint at a kid's art easel."

"Landscapes or portraits?"

"Portraits mostly. Your turn."

"I still watch 'Scooby Doo'."

"Hallmark commercials make me cry."

"I had a huge crush on you when I was ten."

The room went very still and we stood there staring at each

54

other. "I shouldn't have said that. I'm sorry."

"No, it's fine. It's fine. You're not ten anymore. Heck, I'm not thirty anymore."

"I have changed considerably. You haven't. Not really. Not that much." He turned towards the shoes. "So, how many boxes do you think your trunk can hold?"

Chapter Eight

Fear Of Flying

I went to see Vaughn the following week. Allie declined to work with her father, but did go to have dinner with him. Tom had been contrite, and in that spirit said if I was sure I wanted a divorce, he wouldn't stand in the way. And that if I agreed to arbitration, he'd give me the house and the lion's share of our joint assets.

"So, arbitration?" It sounded like something ominous coming from under Vaughn's neatly trimmed beard.

I picked up the photo on Vaughn's desk: his only daughter, Claire, holding a horse by its withers. "How old is she now?"

"Eighteen. Her horse, Dixie. We bought it for her last year. She loves that horse." Vaughn looked at the picture with obvious pride. "She's spending a semester in London."

"You miss her."

Vaughn took the picture from me and set it back on the desk. "You didn't come to chat about Claire," he said. He looked at his watch. In ten minutes I had already overstayed my welcome.

"I forgot that you charge by the minute," I said.

"India, please." He indicated the chair across from his desk. "I always have time for you." The words weren't genuine, though he said them in the same casual friendly voice he always used. He always had time for me. Except when he didn't. Now, for instance.

"So—arbitration?" he said again, crossing his arms and sitting back.

"That's what Tom wants."

"And what does India want? Revenge?"

"India wants advice."

"As your attorney or as a guy who's known you for over thirty years?"

56

"Both. Maybe."

"As your attorney, I'd say arbitration is the way to go. He's willing to give you a fair deal. More than fair. It's a lot quicker and a lot easier than going to court."

"And as the guy?"

"I'd like to hang him upside down and drain the blood out of him."

"Ouch."

"Come on, India. He cost me. First you. Then he nearly cost me my marriage."

There it was, hanging out. The dirty laundry I'd hidden in the bottom of the hamper. The real reason why the Whites and the Othmars did not see each other socially.

"You don't know for sure," I said, still wanting to hang on to the stained notion that it was all just hints and allegations.

"Afraid I do. Danielle confessed. It was a long time ago. I forgave her. You did the same."

I shrugged, not wanting to admit I hadn't forgiven. What I'd done was to close my eyes.

"But you can't keep forgiving. And now you find yourself alone."

Alone. There it was. I was alone. Then again, I wasn't alone. Not really. I had Allie. And Eva. And Patch. And Mitch. I was hardly alone. I told Vaughn as much. He took my hand and caressed it between his own. "But they can't keep you warm at night, can they?"

I was startled by this. Under different circumstances, I might have thought that Vaughn was making a pass at me. But Vaughn, even in his callow and ambitious youth, had never been a man to make passes. I looked at him, flummoxed. Had he been flirting?

Vaughn let go of the hand and sat on the corner of his desk. "Once a woman reaches a certain age it's harder for her to…find companionship."

"Because middle-aged men prefer women half their age?" All the hurt I'd been feeling over Tom's betrayals spilled onto Vaughn's Oriental carpet. We both looked at it as though it were a physical thing, a stain that could be soaked up with club soda.

"You asked for honesty," Vaughn said to the imaginary splotch. "And honestly, yes. Maybe women get to a place where they are no longer…"

I stared at him. He stared back. His eyes, amber and surprisingly bright, carried the hint of the boy he'd been at eighteen. "I didn't mean to insult you, India," he said quietly.

I stormed Eva's house when I got home from Boston. I'd had lunch with Patch and all I could think of was how I'd, as Vaughn suggested, wandered past a certain age into oblivion. I couldn't ask Patch about it. You don't ask your twenty-nine-year-old son if he thinks you're still attractive. I'd stolen a glance in the ladies' room mirror. I needed to lose twenty pounds. I needed dark lighting. Vaughn was right in his diagnosis, but I still wanted a second opinion. Eva would tell me the truth.

She circled me, evaluating me as though I were a house, a fixer-upper that she needed to unload. An antique cape with peeling shingles and squeaky floors. "You can't compete with the Sashas of the world," she said.

This wasn't what I wanted to hear. "What happened to the 'there are men out there' pep talk?"

"Let me finish. Twenty is done. You can't go back. The question is, why in the world would you want to? You are a mature woman. There is something to be said for that."

"Something like what? Comfort in extra flab? Extreme gratitude if a man happens to notice you exist?"

Eva clicked her tongue in an *India, India* kind of way. "Your problem is that you fail to understand your allure."

"What allure? According to Vaughn White, once a woman hits fifty she can bend over and kiss her allure goodbye. And he's not the only one who feels that way."

"The gospel according to Vaughn White," Eva said. "Vaughn is a fool, darling. And so is Tom Othmar." Eva walked over to her office chair and swiveled it in my direction. "Sit," she said.

I sat behind the lovely antique desk that Eva and I had found at an estate sale.

"What do you see?" Eva asked.

I stared at her. I had no idea what she was getting at. "An office?" I said.

"My office. The hub of a very successful real-estate business."

"Okay.".

"I've sold the most houses in the region two years running.

Last year, I won the realtor's award."

"You're very good at what you do."

"Ten years this September since I started this business."

"Ten years? Has it been that long?"

Eva nodded. "Ten years. Ten years since I sat in your kitchen fretting that I could never make it on my own. You said 'go for it', do you remember? You pointed out all the reasons why I'd be great in my own business. You helped me put together a business plan. You researched the best loans. You even found me a desk."

"This business is yours, Eva. I can't take credit for your success."

"This business wouldn't exist if not for you. If not for you, Patch would never have switched from business to pre-law because you are the one who talked Tom into letting Patch do what Patch needed to do. If not for you, Allie would never have had the gumption to go to Africa. Even Tom. Tom would still be working as a sales rep if not for you." Eva put her hands to either arm of the chair. "*That* is your allure. Sasha Peterson can't hold a Bic lighter to that. Sasha is nothing but a pretty package of boobs and legs in nice clothes."

I looked away. She'd made me cry. I didn't want to cry. "You are a wonderful friend," I said. I got up and hugged her.

"You bet your alluring ass I am." She held me out at arm's length. "Now let's find you a man who will appreciate you."

That was how I ended up taking a flying lesson.

If the flying lesson or, more to the point, the flight instructor, was supposed to help my self-esteem, it didn't work. I was afraid of small planes. I'd told Eva as much, to which she'd said that I'd told her I always wanted to fly. To Paris, I told her. In a jet plane. First Class with those little wine bottles. Eva can be pretty convincing, though, and a few Saturdays after school let out for the summer, I found myself in a hangar at the Tamsett Municipal Airport with Red Lansing.

Red looked like an older version of Alfred E Neuman. He had bright red hair speckled with gray and tonsured along the top of his head, a spate of freckles that would have made him cute if he were ten, and ears that probably could have flown the plane. He had a broad Texas accent and he called me little lady. He also informed me, straight away, that he'd already had four wives and wasn't planning on a fifth. "Just for the record," he said.

"Well, little lady, you ever been on a small craft before?"

We were standing next to Red's Cessna. It could have fit in my garage. "No," I said, both an answer to his question and also, no, I didn't particularly want to hop into a small craft with Red or anyone else.

"Well, little lady, climb on in and we'll show you how it's done."

He stroked the wheel as though it were an aphrodisiac. And I gathered from the way he explained all of the other doohickeys that he did have a strong affinity, an attraction, to the Cessna. They were all just doohickeys to me. I told Red as much.

Red chuckled and ran his fingers over what I think was the altimeter. "Don't you worry, little lady, you're in good hands," he said.

Soon we were soaring through clouds stacked like houses of cards, darting in between the layers. I could get used to this, I thought. Maybe there is something to this flying stuff after all. Maybe I'd even ask Red if I could take the wheel, or whatever the steering thingy was called. Maybe...Then the plane stalled.

The engine went dead. My thoughts dropped from high cloud fluttering to thudding doom. We were plunging through the air like a wet rock. I have never been fond of plunging. My stomach did a tango with my toes.

The engine hummed again and we began climbing. "Got to learn how to stall, little lady," Red shouted over the blessed loud din.

"You did that on purpose?" I asked. I was just a tad hysterical, but Red didn't seem to notice. He looked downright pleased with himself.

We swooped over the Tamsett River. Red dipped the plane sideways, making me grateful for the window glass because it was the only thing between me and oblivion. There were two men fishing in a row boat. We dipped close enough for me to read the Orvis brand name on the boat's side.

Red whooped. "How you like it so far?" he shouted.

The Cheerios I'd had for breakfast were sloshing around with the coffee I'd drunk to chase them down. It must have been terror that kept it all in check, because as soon as we hit the tarmac, I felt the gorge start to rise. I made a beeline for the hangar bathroom.

I'd like to say that I made it to the hangar bathroom. But the truth is another matter entirely. Not only did I not make it to the hole-in-the-wall that passed as a bathroom at the back of the hangar, in my haste I also managed to slip on some oil near the bathroom door. I landed on my right arm. A terrible shock of pain went through me and my already compromised stomach gave itself up all over the front of my crisp white blouse. I sat in the grease stain. My ruined clothes seemed beside the point. I wanted to board a real plane to Paris and start life anew on the Left Bank. I didn't want Red Lansing to saunter over and wrinkle his freckled nose at me.

Red handed me a dirty rag and pointed the way to the bathroom as though I hadn't understood that it was right behind me. I got up, my wrist throbbing, and hobbled through the threshold. I did the best I could to clean off my blouse left-handed, using borax and rust-colored water. Then I threw up in the sink for good measure.

Red stood at the door. "Little lady?" I was busy examining my wrist, which had turned an interesting shade of purple.

"I think I might need to go to the hospital."

Red eyed my arm from the door. "Hospital?" he asked as though he'd never heard of such a thing. He shook his head. "I can't leave. I got another lesson coming in." I looked at my arm, and then at Red. My horror must have shown, because he flushed the color of his thinning hair. "I'll call you," he said. "Make sure you're okay. It's probably nothing. Just a ding. A little ding."

I walked out of the hangar without saying goodbye. "You don't have to be ashamed," Red said to my retreating back. "Lots of folks lose their lunch the first time out. Happens."

I got into my Camry and drove to the ER, steering left handed while cradling my right hand on my thigh.

Mitch was on duty and he took me in right away. "You drove from the airport?" he asked.

"It's an automatic transmission," I explained.

"That must've hurt."

"A little." He touched the swollen spot and I said "Ouch," as though to illustrate.

Mitch had the arm x-rayed. He put the x-ray up so we could admire it together. "Chipped the bone," he said, "right here." He pointed to a tiny spot on an island along the archipelago of bones that was my wrist. "How did this happen again?" I retold the story, trying not to wince, as he splinted.

Chapter Nine

Days Of Percodan And Garlic

"Thanks," I said to Mitch when he'd finished. I stood up and headed for the door.

"Where are you going?"

"Home." I was thinking pajamas. I was thinking a gallon of Vermonty Python. I was thinking of wringing Eva's neck.

"You can't drive home."

"I drove here."

"That must've hurt," he repeated. "I'll get you something that might help." A minute later he came back with a blister pack of pills and a bottle of water. "Free sample of Percodan for dropping by," he said, handing it over.

"How am I going to get home if I take this?"

"This is a full service hospital. I'm calling you an ambulance." He caught the horrified look that must have crossed my face. "Seriously, I'll bring you home when my shift ends. Fifteen minutes and counting."

My wrist throbbed after all the handling and splinting, much the worse for wear. I swallowed down the pills. Sometime later, I floated around on the passenger seat of Mitch's car. It felt a little like an airplane ride. The pain was still being duly noted somewhere in my brain, but the rest of me didn't much care.

"Thank you so much," I said to Mitch, though the words kind of twisted and came out crooked. I opened the door to get out. The driveway was a long ways down and my legs didn't seem to reach.

"Whoa, there." Mitch came around to grab me under the arm in the nick of time. "Let's get you into the house before you break the other wrist."

We staggered to the door together. "Thank you so very much,"

I said.

"Did you take both pills in the pack?" Mitch asked.

"Why, yes. Yes, I did indeed."

"Ah. I didn't say one now, one later, as needed?"

"I don't recall."

"Oh, God."

"Problem?" I couldn't imagine that there would be or ever had been a problem.

"Mom?" Allie, by the look of her sweatshirt, had been in the garage working on Project Planter. Horace had declined our offer of fifty shoe planters, but Allie was excited enough by the idea to convince me to do a few prototypes. We'd shown them to Eva, who'd been delighted with our whimsy and had gotten us a table at the Caramel Mountain Crafts Fair. The problem was that whimsy came at turtle speed. Each shoe had to be lined in plastic and the plastic had to be fitted individually and glued in a way that didn't show. From there we filled each new planter with soil and flowers. Martha Stewart would have thought the whole thing labor intensive. We decided on one hundred planters for the crafts fair. At the current rate, we'd be ready for business in the year 2030.

It occurred to me that if it was time consuming to turn shoes into planters with two hands, it would be at least twice as time consuming to do it one handed. Though, truth be told, in my current Percodan-addled state, that didn't seem like much of a problem, either.

"Oh, dear," I said anyway, wondering how to tell Allie about my wrist. Not realizing that the splint might be a dead giveaway.

"What happened?" Allie asked as I let go of Mitch, or Mitch let go of me, and I sprawled onto the couch.

"I'm fine, honey. I'm just hunky-dory, okey-dokey? I could use a teeny nap, though." The couch went a little fuzzy as my head crashed into it.

I woke up with my head in a vise, my wrist on fire, and a giant hamster gnawing at my stomach lining. The good news was that the couch was no longer fuzzy. I heard voices and I followed the sound like bread crumbs through the dark forest. I was rewarded by my tribe, Allie and Patch and Mitch, all bustling around my kitchen.

"We heard you had a rough day, so we cooked," Patch said.

He pointed to a pot of goo bubbling on the stove. "It's supposed to be chicken soup."

"I told him we should have opened a can," Allie said.

Patch shook his head as he stirred the brew. "It had to be the real thing. I found Granny's recipe in that file you keep."

"Granny Smirtoff's recipe? You cooked?" If it weren't for the throbbing of my head and wrist and the fact that the smell inside the kitchen would ward off vampires for a hundred-mile radius, it would have been one of life's perfect little moments.

"Can you excuse me?" I said. I'd taken a step closer and the smell had assaulted my nose. I barely made it to the bathroom. When I looked up from where I knelt by the toilet, there was Mitch standing by the door.

"Overdose," he said. "You were only supposed to take one of those pills."

"Oh, dear God." I sat down next to the bowl.

"Head throbbing?"

"Yes. And my arm, too. My stomach feels better, though."

Mitch rooted through the medicine cabinet and pulled out some Tylenol. "These should help," he said.

I waved away his hand. "I'm done with drugs. They ruin your life."

"You don't look ruined," he said, taking out two pills and handing them to me. "It's been at least four hours, so a couple Tylenol won't hurt you."

"Four hours?" I took the pills and the water Mitch handed me.

"I don't think I can face the soup," I confessed once I'd swallowed.

"I'm not sure what they did to it," Mitch said. "but I take it you didn't teach your kids to cook."

"No," I said. The smell wafted into the bathroom. "At least it's not making me sick anymore."

"There's a great endorsement. Our soup won't make you heave."

"Did you help?" I asked, feeling terrible about feeling terrible.

"Hell, no. I watched you sleep and made sure you didn't lapse into a coma."

"That was very kind of you," I said.

64

Allie ladled the soup into bowls and placed them on the counter. I sat and played with my spoon while she dipped hers in and took a tiny sip. "It tastes a little funny," she said.

Mitch and I looked at each other. He hadn't sampled his bowl, either. Patch took a sip and looked as abashed as Allie. "I followed the recipe," he said. "You don't think Granny left something out, do you?"

I'd made that soup a hundred times. It was the best chicken soup anyone could make. Good for what ails you, Granny used to say. I took a sip and nearly had to take another trip to the bathroom. "Garlic," I said, grabbing the glass of water and chugging some. "It's a little heavy on garlic."

"I told you," Allie said.

"I followed the recipe exactly," Patch said.

"It's okay," I said, making ready to endure another sip.

"Don't eat that." Patch snatched away the bowl. "Allie's right. It sucks."

"How much garlic did you put in?" I said, sticking a toe into the raging waters of soup-making.

"One clove," Patch said.

"That sounds about right," I said. Then it hit me. "One clove or one bulb?"

"Bulb? Clove?" Patch looked puzzled.

"Honey," I said as gently as I could. "One bulb is about thirty cloves."

"Thirty?"

"Give or take," I said.

"Jeeze, Patch," Allie said. "A whole bulb? Even I know better than that."

"If you're so frigging smart why didn't you say something?"

"Somebody had to pick up the prescription." Allie marched over to her purse and pulled a cylinder of pills from it. "Percodan," she said, setting the bottle next to my water glass. "Want some?"

My stomach settled despite the soup. I wanted for nothing. My wrist throbbed, to be sure, but really, it didn't matter. I had Patch and Allie and Mitch to cook for me and buy me drugs and make sure I didn't lapse into a coma. What else could I possibly need or want? The thought brought tears to my eyes.

"Mom, are you okay?" Allie asked.

All three of them looked at me with concern and— dare I say

it— love. "I'm really, really happy," I said. And I started to cry all the harder.

Chapter Ten

The Great Shoe Caper

"We'll never make it," I said to Allie. We were staring at ten shoes, sneakers all, lined up on the work bench in our garage turned potting factory.

"Only eighty more," Allie said. "We've got three days."

I picked up one of the sneakers with my good hand. We wouldn't get eighty done in three months, even if both my arms were functioning. The best I could do one-handed was scoop dirt into the plastic-lined opening. Allie was game, but it had taken an hour to do three shoes, an entire day to do twenty counting those three shoes. I was starting to feel like the princess in *Rumpelstiltskin*. Where was that little guy when you need him, anyway?

It wasn't Rumpelstiltskin but Eva who came to our rescue. Dressed, as always, to the nines in cream slacks and a dark shirt with heels to match, she surveyed our Armageddon. "This whole Martha-Stewartness goes against my beliefs," she said "but, hell, I did have a hand in creating this monster."

"And breaking my Mom," Allie added.

"I did not break your mother."

"It wasn't Eva's fault," I incanted at the same time.

"Who made her take that stupid flying lesson?" Allie said, jumping to my defense. I'm not sure that I wanted defending.

"No one held a gun to her head," Eva said. "I was just the facilitator." She turned to me looking somewhat apologetic. This was Eva, though, and apologies were as against her beliefs as Martha-Stewart-type projects. "I hate to bring this up," she said, "but Red wants payment for the lesson."

"The first lesson is free," I said reciting what Eva had told me. "A free flight to see if you like flying."

"Apparently, that's only if you actually like flying and sign on to work on your pilot's license."

"Since when?" I said.

Eva shrugged. "Fine print, I guess."

"You should sue him," Allie said, " for pain and suffering."

It was true, Red Lansing had caused me to suffer. But then again, so had J. Hank Sorenson. So had Thomas P. Othmar and so had Vaughn White. It seemed like the entire male over-fifty population of Massachusetts was out to cause pain and suffering to poor, unsuspecting, mature women like myself. And I was not planning on suing any of them. What would be the point? I didn't want to sue Red Lansing. I wanted to forget Red Lansing.

And I would have forgotten Red Lansing if he hadn't called the next day.

"How's that hand, little lady?" he asked.

"Broken," I said.

"No!" he said. As if he didn't know. As if he hadn't spoken to Eva and heard that I'd be in a cast for the next six weeks. "I hate to bring this up, you being one-armed and all," he said. Then he brought it up anyway. The flying lesson. He had overhead. Airplane fuel didn't come cheap.

"Take it up with my son. He's a lawyer," I said, bluffing. I didn't want to sue, but I wasn't beyond threatening small claims court. At the very least, I figured it would get Red off my case.

It didn't. The very next day he showed up at my house. The craft fair was one day away and Eva and Allie were working harder than Santa's elves on Christmas Eve to make one hundred shoe planters a reality. I'd been assigned to fetching iced tea and cookies, something I could do one-handed.

"Let me help you out there, little lady." Red took the pitcher of iced tea from me once I'd already made it and was carrying it out of the house. Then he reminded me again of the three hundred dollars I owed him. "I got overhead," he said. "Jet fuel costs money."

"So I've heard," I said. We, or Eva and Allie, were on planters number eighty-one and eighty-two. The finished products were lined proudly on the garage shelves, waiting to be brought to market.

"What's all this?" Red asked, surveying the enterprise from the garage door.

"Santa's workshop," I answered. And it did look a little like the North Pole, or some other beehive of activity, what with potting soil spilling from the workbench, and singleton shoes stacked in every recess, and flats of petunias and geraniums littering the floor. In the middle of the bustle were Eva wielding a staple gun and Allie with a garden trowel.

"Well, this is wonderful." Red went over to inspect the finished product. "You little ladies got yourself a gold mine right here."

"Why, Red," Eva put down the gun and went into charm mode. "I'm so glad you like our work."

"Like it? Why, it's pure genius!" Red eyed my daughter as she placed a petunia into a waiting Mary Jane. "And who, may I ask, are you?"

"That's Allie," Eva said, being eternally helpful.

"Well, well, well. Allie. Aren't you about as pretty as those flowers?" Red stood behind her, put both arms around her and took the trowel. "Maybe you could show me how it's done," he said.

Allie, annoyed, stepped out of his way. I had a more visceral reaction. A deep-seated angry sort of reaction that rose from somewhere in the vicinity of my diaphragm. I grabbed the garden trowel from Red with my good hand and shoved it into his chest.

"Get out of my garage," I said, holding the point of the spade to his heart.

"Now, little lady," Red said. "I was just flirting. I like flirting."

I pushed the tip of the spade. "Out now."

Red raised his arms as though the spade were a pistol. "Fine," he said. "I'm going. But you ain't got much of a sense of humor there, little lady." He turned around at the mouth of the garage. "Three hundred dollars, darling. I know you won't forget."

"Yikes," Allie said.

"You're not going to pay him, are you?" Eva asked.

I surveyed the garage. I'd had an idea. An awful, terrible, wonderful idea. "Oh, I plan on paying," I said, "only not in cash."

"You want to do what?" Patch asked. He and Mitch were loading the planters onto the back of the truck we'd borrowed from Eva's latest man, Dave, who ran his own construction firm.

"Is it legal?" I asked. "I mean, could I get in trouble?"

69

Patch thought about it. "I don't see how," he said. "Though I don't think that four thousand nine hundred single shoes count as legal tender."

"Maybe they could be considered raw material," Mitch held up one of the finished planters. "These things are really nice."

"If he wants planters, he's going to have to make them himself," Allie said, holding up a blistered hand.

Allie's blisters were not for naught. As it turned out, Mitch wasn't the only one who thought the planters were nice. All one hundred of them sold on the very first day of the two-day craft fair. One of the buyers was Luce Morgan, the eighty-year-old matriarch of Morgan Family Farm. "I could sell a hundred of these at the farm stand in a month," she said in a voice painted with gravel.

"Really?" asked Allie, looking fresh-hatched next to Luce.

"We can't make anymore," Eva said.

"Actually," I said, "there is someone who may be interested in taking over the business." I had Allie write Red's name and Fly Rite Flight School on a piece of paper. "He's in the yellow pages, under aviation." Luce stashed the name in her beaded purse and walked off.

Allie picked up a red pump planter with purple petunias. "Mr. Lansing did say it was a million dollar idea," she said.

"And we're donating the raw material. Gifting, you might say," I added.

By day's end, we'd passed Red Lansing's name along to six more customers, all of them small-business owners who wanted to feature shoe planters in their stores.

Stealth delivery of four thousand nine hundred singleton shoes to an airplane hangar was no easy proposition. Luckily, Red was out giving another g-force demonstration to an unsuspecting prospect. We managed to pile the shoes into the hangar without being discovered. As a bonus, we left potting soil and sheeting. A gesture of good will, you might say.

Red didn't take it as a gesture of good anything. He came to my door that evening in a less than jovial mood. I wasn't in the best of spirits myself. Allie and I had just sat down to dinner and I was having the usual trouble eating left-handed.

"Can I cut it for you?" Allie asked.

"It's salmon, Allie. You don't cut salmon."

My daughter rolled her eyes at me. "Can I fork it for you?" she said. I rolled my eyes at her. All of this eye rolling would surely have gone somewhere if not for the incessant knocking on the front door. Banging, actually, is a better way to describe the noise. Incessant banging followed by leaning in on the door bell. I stopped rolling and started to wonder if I should answer. It sounded like assault come to call.

I did, of course, get up and go to the door. And there stood Red, his face giving meaning to his name. "Mrs. Othmar," he said, the formality coming from between clenched teeth like froth.

"Mr. Lansing," I said. The screen door was shut between us. I thought twice about opening it. In fact, I was relieved to see that it was locked.

"Well?" he asked, stamping his feet on the welcome mat like a bull about to charge.

I checked the little lock again. "Well," I said.

"I ought to have called the police but I'm too much of gentleman for that. I don't like to see a lady go to jail."

"Go to jail? For what?"

"You know damned well," Red said. The words exploded from his mouth.

"You didn't like my gift?" I said.

That did it. He charged the door with a fierce blinding rage, nearly taking it off the hinges. It reminded me of that old story about huffing and puffing and blowing the house down. Only this was more like rattling and stomping and shaking the screen door down. Red actually shouted, "Let me in."

The noise sent Allie running in from the kitchen. "Call the police," I told her. My voice was a lot less quivery than the Jell-o my body had turned into. I silently thanked the makers of the screen door for manufacturing such a sturdy product.

At the word police, the rattling stopped. Red stood staring at the two of us, me backing from the door, Allie behind me with her cell phone at the ready. The bluster in his face drained as though a plug had been pulled somewhere in the vicinity of his neck.

"You wouldn't dare," he said.

"You are battering my door. You are threatening me and my poor defenseless little daughter." If Allie hadn't been so shaken she would have rolled her eyes at me.

"You. You." Red didn't finish. I guess it was to his credit that

71

he wouldn't call a woman lewd names, even if he wanted to with every fiber of his being. "You will hear from my lawyer."

"My son's a lawyer," I said, one-upping him as though this were a hand of Texas Hold 'em.

"Humph," he said. He muttered something under his breath as he turned and stomped off the porch. His pants caught on the rhododendron on his way down the stairs. He stumbled and did a little pirouette to recover. Then, hunching his shoulders against some unseen strong wind, he huffed off into the wilds of Easterly Street.

"He could have hurt you," Patch said when I told him about it the next day.

I raised my arm. "He's already done damage. What I want to know is, does he have a case?" Patch bit his lip. "Oh God," I said. "he's going to sue me."

"I'm not sure that he can. I've just never come across a case of..."

"Joking?" I said. "I mean, it might have been a little mean, but it counts as a practical joke, right?"

Patch bit his lip again.

Chapter Eleven

Parts Is Parts

I spent the next few days worried. It was Eva who saved me from certain despair. We were out on our usual walk. She was talking about her ten year anniversary. "There's this wonderful new martini bar," she said. "You and I are going to go there to celebrate. My treat. So mark your calendar."

I mumbled something like that would be fun.

"Are you still fretting about Red Lansing?" she asked, as we chugged up the hill on Newman Street on the last leg of our morning walk.

"I hate the idea of going to court. Bad enough that I'm getting divorced. Now I'm getting sued."

"The man is all bluster. He won't sue."

"How can you be so sure?"

Eva smiled beatifically at me. "He won't sue. He's got too much pride for that. Do you think that he wants to admit that he's been bested by a little lady? The shoes would humiliate him, were it to become public. That's the kind of man he is."

"What if you and I have no idea what kind of man Red is?"

"Then there's the Canada matter." Eva took a dramatic pause, waiting.

I knew my line. "What Canada matter?"

"It seems that our Mr. Lansing has imported a few prescription drugs from our neighbors to the north. Nothing too serious, but enough to get him into some hot water. So I do think he's going to be a good boy."

I didn't want to ask where Eva had gotten her information. She had a better network than the CIA. We were just turning the corner of Easterly. I could see our houses through the broad maples that lined the sidewalk. And there was something else, something twinkling between the leaves and boughs. "What in the world?" I said, breaking into a jog. The sun poked through the clouds. The twinkle brightened. Eva jogged behind me. We both stopped short at my front yard.

"Holy shit," Eva said. "It's a car graveyard."

My front lawn was littered with bright and shiny metal objects. I'm not handy with engines, I couldn't have told a carburetor from a muffler, but you didn't have to be a mechanic to recognize that these were engine parts. Big engine parts, from what I'd guess were big engines.

Eva and I picked our way through them, a minefield of big honking engine parts. "Holy shit," Eva said again. Which, really, was about the only thing that could have been said.

A post-it note was stuck to my front door. *A little gift*, it said, *from me to you.* It wasn't signed. It didn't need to be.

Eva started to laugh. "Touché," she said. "you've got to hand it to him."

I was not nearly as amused. I picked up my cell phone then stuffed it back into my pocket. "I won't give him the satisfaction," I said.

"I think he likes you," Eva said.

"I think he's an asshole."

"Shocking language for a kindergarten teacher."

I plopped down on the front step and surveyed the damage. "How am I going to get rid of this stuff?"

"Don't worry," Eva said, "I know someone."

An hour later, two guys from Rick and Nick's Used Auto Parts drove up in a dusty red truck. They jumped from the cab and surveyed the front lawn as though Santa had lost track of time and had hit my house mid-summer.

"You the lady who called?" asked the shorter of the two.

"That would be me." The taller one smiled. He had no front teeth. "India," I said "India Othmar." And I offered up my hand.

The short one rubbed his hand on his shirt before taking mine. "I'm Rick. This here is my brother, Nick. So, you got some parts for us?" he asked, as though he hoped there were more in the basement.

"There they are," I said, opening my arms to the bounty on the lawn.

Rick and Nick walked around the parts, poking and prodding, then stood at the far end of the lawn with their heads together. Rick ambled back towards me.

"Problem," he said.

"Problem?" I asked.

He nodded. "Problem."

"What problem?"

"These here, they ain't standard auto issue."

"Standard auto issue?"

"They ain't your standard auto parts. Fact is, they probably ain't auto parts at all. Nick there, he thinks they come off a plane." Rick nodded to Nick, who nodded back.

"A plane?" I said.

"A plane. We don't deal in plane parts."

"No plane parts?"

"No plane parts."

I was going to ask why not, but it seemed kind of pointless.

"But," Rick said, "as you seem to be a nice lady and all, we can take them off your hands at cost."

"At cost?"

Rick held up a hand as though to stop traffic and ambled back over to Nick. They bowed their heads together again, then Rick ambled back over to me. "Three hundred dollars ought to cover it."

I was in no position to haggle. I had a truck load of plane parts fertilizing my front lawn. "Fine," I said. "I'll write you a check."

"No checks," Rick said.

"No checks?"

"No checks. We got a cash-only business."

"I don't have that much cash," I said.

"We can come back at a more convenient time. Next week, maybe."

"Next week?"

"We only do pickups on Thursday. Today being Thursday and all, I guess you could say you got lucky."

"Thursdays only?"

Rick shrugged towards Nick. "We only got the big truck on Thursdays. Long story…"

"Okay. Okay… Wait right here. I'll get you the money. Wait here." I sprinted into the house and riffled through my purse. Forty two dollars and fifty-four cents. "Wait right there," I said. I dialed Eva.

Eva was on the other end of town, doing what's known in the real estate business as a caravan, where all the realtors get together and tour houses new to the market. "Cash?" she asked for the second time.

"Cash," I said. I heard her slam the car door, the radio on in the background.

"Sorry, honey. Cash is so twentieth century. I can't believe they don't take plastic. Everybody takes plastic."

Eva, it seemed, had already stepped up to the plate once for operation cleanup and was about to sit the rest of the operation out in the dugout. Or in a 4BR with Jacuzzi colonial on Brandt Street.

I hung up and waved at Rick and Nick. Allie was in Boston interviewing for a job at the Franklin Park Zoo. Patch was working, also in Boston. Piggy bank? Nope, not three hundred dollars worth. I'd already deposited the shoe money. In a last-ditch desperate move, I called Mitch Tinker.

Mitch, it turned out, had worked a double shift at the hospital and was spending his Thursday morning sleeping.

"I'm sorry. Did I wake you?" I asked, as though his groggy hello hadn't clued me in. "It's India."

"Yes, I know. And yes, you did wake me up."

"This may sound strange..." I began. There was a patient silence at the other end of the line. I thought I caught a yawn. "This may sound strange..." I said again.

"India?" Mitch asked. "did you want something?"

"Do you have any cash?"

"Cash?"

"Yes. Cash. Money." The phone clunked. I heard fumbling. "Mitch?"

"Still here," he said. "checking my wallet. Twenty-five dollars."

"That's all?"

"Twenty-five dollars and two singles in my jeans. Twenty-seven dollars."

"Oh no," I said. I waved to the auto guys.

"Problem?" Mitch asked.

"I need three hundred dollars."

"Flying lessons?"

76

"A related issue," I said.

"I've got a bank card," he said.

"They don't take plastic. Cash only."

"Who are they and why do they want three hundred dollars in cash?" It sounded as though Mitch were fully awake now.

"Rick and Nick. They only take cash."

"Of course they do." There was a slight pause. "I'll tell you what. I'll drop by the ATM on the way to your house."

"Could you? Oh, God, Mitch. That would be stellar. That would be fabulous."

"India? Who, exactly, are Rick and Nick?"

"Nice porch you got here, missus." Rick said. Nick nodded. "Pretty yard, too." I looked around. A lot prettier without the shiny engine parts, but I guessed that pretty is in the eye of the beholder. I'd held Rick and Nick off for twenty minutes, offering up lemonade and cookies, when the posse, AKA Mitch in his shiny blue Honda, arrived with three hundred dollars in crisp twenties fresh from the ATM.

The bills were counted and deposited into Rick's shirt pocket. And Rick and Nick began Operation Spare Parts Cleanup.

"I owe you big time," I said to Mitch as the last of the airliner was collected and Rick gave a friendly tug of his John Deere cap before hauling off with Nick riding shotgun.

"You owe me three hundred bucks and lunch at Friendly's, " he said.

"Lunch at Friendly's? You're easy."

He opened the passenger side of his car. "I got me a hankering for a Buffalo Chicken sandwich, little lady," he said.

We stopped at the ATM, mine this time, at my insistence. I took out three hundred in cash and handed the money to Mitch. "This ought to cover lunch," he said.

"No way. I owe you lunch," I said.

"No way. You are tapped out." He was joking, but it was true. It burned my bottom that I'd ended up paying for the flying lesson anyway.

It also burned my bottom that I had trouble picking up my tuna cheese melt with my left hand. Tomato dripped from the side. Mitch told a story about a guy who came into the ER to get his nipple pierced. "Can you imagine?" he said, "One hundred dollar co-pay and he thinks we're the Piercing Pagoda." Mitch looked up. I was embarrassed by the drippy mess I'd created. He grabbed the plate from me, deftly cut the sandwich into bite sized pieces, and handed me a piece.

"I hate this," I said, feeling nearly frustrated enough to cry.

"A few weeks and you'll be able to cut your own sandwiches again," he said.

"A few weeks. I can't even imagine what I'd do if it were permanent. School starts in a few weeks. I can't imagine managing a roomful of kindergartners left handed." I delivered the sliver of sandwich to my mouth. Mitch handed me another piece. Our fingers brushed and I felt this little jolt travel up my arm. Stop it, I told myself. Much as I'd told myself to stop it every time that happened around Mitch Tinker. I valued Mitch's friendship. I'd come to count on it, really. And harboring a school girl crush was not good for that friendship.

I took the sandwich piece from him. Mitch, maybe sensing my discomfort, slid the plate back to me. "You did a fine job with the tuna melt," I said to cover the awkward moment that started to bloom between us.

"Thank you, little lady. I aim to take good care." His head dipped towards his salad.

"You have been, haven't you? Taking care of me?" I asked.

He looked up at me with such tenderness that the awkward moment threatened to make a comeback. "What I mean is, you and Patch and Allie and Eva. I don't know what I would have done without you these past few months."

Mitch speared a piece of chicken and the awkwardness budded a little.

"I'm not saying this very well. What I mean to say is thank you. Your friendship means the world to me."

Mitch put down his fork and took my hand. His eyes, and the feelings I had, that I wanted to dive into those eyes, made it hard to look at him without coming undone. "You mean the world to me, too," he said.

Chapter Twelve

Outed In Africa

Allie was home from Boston by the time Mitch and I got back from lunch. "Guess what?" she asked as Mitch drove away. She was as excited as an eight-year-old with a new bike.

"What?" I asked, squeezing her shoulder. We walked into the house together.

"You are looking at the new elephant lady at Franklin Park Zoo."

I didn't want to burst Allie's happy balloon, but two months ago, she'd been teary eyed with hatred of elephants and their ilk. "I thought you were through with elephants," I said.

"I guess it wasn't the elephants. I kind of like the buggers. It was Africa. Or, more to the point, what happened in Africa."

"What happened in Africa?" I considered the worst. I'd seen the movies and read the articles. Africa was rife with insurrection. Twelve-year-old boys carried Uzis and machetes. There were starving babies in fly-infested hovels, their mothers thinned by AIDS. When Allie had first told me about wanting to go to Africa, I'd been afraid for her. But Allie had been so wide-eyed and passionate. Allie had been so ready to go that I packed away my misgivings and helped her pack her bags.

"What happened in Africa is complicated," Allie said. I poured us each a lemonade and we sat at the kitchen table. "I met someone. In Africa."

That was complicated. And simple. Oldest story in the world. "And it ended badly," I offered.

"It's more than that," Allie said. She was looking at me as though I'd never in my life known heartache. I was deciding whether or not to bring up Tom and the thirty-odd year marriage that had been set on fire and left to smolder in ruins, when she said something so unexpected that I nearly spilled my lemonade. "That someone, in Africa? Her name was Lydia."

"Lydia?" I said. I tried to wrap my mind around this new development. In truth, I think I'd always know about Allie's leanings. It was one of those things I'd known without really knowing. In the same way that I'd known Tom had cheated on me any number of times. The signs were there in both cases. In both cases I'd blithely ignored them, telling myself that I was just being silly. By the look of Allie, she'd been nearly as surprised as I was. And not surprised at all.

"Lydia was the head of the research team," Allie said as though that explained everything. "Only, her, shall we say, romantic interests were different from mine. She fancied a bush pilot. Luis."

"Luis?" I asked.

"I never told her how I felt. I mean, why humiliate yourself, you know? But I couldn't stay. I couldn't stay and share a tent and stare at elephants all day as though nothing had changed."

"So you don't hate elephants?" I asked, mostly because I didn't know what else to say.

"No. I mean, Lydia and Africa and elephants were all tied in together, you know?" Allie stirred her finger through her lemonade. "I know this is a lot to take in," she said, as much to herself as to me. I nodded. Maybe my little girl had found herself. In her own way. What I wanted was for Allie to be happy. Then I thought about Mitch. And I started to laugh.

"What's so funny?" Allie asked, looking offended.

"Mitch," I chortled. "I thought you had a crush on him."

Allie starred at me. Then she started laughing, too. When we finally stopped giggling, Allie said, "Mitch is the one who introduced me to Liz."

"Liz?"

"Zoo vet at the Franklin Park Zoo. She and Mitch were college buddies."

"Zoo vet? Liz?"

Allie nodded slowly. "She told me about the job?" When I still didn't get it, Allie said, "After we went out for drinks. Together." She was still nodding at me.

The shoe finally dropped. "Oh, drinks. Together. You and Liz."

We sat in an awkward silence again. "So, you like her?" I finally ventured.

"She's terrific," Allie said.

"And Mitch introduced you?"

"He's got a future at Match.com if the whole medical thing doesn't work out," she said.

"So I guess I shouldn't hire the DJ for your wedding to Mitch," I said.

"Not going to happen," Allie said, smiling. "Though maybe you could marry him."

I nearly knocked over my lemonade again. Allie laughed. "I'm kidding, Mom. I'm kidding."

Chapter Thirteen

Free At Last

My cast was scheduled to come off the day before school started. This was a good thing, a very good thing, because I don't know how I would have managed two groups of twenty-two brand-new-to-school kindergartners with a broken wrist. Allie started her new job, Eva was showing houses to a couple from Philadelphia, and Patch was on another trip, to Dallas this time, on the appointed day, so I drove myself over to the hospital.

The x-ray showed complete healing, the technician sawed through the cast, and eureka! I was a two-handed woman again. I don't think I've ever been as grateful for working body parts.

I felt downright euphoric, and because I wanted to share the joy with someone and because Mitch happened to work on the first floor, I sauntered down to show off my new arm. The ER crawled with the sick and wounded. Activity whirled around me. I spied Mitch's head behind an examining curtain seconds before I ran into a nurse. The nurse had, unfortunately, been carrying a tray of something I'd guess was suturing stuff. The tray upended and everything on it clattered to the floor. I stood there in shock for a minute, then crawled under the main desk to retrieve a pair of scissors that had taken refuge under the counter.

I looked up to see Mitch standing there, a bemused look on his face. I held up my right arm. "Got the cast off," I said.

"Nice," he said as he helped me up.

I handed him the scissors, then began apologizing profusely to him, to the nurse I'd run over, to the man waiting behind the curtain. I would have apologized to the entire waiting room for being a wrecking ball had I been given the chance. "I'm going home before I cause any more damage," I said in conclusion. I nearly backed out of the place. I kowtowed to the door and made a break for the car. Home. That was exactly where I would go.

I'd go home and I'd finish getting ready for my kindergartners. Maybe we could do a hospital field trip. Twenty-two five year olds could not possibly cause more chaos than their teacher just had.

After planning out opening day, without the field trip, I made beef stroganoff using Granny Smirtoff's recipe. I made it just because I could. I looked forward to eating it with two hands. I called Eva and asked if she wanted in on good food, but she had a date with Dave.

I set a pretty table for Allie and myself, good china, the real silver flatware that I polished to a sheen, a linen table cloth. We would have an elegant girls' night in. Allie called as I was cutting bread. She'd be late. There was an elephant emergency.

"One of our females has an ingrown toenail," she said. "I need to stay with her."

"You're a good elephant lady," I said.

"Oh, gosh. Your cast. How did it go?"

I told her it went swimmingly, but I could tell that she wasn't really listening. I didn't tell her about the stroganoff. Why ruin an elephant toenail emergency with guilt?

I sat down to eat all by my lonesome, feeling pretty darned sorry for myself, even if that self could use a fork and cut her own meat. I was about halfway through when Mitch rang the doorbell.

I'd embarrassed myself so completely at his workplace that I apologized yet again when I let him in. "Made my day," he said. He held out a bottle of chardonnay. "Little-get-the-cast-off gift." We brought the wine into the kitchen. Mitch lifted the lid off the pot. "That smells terrific," he said.

"Beef stroganoff," I said. "To celebrate my new found independence."

"Ah, glad I had the foresight to bring wine," he said. Then he glanced toward the dining room. "Sorry," he said.

"About the wine?"

"About interrupting."

"Oh. Also new found independence. Only Allie couldn't make dinner."

"Allie?"

"I considered just not. I hate eating alone. But school starts tomorrow and my arm is all better and I cooked." Mitch looked at me curiously. "Have you eaten?" I asked. It occurred to me that he probably hadn't. That he'd probably had to stay late at the hospital re-sterilizing the stuff I'd dropped.

"No, actually, I haven't," Mitch said, confirming my suspicions.

I opened the wine with my two dear, good hands and poured us each a glass. "I'm really glad you happened by. Did I mention I hate eating alone?" I handed Mitch one of the glasses. Another thought occurred. "Oh, God. You didn't have plans, did you? I mean, you don't have to keep me company."

"I did have plans," he took a sip of wine. "Big plans. I was going to zap an entire package of bagel bites and watch *CSI* reruns."

"No kidding? That's what I have planned for tomorrow night." I said.

Mitch raised his glass. "Here's to good company," he said.

We were just finishing dinner when the doorbell did an encore. A puffy sleep-deprived version of Red had replaced the angry version I'd seen after the great shoe incident. Which was, of course, followed by the big mechanical dump. I hadn't seen Red since that night. I wanted to let bygones be bygones. I figured we were even and that he'd gone back to importing contraband from Toronto and other exotic places. Needless to say, I was less than thrilled to find him gracing my threshold yet again, especially considering the fact that he was staring at me like a rabid raccoon.

"What are you trying to do?" he said, before I could even say howdy.

"You're interrupting dinner," I said.

"I can't sleep at night waiting for the other shoe to fall. You got your revenge. You got your payback."

"Payback? Revenge? What are you talking about?"

"You know damned well those parts were from me," he whispered.

"You got me good, Red. Cost me three hundred dollars to clean up the mess."

"Not less than you deserve, little lady. I couldn't get my plane into the hangar for a week. And then there were the calls, at least a dozen of 'em, from crazy women all over the state wanting to order planters. I had to change my damn phone number. And I still haven't seen the three hundred you owe me."

"Please tell me you're kidding about the three hundred," I said.

"It'd be worth three hundred to me if you call it off," he said.

"Call it off?"

"Whatever it is you got planned."

I worked hard at keeping a straight face. "Deal," I said. "And no guff about the three hundred dollars. I'm a teacher. I don't make a fortune, you know." I threw him a hard stare. He actually backed up a step.

And that's when Mitch came up to the door and asked if I wanted any more wine.

Red's jaw dropped towards the porch floor. "Good God, little lady," he said.

"Something wrong?" I asked.

"*This* is the dinner I interrupted?" he asked. "I mean, I know that you've got needs and all, what with your husband throwing you over for some little hoochie-coochie. And God knows you got a revenge streak wide as the Mississippi Delta, but Holy Dear God, you're playing with boys now? Je-sus."

I glanced at Mitch, who looked as though Red had set him on fire. I held up a hand, because I thought a fight might break out. And I didn't need any more scenes. Besides, I could fend for myself. "Go home," I said, as though commanding a big dog. "Don't ever set foot on my property again or shoes in your hangar will be the least of your troubles."

"You don't scare me, little lady," Red said.

"INS," I said, "FBI, FDA, CIA." I almost spouted CSI, but Red said that I was totally insane and took off before I could.

"Remind me never to cross you," Mitch said, as we watched Red's truck pull into the night.

I was nearly too embarrassed to face Mitch. Upending a suture kit had been bad enough, but this… I mean, here we were having a friendly dinner. And here was Red, turning it into something sordid. I did face Mitch though. I owed him an apology.

"That bit about…You're not a boy," I said.

Mitch smiled. "Nice of you to acknowledge that."

"And Red Lansing is an idiot. An idiot who jumps to conclusions." I could feel my face go hot. Mitch grinned at me. "I guess it is kind of funny," I said.

"I don't think it's funny at all." Mitch took my hand and

kissed the place where the cast had been. Which, had I wanted to delude myself, could have been misconstrued as a friendly kiss. The next kiss, though, was a direct hit. On the lips, with feeling, and there was no misconstruing that at all.

Mitch took my chin in his hand. "I've wanted to do that ever since you showed up in my ER," he said.

"I don't know what to say," I stuttered out.

"Maybe you should think about it," Mitch said. "I'll go home and you can think about it." He fished his car keys from his pocket and let himself out the door. Halfway down the stairs he stopped and turned. "Don't think too long," he said. Then he was gone.

I did think about it. I thought it about it up and down and sideways. I thought about Red's reaction, not that it mattered. I thought about what Patch would think, which mattered a whole lot. I thought about Eva and Allie and even about Tom and Marissa. I thought about everything except the one thing I wouldn't let myself dwell on: that when Mitch had gone out the door I'd wanted to say *Wait*. I'd wanted to hurl myself at him and tackle him in the rhododendrons. That kind of thinking was far too dangerous and I wouldn't let my mind wander there. Not much, anyway.

When Allie came home a few hours later, I was sipping the last of the wine and still thinking about it.

"Celebration," I said, when she asked about the leftover feast on the table. I held up my new good arm.

"Oh, God. You did this for us, didn't you? I'm sorry."

"Oh, it's fine. Besides, you wouldn't want to have missed out on an elephant toenail emergency."

"It was pretty intense," Allie said. I reheated leftovers and she talked a mile a minute about Liz and the elephant. "And then there was all this blood. From a toenail. Liz says it's…" And she stopped.

"What did Liz say?" I asked.

"Why are there two used plates? And two wine glasses?" Allie asked.

I stuffed the incriminating evidence into the dishwater. "Oh, this," I said, trying to sound casual despite the coronary. "Mitch dropped by. I fed him."

"You got him drunk." Allie picked up the empty wine bottle.

I grabbed the bottle from her. "I did not. We had dinner. He

86

just happened by, that's all."

"Okay." Allie picked up a dishtowel. "You're funny when you get flustered."

"I am not flustered."

"Right," Allie said. Then she launched into another chapter of Liz and the elephant toe.

I woke up in the middle of the night, whatever dream I'd had lost to consciousness but still spinning my heart. After five months of sleeping alone, I had finally started sleeping again. I'd finally stopped the Tom tape that looped nightly through my brain. Or, more to the point, the Tom and Sasha tape. I'd replayed, over and over, that day last winter. It had been a Saturday. I'd gone shopping in Boston. Things had been a little tense with Tom and me; he'd been working long hours. There was a distance between us, a distance I thought I'd created and that I should remedy. I'd surprise him; we'd go out to lunch. So I'd gone to his office. Surprise! No one in the front office, so I'd gone right to Tom's door. Only the door was locked. There were noises. Stupid India, even then all I thought was who is using Tom's office for illicit sex? I knocked on the door. The noise stopped. I said *"Hello?"* There was shuffling. Tom answered. His tie was off. His collar askew. There was Sasha sitting in the chair by his desk, her hair a mess. "India!" He sounded almost angry. As though I was the guilty party. I ran out. He shouted that he could explain. He could explain.

That night, he came home as though nothing was wrong. I'd packed his suitcases. I had them by the door. I was sitting in the living room, drinking scotch on ice. I don't even like scotch. "I can explain," he said again.

"How long has this been going on?" I asked. It occurred to me that this was a song lyric.

"India," he said.

"How long?" I demanded.

"Don't do this," he said. But it was too late. Too late. I threw the Waterford glass at the wall near the door and buried my face in my hands so I wouldn't have to look at him. I heard the glass shatter, a sound my heart might have made had it been audible.

"Do you love her?" I asked. He didn't answer me. I heard the front door slam. I heard the car start.

I'd played that movie a thousand times. I'd finally gotten it to stop being the feature presentation. And now, here was a new movie. The Mitch movie. Mitch kissing me. Mitch telling me that I could think about it. And me, seesawing like a three-legged rocking horse, yes, oh yes, and no, my God, how could I? Back and forth.

Chapter Fourteen

Bad Dates And Good Weed

Lack of sleep is not a good thing when you are introducing yourself to a roomful of kindergartners. There they were, all bright-eyed and eager. And there I was, Mrs. Othmar, teacher and part-time zombie. Luckily, I'd had this gig for twenty years. I could fake it if I had to.

I nodded my way through both the AM and the PM sessions. It was a wonder that I made it up the porch stairs at day's end. I left a note on the refrigerator for Allie: "Take out, leftovers, or just skip it." Then I slogged up to the bed I hadn't made. I took off my skirt and blouse, climbed in, and pulled the quilt up over my shoulders. I closed my eyes. A new movie started, this one staring Patch. "And by the way," I told him in this version of India, film at eleven, "I'm thinking of having an affair with your best friend."

Affair? The word had popped into my brain unbidden. Was I, India Paige Othmar nee Smirtoff even capable of having an affair? Affairs were for women of a different ilk, women who wore black leather slacks and smoked Virginia Slims. Women who were young, or at the very least beautiful, in a *Cosmo* meets *Vogue* sort of way. Women like me didn't have affairs.

But would it be an affair? Tom and I were legally separated, hammering out a divorce. I owed Tom nothing. Patch was another story. Patch might be thirty, but he was still my little boy. And Patch had been through enough. Poor Patchie threw himself into work. As far as I knew, he had no social life at all. He lived in Mitch's basement. Well, okay, it was a nice apartment, but still. From what I could see, Mitch was his only friend these days. And I was thinking about an affair? Was I thinking about an affair?

I'd finally managed to turn the brain mess off and fall into a deep and blissfully dreamless slumber. The phone jarred me back. I answered still in a fog, not yet touched down in the real world.

"You ready to go paint the town?" Eva asked on the other end.

I pulled enough cotton from my brain to remember what I'd forgotten. The ten year celebration. That was tonight?

I had nearly managed to stumble out of bed when I heard her clomp up the stairs. Then there she was, standing in my bedroom in a slinky, short black dress and five inch heels looking like a woman who had affairs.

"You're not even dressed," she said.

"I'm sorry. I thought it was tomorrow night."

Eva put her hands on her hips and looked at me, perturbed. "It's been on your calendar for over a month."

"Sorry," I said again. "Maybe we could change it? We could go tomorrow."

"I made those reservations when you put the date on your calendar. Those reservations are nearly impossible to come by. You cannot stand me up."

"Okay. Okay. What time is the reservation?"

"Seven," she said, pulling the black dress from my closet. "We can still make it if you get a move on."

I pulled on some pantyhose and reached for the dress. "Where's the Spanx?" said Eva.

"Do I really need Spanx? We're past the first date stage here, are we not?"

"We want you to look fabulous here, do we not?" Eva fished the girdle-contraption from my dresser drawer and tossed it to me.

I would have argued the point but I was already in Eva's dog house. If Spanx would appease her, then I was willing to go with it. I should have known that she had ulterior motives.

Arlan's Martini Bar was the new hot spot in eastern Massachusetts. The *Boston Globe*, in an article in the Sunday Living section, had described it as intimate. Which, looking the place over, I construed as meaning tiny. It had all of ten tables. Apparently, people drove from the far reaches of New England for the privilege of sitting at one of them. As Eva had said, even on an ordinary Wednesday night like this one it was nearly impossible to get a reservation.

She shepherded me over to a table near the window. Two men were already sitting there. I recognized Dave. Across from him sat an elderly gentleman with a hooked nose and no hair to speak of except for the ones growing from his ears. I gave Eva what I hoped was a dirty look. She kept her hand squarely against my back and gave me the tiniest of shoves.

"India, my sweet. You know Dave. And this," she made a flourish towards the elderly man, "is Henry."

Henry, it turned out, was Dave's uncle. He was eighty-two years old, he was a widower, and he lived at a place called River View, which he described as a community for mature adults. I might have known. How could I expect any less from Eva?

I did my level best to curtail my anger. I smiled, made polite conversation, and toasted Eva's success.

Henry was, it turns out, not so easily fooled. "You seem a little preoccupied," he said. We had finished dinner and moved to the famous martini bar for a farewell famous martini. Eva and Dave were snuggled together a few stools down, whispering like a pair of teenagers.

"Do I?" I said, giving Henry my best charming smile.

Henry put his hand on my thigh, which did nothing to decrease my level of discomfort. "No worries. I've got a little present for you."

I could just imagine. A picture of Henry in boxers jumped into my head. I put my hand on Henry's, moved it gently away, and said, "Oh?"

Henry reached into his pocket and pulled out a baggy. "Open your purse," he whispered. He buried the baggy under my wallet and winked at me. "Prime stuff," he said. "Maybe you'll share it with me later."

Flustered, I pulled my purse into my lap and put my arms around it. What exactly, does one do when an eighty-two year old man hands you a packet of weed? Did Miss Manners have some protocol for this?

"Thank you," I said. I was uncomfortable in Spanx and heels, slightly drunk, though the martini had done nothing to make the headache I was working on go away, and I was ready to bonk Eva on the head and take the keys when she finally relented.

"What is the matter with you?" she hissed as we got into the car.

"Me? What is the matter with me? You set me up on a date with Uncle Henry and you ask what is the matter with me?"

"He's a nice man, India. A nice older man. A little more your speed. Good God, I give up trying to help you."

"Thank God," I said. I crossed my arms and stared out at the trees whizzing by on the highway. Then it hit me, what she'd said. "My speed?" I said. "I might not drive or date like a demon but my speed? My *speed*? "

"Henry is lonely. He is a mature man who is going to look at you like you are a sweet young thing. Which, by comparison, you are. It wouldn't have killed you to be a little nice to him."

"A little nice?" I could not believe what I was hearing. Had I not spent the entire evening trying to be nice? I was the poster girl for nice. Unlike my hard-driving friend. "How would you know if I were nice or not? You were too busy playing 'tickle me, Dave.'"

"A little flirtation might do you good, India."

I was thinking hard for a comeback and coming up blank when I saw the blue flashers. "Great," I said. "A perfect end to a perfect evening."

The policeman who pulled us over was a middle-aged stocky guy. "Don't worry," said Eva, checking him out in the rear view mirror as he walked to the car. "I can handle him." She rolled down the window. "Problem, Officer?" I swear she batted her eyelashes.

"Any idea how fast you were going?"

"Why, no."

"Eighty-five. The speed limit is fifty. May I see your license and registration, please?"

"Eighty-five," Eva said. "Imagine! My friend and I were just chatting away. I guess I wasn't paying attention."

"License and registration. Please."

I reached into the glove box to pull out the registration while Eva rooted through her purse. "Oh dear," she said. "I'm afraid I can't find my wallet. My license is in my wallet."

"That's just perfect," I said, only slightly under my breath.

"It's in my other purse, I'm afraid."

"Step out of the car," the officer said.

"Officer, what did you say your name was? It's just an oversight. I left my wallet in my day purse. You know how we gals are with our purses."

"Please step out of the car, ma'am." Officer Stocky was not buying. I figured we didn't stand a chance. But Eva charmed and flirted and cajoled. And Officer Stocky, whose name turned out to be

Mike Hanlon and whom Eva was soon calling Mike, let us off with a warning. "But your friend's going have to drive home," he said, nodding at me. "You do have a license, don't you?"

"License? Yes. Of course." Eva may have been enjoying our brush with the law, but I was totally frazzled. I pulled my wallet out of my purse and out dropped Henry's present.

Chapter Fifteen

Busted

"What is that?" asked Officer Mike.

"What's what?" I said, taking a cue from Eva. My skills were limited. "It's a gift."

"May I see it?"

What could I do? I handed over the stash. Officer Mike opened the baggy, sniffed the contents, and sighed. "Out of the car, please," he said.

"Oh, not again, Mike. Really," said Eva

"I'm afraid that you are both under arrest."

"Arrest?" I said. Another A word. A lot scarier than affair.

"Possession of an illegal substance, ma'am."

I could not believe I'd gotten arrested. I couldn't believe an eighty-two year old man had given me weed and gotten me arrested. Eva couldn't believe it, either. But there we were, sitting at the Tamsett police station. Officer Mike had been kind enough to let us sit on a bench in the office rather than go to lock-up.

Bail was set at three hundred dollars, a figure that was getting to be legendary in my life. Eva joked about calling Red, which I did not find the least bit funny.

"Call Henry," I said. "This is his fault."

"We can't call Henry. He would get into too much trouble."

"Call Dave, then."

"We can't call Dave. Henry is Dave's uncle. That would be just as incriminating as calling Henry."

By Eva's logic, we'd just have to sit on the bench at the police station until the hearing. The hearing! I hadn't thought about the hearing. I would be heard. I would be heard about, since I was the one with the bag. The nickel bag, Officer Mike had said.

"Call one of your kids," said Eva.

"The last thing I want is to get my kids involved. I'd rather they didn't find out about this."

"Get real," Eva said. "There will be a hearing. They are going to hear about it."

"Oh, God." I put my head in my hands. I tried, all my life, to be good. I tried to be a good wife, a good mother, a good teacher. And here I was, fifty-one years old, on the verge of divorce, about to be convicted of possession. It was more than I could bear.

"Besides," Eva ignored my anguish, "Patch is a lawyer. It would be good to have a lawyer."

"Patch does tax law," I said. "And I don't want my son bailing us out of jail."

"I don't think we have a choice," Eva said.

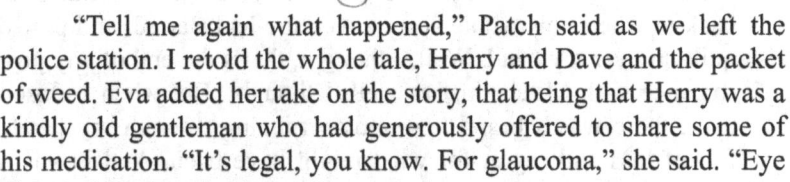

"Tell me again what happened," Patch said as we left the police station. I retold the whole tale, Henry and Dave and the packet of weed. Eva added her take on the story, that being that Henry was a kindly old gentleman who had generously offered to share some of his medication. "It's legal, you know. For glaucoma," she said. "Eye disease is serious business."

I rolled my non-diseased eyes at her. Patch let out a snort.

"What am I going to tell Allie?" I fretted.

"Don't worry. I already told her," Patch said. "We agreed to visit you on alternate Sundays at the big house."

"Oh, my God. I could go to prison for this."

"I, for one, am not going to prison," Eva said. "I'm just an innocent bystander, after all."

"I could go to prison."

"We'll get you a good lawyer. I can probably get you a speedy hearing. Most of the judges in the county have a pretty good sense of humor," Patch said.

Eva and I went our separate ways once we hit my driveway. "Don't worry," she said for about the fourth time. Eva had nothing to worry about. She was right, she wasn't the one with the nickel bag. And Eva was Eva. Mike Hanlon had already offered to come get her in the morning so she could pick up her car.

95

There was a yellow ribbon tied around the porch rail. Allie ran out to meet us as we came up the steps. "I was going to bake a cake, but I couldn't find a file," she said as she led us toward the kitchen.

"I'm glad you're all so amused," I said to my children. I'd almost gotten to the place where I could find it funny. Almost. I might have started laughing if Mitch hadn't been sitting in the kitchen.

"Mitch knows?" I whispered to Allie and Patch.

"He stopped by. Wanted to know where you were," Allie said.

"Here she is, our own jailhouse mama," Patch said as we walked into the room. Mitch smiled, all except his eyes. His eyes were full of question marks. Questions with a hint of anger and a hint of hurt, all aimed at me.

"Wait until you hear this," Patch said.

"Maybe we don't have to tell the story again," I said.

"Oh, but we do. We really do."

"Fine," I said, not daring myself to look at Mitch again. "You tell it. I'm going to bed." I couldn't have stayed. I went upstairs, back to where this whole sorry adventure had started, and pulled my quilt up over my head. Well, I thought, that's the end of any possible romance with Mitch. Just as well, I thought. But when I closed my eyes, there was a brand new movie running through my head, one full of loss and regret for what might have been. And it was not a nice picture.

I managed to get up and walk with Eva the next morning. With a full night between us and jail, Eva managed to turn the story in our favor. "The whole thing is ridiculous," she said. "They'll drop the charges, you wait and see."

After that, I managed to get through two more sessions of kindergarten. Five-year-olds have a way of putting you in another place and time. For a few hours, I was Mrs. Othmar, kindergarten teacher. Mrs. Othmar was a comfortable and competent woman. She could teach you to tie your shoes. She knew all the words to the ABC song. She knew which cubby had your name on it. Mrs. Othmar was bright and cheerful and not in trouble with the law and not fantasizing about unattainable affairs with men half her age. India, however, was another story.

Chapter Sixteen

Bargain Basement Lawyer

I was a big mess. Impending divorce. A mother-in-law who called weekly to see if I'd come to my senses. A hearing, scheduled at the end of the week. And Mitch. It'd been nearly a week since my brush with the law and Mitch had all but disappeared. I hadn't tried to contact him. I didn't know if it was pride or shame. Or just the fact that I was fifty-one and having regular hot flashes that seemed to point the way to crone-hood. The last thing Mitch needed, I reasoned, was an overheated old woman. As for me, maybe it was just raging hormones, some re-worked adolescent stage I was going through that made me think about having an affair.

As though to confirm this theory, on the Wednesday before the hearing I went home in a state of overheat, thinking that a cold shower would cure my ills. My avoiding Mitch was a cold shower on any bud of a relationship. It was for the best, I told myself for the hundredth time. And yet when I saw a car parked in the drive my heart rate doubled. Only to plummet again when I identified the car as Patch's.

Patch stood at the front door as I came up the walk. It gave me a start, him standing there like that. This was the future: Patch with some lovely young woman, a woman nicer than Sasha, at any rate, raising a new batch of children in the family home whilst I was tucked away alongside the likes of Henry and other mature adults. The thought was a sobering one.

Patch waited as I unlocked the door, and followed me into the kitchen. I was so caught up in my hot flash and my maudlin thoughts that I didn't notice until I put my canvas bag of kindergarten projects on the counter that he was biting his lip. It occurred to me that Patch worked eighty-hour weeks. It was three o'clock on a Wednesday afternoon. He should be in his office. Mother panic, the kind that always assaulted me whenever the kids came home after curfew when they were teenagers jumped out from behind the pantry door and yelled "oooga booga." "What's wrong?" I said.

"Nothing's wrong," Patch was chewing and tapping his toe. Chewing and tapping were bad signs. Also, his neck was developing a little rash. "Can't a guy drop in on his mom?" He ran his fingers along the island counter. "How's Tim Jensen working out?"

Tim Jensen was the lawyer Patch had recommended to me. He seemed like a fine and competent man. I told Patch as much. "But that's not why you're here," I said.

"I told you, I wanted to see how you were doing," Patch said. I didn't argue the point. I knew my kids. Patch would get around to it soon enough. Instead, I did what any good mother would have done. I offered him a sandwich. And like the good son he was, Patch accepted the offer of turkey on rye, though he did say that he was quite capable of making his own.

"I'm aware," I said, pulling out the bread. Patch got milk from the fridge and poured us each a glass. "So. How are you?" He bit his lip again.

"I'm okay, I guess. Arrests aside, I'm hanging in there. How are you?"

"Hanging in there," he said. We sat down to sandwiches. "I'm seeing someone," he said. "She's…nice. I think she's nice, anyway. She works with Mitch in the ER. Laura Rosetti." He looked at me uncertainly. "I'm glad," he blurted, "that you're, you know, moving on too."

"Oh," I said, not knowing what to say to this strange turn.

"I mean, you go out. You get yourself arrested. You try to have fun."

"I have Eva to thank for that. I'm not sure if I should thank her or kill her." I smiled.

Patch smiled back. "I quit my job," he said.

I dropped the sandwich. "Quit? Your job?"

"Quit. My job."

"With Vaughn White's firm?"

Patch took my hand. "I know that Vaughn White is like this old family friend. But the firm, it just isn't what I'm about. I can't see myself working hundred-hour weeks to keep corporations from paying taxes for the rest of my life."

98

"Quit?" I said again. Patch had been so proud of landing a job with one of the best law firms on the East Coast.

"The money's great. But, so what? I mean, I spent a bundle on Sasha. That apartment. Four Armani suits. But the truth is, I'm happier living in Mitch's basement. I want to set up my own practice, here. Help poor desperate woman get off from drug charges."

"So you just hang out a shingle."

"I've talked to Tim Jensen. He's looking for a partner. I'm it."

"Well," I said. "Congratulations."

Patch took a big bite of sandwich and said I made the meanest turkey on rye this side of the Mississippi.

"You trying to get on my good side?" I said.

"Actually..." Patch poured himself another glass of milk. "I have a favor to ask. Tim and I are going to hunt for a better office. His is too small." Patch was right about that. Tim's office was a rabbit warren above a shoe shop. Very different from Vaughn White's glass tower in downtown Boston. "There's a great space in the newspaper building. And a few uptown. We're going to look at them over the next few weeks. But in the meantime, I was hoping I could use Dad's old office."

"You want to practice law in the basement?" I said. Tom had a little office space carved out next to the water heater. He'd used it mainly for storage. I'd spent a good deal of time down there in the last few months, sorting through receipts and tax returns and all the other detritus collected over thirty years of marriage.

"Thomas Othmar, Jr., The Bargain Basement Lawyer. Has a good vibe, don't you think?"

I laughed. "It's yours for the asking," I said.

I turned on the light at the head of the basement stairs and down we plunged. The office was fairly neat in a disorganized way. If I thought about it, this was exactly how I would have described Tom, always careful about appearances, but just under the surface there was a lot of chaos. There were folders everywhere, papers peeling out of the sides. I'd sorted through about half of them by now; the ones I'd finished were stacked more neatly off to one side of a bookshelf.

Patch picked up an unsorted folder. A loan agreement for a car we hadn't owned in twenty years fluttered out. Circular file, we both agreed. I'd filled several trash bags already.

99

"It's a little overwhelming," I said.

"I can help you go through it if you want," he said, picking up another folder. "There is an awful lot of..."

"What?" I asked.

"Nothing," He snapped the folder shut.

"What," I asked, grabbing for the folder. He wouldn't let go his end.

"Nothing," he said.

"Patch," I yanked at the folder and out flew an old Polaroid snapshot. Patch grabbed it and held it to his chest like a poker card.

"It's a blurry picture. Not very good." I gave him an exasperated look. "It's a girl, okay. She's really young and really pretty." He glanced at the picture. "Oh, my God," he said.

"What?" Despite everything that had happened between us, the last thing I wanted was more proof of Tom's infidelity.

"It's you," Patch said softly.

It was me, faded, a little fuzzy and smiling brightly for the camera. For Tom. I was eighteen, he was twenty, both of us younger than the children we'd have together. "Skating," I said. "That's how I met your father." I'd been with friends, my first year at BC, and we'd gone skating. "I was a good skater and I was pretty pleased with myself. I twirled and glided over the rink, forward then backwards then right into your father."

I remembered it with painful clarity. The laughter, the bump, the hard bruising of ice against my thigh. Tom stumbling and grabbing for a bench. I stuttered apologies. He could have been angry, I would have knocked him flat if not for the bench. But he laughed and let me buy him a hot chocolate. Then he asked me out for coffee. I'd been dating Vaughn White. I had been Vaughn's one-girl fan club. A wide-eyed admirer of his big ideas. But that sort of admiration wears thin and by the February I met Tom, Vaughn and I had both grown tired of it. I had anyway.

"We skated together twice a week after that," I told our son. Thirty-three years ago, skating together had been everything. Now we skated apart. Tom had found someone new. Someone different. Someone better.

"Let's go back upstairs," said Patch, taking the photo from me. He looked stricken and I realized I had started to cry.

I thought I was done crying over Tom. I'd cried long and hard the first month. But since? I picked myself up and dusted myself off.

100

I went flying and got arrested. A much younger man kissed me. I figured out how to be alive all over again. Or had I?

Chapter Seventeen

On Being Heard

"It was best that Mitch didn't call" became my new refrain. It was best that we kept a careful distance before one of us (me, most likely) did something that we (I) would regret. It was better to move past this little infatuation. He knew where to find me.

And why, oh why, didn't he find me? When my arm was broken, he'd come by nearly every day. I'd teased and said he was checking on me. I'd flatter myself to think it had been otherwise. But hadn't it been otherwise?

Such were the boiling thoughts in my head. Finally, it got to me. On Thursday , I drove over to Mitch's house under the pretense of seeing Patch. It was a thin excuse at best, because Patch was setting up shop in my basement. But it was the night before the hearing and I was more than a little fidgety and I told myself that I wanted to go over my defense one more time. And I couldn't call Tim Jensen because it was too late in the day. Mitch's house was dark, at any rate. At any rate, I decided to get real and admit to myself the reason for refreshing my makeup and driving over. I got back into my Camry and drove to Tamsett Memorial.

"Mitch Tinker, please," I said to the triage nurse, trying to make myself sound business-like and efficient.

"What seems to be the problem?" asked the nurse.

"Never mind," I said.

"Why don't you have a seat." Having looked me over, she had apparently satisfied herself that I was not in need of immediate medical attention.

I beat a hasty retreat to the door. I was an old fool, I told myself.

"India?" Mitch bounded towards me. "You okay?" He looked

a little concerned.

"I'm fine. Everything's fine." Twenty more feet and I would have made it to the parking lot.

"Are you sure?"

"I'm fine. I just dropped by." What was the use? I might as well come clean. "To see you."

"To see me?"

"To see you." There. It was out. My face felt hot. My tongue got twisted into a knot. I couldn't have said anything else if I'd tried. We stood staring at each other for an uncomfortable amount of time.

"Well," Mitch said, finally. "You've seen me."

"Yes, yes. I have," I said, twisting my tongue back to normal. "Are you okay?"

"I'm fine."

"Fine?"

"Yes, fine."

Apparently, the gift of gab hadn't made a full comeback. There was another long silence. " I should get back. To work," Mitch said, again breaking over the barrier.

He was blushing. Something about that untwisted things. "You should drop by," I said.

"Why?"

"Why?" He had me there. "Because. Because you always used to come by? And because we'd like to see you?"

"We would?"

"Yes. Yes, we would."

"We're kind of busy, aren't we? Skirting lawsuits, going to trial, dating geezers. We don't really have time to visit, do we?" He said it as a joke, but there was the slightest hint of anger or disappointment.

"We're not that busy," I said. "And we miss you."

"Miss me?"

I nodded, my tongue splayed out again.

"I guess we need to figure this out then," he said. He was giving me an opening. But not much of one. "But right now, some of us have to go back to work. Why don't we call so that some of us will know where we stand?" He turned to go back into the brightly lit waiting room just beyond the revolving door. Full of people who needed him more than I did.

If I'd let him go through that door, we might have remained

friends. But whatever this was, this budding thing between us, would have come to a screeching halt. I hadn't driven to the hospital on a Thursday night to see that happen. "Mitch?"

He stopped and turned. Maybe he'd wanted all along for me to stop him. God, I hoped so. Because if he didn't, what I did next really would have made me seem like a fool. I ran up to him, put my hands to either side of his face, and kissed him. I kissed him hard, like I meant it. I did mean it. He kissed back. Thank God, he kissed back. Like he meant it, too.

"We have thought about it," I said softly. "It's taken up a good deal of think space."

He smiled and ran his finger over my cheek. "We've been thinking about it, too. God knows, we haven't wanted to, but it's not easy not to think. Have dinner with me tomorrow."

"Tomorrow?"

"Friday. Tomorrow. I've got the night off."

"Okay. Tomorrow."

"Wear that dress you wore for the geezer," he said.

A dark thought punctured the rosy cloud I floated on. "The hearing. My hearing is tomorrow. Oh, dear Jesus, I might be in jail tomorrow night. Oh, God."

"I'll swing by at seven. If you're not there, I'll come visit you in the pen."

"You'd visit me?"

"Sure." He kissed me again. "But India?"

"Um hum?"

"Wear the dress."

I did not wear the dress to the hearing. I wore a lovely dove gray jacket with matching pants and a white blouse. I accented with dove gray flats and a string of pearls. I could have campaigned for office in that outfit. I could have picked up an award as teacher of the year. Or defendant of the year.

My lawyer, Tim, gave me an approving once over and declared the outfit perfect. Tim, at first glance, looked a little shy of perfect. He made up for a spreading bald patch with a thin gray ponytail tied with a ribbon. He wore a gold hoop in his right ear. The gay ear, he'd told me when we'd met. And yes, he said, was the answer to my question. Patch assured me that Tim was a fabulous trial lawyer. He had a terrific track record. He was smart. After a single meeting with Tim, I came to see why Patch believed in him. And I'd come to believe in him, too.

Patch and Tim had both given me court dressing tips, hence the outfit. They'd given Eva tips as well, but Eva apparently misplaced the memo. She showed up in court wearing a see-through tuxedo blouse tucked into a short black leather skirt, sporting a pair of boots with nose bleed heels and a toe box pointy enough for the Wicked Witch of the West. Not a good candidate for defendant of the year outfit. But this was Eva. Eva could pull it off. And when we walked into the courtroom with Tim, it was Eva who looked as though she was in charge.

Judge Rawlins was a tall man with skin the color of night, whom I would have pegged as being a few years short of retirement. He made quick work of the case before ours, a man who'd allegedly torn his girlfriend's front door off its hinges and used it for kindling. I wondered that anyone would do that kind of thing. Then I reminded myself that I'd done a few strange things in the past few months. Judge Rawlins looked as though he were bored with the man's story and told him that he'd have to go to trial if he insisted on pleading not guilty. He set a trial date and banged his gravel. Signed, sealed, delivered.

We were next. "State versus Othmar and DeSantis," the bailiff boomed. I nearly curtsied before crossing the bar.

"Approach the bench," the judge said. A new feeling hit, not unlike Dorothy at the castle in Oz. I quaked in my dove-colored flats and, dear God, what a time for a hot flash. Only it wasn't a hot flash, it was me—profoundly embarrassed and ashamed and trying hard not to let it show.

The judge looked down over half-moon glasses at the pair of us flanking Tim Jenkins. His eyes puckered with amusement and traveled over to the assistant DA, a sweet looking blonde who looked to be about Patch's age. They journeyed back to me, then to Tim, and came to rest on Eva's see-through blouse.

"Eva, Eva, Eva," the judge said.

"Yes, Martin?" Eva said.

"What have you done this time?"

The judge took the four of us into chambers and asked if we wanted coffee. "Water," I said. "Water would be nice."

The bailiff came back with ice water, coffee for the judge, and a few brownies that the court reporter had baked last night. The brownies and water were a great medicinal. The hot flash disappeared and I started to relax.

Judge Rawlins took a sip of coffee and then asked me to tell my story. Tim objected. "With all due respect, your honor, this is highly irregular."

The judge raised a judicial hand. "With all due respect, Mr. Jenkins, this is my court. And I would like to hear what Mrs. Othmar has to say."

"Fine," Tim crossed his arms. I think he would have liked to stamp his Gucci-covered foot, but he didn't dare. It was, after all, Judge Rawlins' court.

I took a second sip of ice water and a deep breath and started in: the blind date, the gift I'd been given. How, because of politeness and the giver's advanced age, I hadn't wanted to refuse said gift. "It's no excuse though, is it?" I said in conclusion.

"This date was Ms. DeSantis's idea?" the judge asked.

"Yes, but..."

"That figures," he said looking pointedly at Eva, who looked pointedly back.

"Yes. But," I began again.

The judge ignored my stammering and turned to the prosecuting attorney. "Ms. Carson, do you want to go to trial with this?"

"I don't want to prosecute unless I have to, your honor." Ms. Carson turned her pretty pink face in my direction. "You don't remember me, do you?"

I looked at her long and hard. "I'm afraid I don't."

"I had brown hair then. And I wasn't Cynthia, I was Cindy.

It dawned on me. "Cindy? Little Cindy Carson?"

"That's me." Cindy Carson had been in my AM class the first year I taught kindergarten. It was no wonder I hadn't recognized her. She'd been a chubby little brown-haired girl. She liked to eat paste. And crayons.

"You've changed," I said.

"Mrs. Othmar was the best teacher I ever had," Cindy said to Judge Rawlins. "I'm not inclined to send her to jail on a trumped-up charge."

"Agreed," the judge said. "Plead guilty to the misdemeanor driving charge, and I'll let you off with fifty hours of community

106

service," he said to the two of us.

"Community service!" Eva said, just as Tim said, "Guilty?" They made it sound as though a prison sentence might be preferable.

"Unless you'd rather go to trial," the judge said.

"Community service will be just fine, thank you," I said.

"Couldn't we just pay a fine?" Eva asked.

"Community service," the judge said. "Fifty hours each, at the Darrow Street Shelter."

"Darrow with the derelicts?" Eva asked. "You have got to be kidding."

The judge beamed at both of us. "It's my court," he said.

Chapter Eighteen

The Hazards Of Group Dating

I was so giddy at having escaped a prison sentence that I nearly waltzed over the box that sat next to the front door. Inside was a single daisy laced with baby's breath. The card said: 'Don't forget. Black dress.' Romance and justice served all in a single day. "Thank you!" I shouted, though no one was home with me. And then, because no one was home with me, daisy in hand, I spun around a few times and shouted thank you some more.

I took my time getting ready for my date. It had been a long time since I'd done girly things and I did them all now. I took a lavender scented bubble bath, submerging deep into the hot water until it cooled. I exfoliated with the peach exfoliate I had bought and never used. I pumiced my feet and put two coats of pearly pink nail polish on my toe- and finger-nails. I hot-curled my hair. By the time I came downstairs in the black dress, Spanx in place underneath, several hours had passed. I twirled around a few more times and checked myself in the hallway mirror and decided that laugh lines weren't such a bad thing. Finally, I sat on the couch and waited. And jumped up when I heard a car pull into the drive. And sat down again. I told myself sternly not to run to the door.

I heard the door open. "Mom?"

"Allie! In here!"

Allie came into the living room with a small and very pale woman at her heels. "Mom," she said, "this is Liz."

Ah, Liz. Allie's new friend. Girlfriend. Friend who is a girl. I held out my hand and wished my awkwardness away. There was nothing to be awkward about. Nothing at all. Though I do wish that Allie had said something about bringing Liz by. Today of all days.

I said all the right things: *nice to meet you* and *I've heard so many good things about you* and *the weather's been lovely, hasn't it?*

Allie stared at my dress. "Patch told you," she said

"Told me what?"

"I can't believe he told you. It was supposed to be a surprise."

"Surprise?" I was acting, I guess, kind of surprised. I had no idea what Allie was getting at.

"You can drop the act, Mom. You got all dressed up. It's obvious that he said something." Maybe because I had been surprised that Allie had brought Liz home I hadn't noticed that Allie wore a dress. Liz wore a dress, too. They had presumably come here from work. I was pretty sure that pulling elephant hangnails wasn't the kind of work you got dressed up for. Before I could question them on this point, the doorbell rang and there stood Mitch with a bouquet of daisies looking like he'd done the male equivalent of the girl thing.

"You look fabulous," he said, handing me the flowers.

"You clean up pretty nice yourself," I said, just as Allie skated in behind me.

"I didn't know you were coming," she said. "It's okay. The cat's out of the bag." She looked over Mitch's shoulder to where Patch had just pulled up into the drive. "And here comes the cat liberator now."

Patch, too, was all dressed up. "Congratulations," he said kissing me on the cheek and handing me the bouquet of daisies he carried. I was beginning to feel like I was in a beauty pageant, what with all the flowers.

Patch looked at Mitch. "You got my message, I see."

"Message?" Mitch asked.

"You can stop the bewilderment bit. Mom knows," Allie said.

"She knows?" Patch asked. "You told her?"

"Told me?"

"Forget it, Mom. It's okay. Are you ready to go?" Allie asked.

"Go?"

Allie rolled her eyes. "To the restaurant for the dinner Patch and Liz and Mitch and I were going to surprise you with. To celebrate your reprieve from prison."

Mitch looked as befuddled as I felt. "Surprise?" he said.

I shrugged. "Surprise." And there we were, the five of us about to go out on our first date. It would have remained at five if Eva hadn't happened by.

"Can you believe this?" she said coming up the walk, ignoring the fact that there were five well-dressed people standing on the front porch as though ready to get a prom picture taken. "He not only cancelled our date, he dumped me. He dumped me! 'I don't get dumped,' I told him. 'I am the dumper.' 'Well,' he said, you might have thought of that before you told your little story to the judge.' Honestly, like I would rat out anyone." She cast an aggravated look in my direction. "You're wearing the dress," she said.

"We're going out. To celebrate," I told her.

"Celebrate what?"

"Not going to prison," Allie said. "You're all dressed up with nowhere to go, why don't you come with?"

"I suppose," she said, eyes floating between Patch and Mitch. "Two handsome young bachelors. Might be fun. Of course, those of us who are more mature will end up being chaperones."

"Liz, this is Eva," Allie said. "Eva, this is Liz. My girlfriend Liz." Allie waited for the light to switch on. Eva was a pretty bright bulb, but it took a minute.

"Girlfriend!" Eva said, switch flicked. "Your girlfriend. It's terrific to meet you, girlfriend!" She moved a few inches closer to Patch. "So, where are you taking us?" she asked him.

"The Palms. In Boston," Patch looked awfully proud of himself as Mitch and I stood wordlessly by. Mitch and I did manage to ride together in Mitch's car to the appointed restaurant. Mitch drove and Eva got into the passenger side before anyone could object. I got in back with Patch.

The Palms was a large place with dark pine paneling. We squeezed into an oversized booth, Liz and Allie with Patch on one side, Eva between me and Mitch on the other. Dating, I decided as the waitress brought menus, was better done by two people than in a group.

Mitch and I didn't get the chance to do much more than cast furtive glances in one another's direction. We did, however, get to hear about the search warrant and consequent search of Dave Sherman's house. The authorities had paid Dave a visit not long after our morning meeting with Judge Rawlins. Dave, as Eva told us previously, had been quite upset and told Eva that he never wanted to see her again.

"No one says that to me," Eva said.

"We did cause him trouble," I said.

"Oh, there's more." A smile played on the corners of Eva's lips. There was nothing she liked better than an audience. "Uncle Henry got a visit. They busted him. Seems he was using his unit at the River View as a greenhouse."

"He was growing the stuff?" Patch asked.

"Oh, yes. He had a regular little garden center, compete with growing lights. It turns out he was quite the entrepreneur."

"He was dealing?" Patch asked.

"Allegedly, my dear. Allegedly. Even so, they've kicked Uncle Henry out of his apartment. So Dave has a roommate."

"No wonder he dumped you," Mitch said.

"Just for that, darling." Eva leaned in to Mitch's ear. "I am not inviting you in for a night cap." It was all I could do not to kick her in the shins with my sling backs.

I rode home in Mitch's car, in the back with Eva this time. Mitch got out and walked us to the door. We didn't get a goodnight kiss, though Patch did slap Mitch on the back. "BC game's on TV tomorrow. I'll supply the beers."

Mitch gave me yet another furtive glance. "I've got to work late," he said. He bade us all goodbye. We didn't ask him in for coffee or a night cap.

The rest of the date broke up soon enough. Patch and Eva went home. Separately. I left Allie in the drive to say goodnight to Liz, climbed up the stairs and out of my little black dress and into my comfy blue pajamas. Then I got into bed and pulled the covers over my head.

Chapter Nineteen

Outed In Tamsett

"Is it her you don't like or that you don't like that she's a she?" Allie asked over coffee the next morning.

"I like her, Allie. She seems nice. Quiet."

"You have a strange way of showing it. You hardly spoke to her at all. You sat there the whole night looking as though you'd lost your favorite dog."

I had been glum, it's true. Group dating has that effect. I hadn't said much to Liz. I hadn't said much to anyone. "I'm sorry, Allie. You're right. I was feeling tired, is all. It was a long day."

"You and Mitch," Allie shook her head, "The pair of you looked like you were on the Titanic and had just hit an..." she stopped. "You and Mitch?"

"How about some omelets? We haven't had omelets in an age." I went to the refrigerator for eggs and diversion. Allie took the eggs from me.

"Mother. Stop it."

"Stop what? You love omelets. I even have red peppers."

"I'm right. I know I'm right. About you and Mitch."

I sat down, eggless. "I suppose you are."

"I'm *right*?" Allie nearly dropped the egg carton. "Holy crap! You and Mitch?"

"Now you stop it, Allison. It was just dinner. Mitch asked me out for a friendly dinner." Which, I thought, was exactly what we'd had. A friendly dinner for six.

"Um hum. Like he came over for a friendly dinner when you got your cast off. The way the two of you always have your friendly little heads together. The way he's always dropping by. Right neighborly of him."

"That's right, Allie. Friendly. We are friends." That wasn't a lie, was it? We were friends, Mitch and I. Amend that, we had been friends. The six person dinner may have put a damper on said friendship.

"Right. Friends. Like me and my dear friend Liz." Allie smirked. I blushed. I couldn't help myself. Allie couldn't help noticing.

"You like him. A lot."

There was at this point no sense in denying it. I did like Mitch Tinker. A lot. And not just because I was flattered that a thirty year old man had taken an interest. I would have liked Mitch if he were Uncle Henry's age. "He's sweet and funny and very considerate and kind of romantic," I told Allie. And he made my heart beat double time every time he touched me.

"Does Patch know about this?"

"No," I said, coming down from the clouds. "I think he'd be awfully upset with me if he did."

"Don't underestimate him. Mitch isn't his girlfriend. There is a difference."

"But it is kind of taboo, isn't it? If I start seeing Mitch, I've broken a code."

"It's good to break a few eggs," Allie said, handing me the carton.

"Are you saying that you're okay with this?"

"If you're okay with Liz, I'm good with Mitch. Deal?"

"Deal," I said, breaking the eggs into a bowl.

It was good that Allie was okay with it. Of course, it didn't matter if Mitch never called again. After last night's outing, I wouldn't blame him if he moved to Alaska, I told Allie. Allie said I was being ridiculous and I ought to call him. I suppose she was right. I should have called.

I picked up the phone about a hundred times that Saturday and, a hundred times, I put it back down again. I wasn't sure what it was I was afraid of. Had anyone asked, I would have said everything.

"Get over it," Allie said as she dressed for her date in the city.

"I can't do it. I know it's dumb. What if he says he doesn't want to see me?"

Allie grabbed my cell phone. "I'll bet you have him on speed dial," she said. She was teasing, but it sounded an awful lot like an accusation.

I sputtered. "For emergencies. It's good to know someone who can handle an emergency."

Allie hit the button and handed me the phone. "This is an emergency," she said.

It rang three times. Then Mitch answered, sounding distracted. That's when I hung up.

"You are worse than an eighth-grader," Allie said.

"I'm better in person," I said.

"Then you better get dressed."

It's a good thing Allie was there. I'm not sure I would have had the fortitude to do it on my own. The black dress came out of the closet. I wasn't ready to put it on for a second night. Really, I should have taken it to the dry cleaners. But a girl's got to do, so I flung caution and one tiny wine stain to the wind and had Allie zip me in.

"You do look good," she said. I looked in the mirror. Not as good as last night, what with all the primping and prodding. But passable.

I tottered, fully heeled, panty-hosed, and Spanxed, to my Camry and made my way to Memorial's emergency room. The intake nurse looked at me like I was an old joke and she still hadn't gotten the punch line. "Let me guess," she said. "Dr. Tinker."

I was developing a weird kind of itchy outbreak on my neck. And a stammer. "Yes," I managed, nodding my head like a bobble-head doll.

"Not here," she said.

"Not here?" I looked around. Maybe he'd pop up from behind curtain number two. "Late. He said. Working late."

"Home. Went home. Half hour ago."

I tottered back to my Camry, overdressed and dejected. Home. He went home. To his house. I knew where that was, didn't I?

A light shone bright in Mitch's kitchen. A light. Somebody was home. Mitch was in the kitchen, cooking eggs or making coffee or…something. I tottered to the kitchen door and knocked.

Patch answered.

"What are you doing here?" we said in chorus.

"I live here," Patch said. Lived here was evidenced by his clothes, or lack thereof. He was wearing boxers. And nothing else.

"You live downstairs," I said. Visions of Patch and Mitch

sitting in their underwear, drinking beer while watching ESPN goose stepped through my head. Only Patch wasn't holding a long neck. In his hand was a bottle of wine. White wine. The other hand held a corkscrew, which he pointed at me.

"You're still dressed up," he said.

"You're not dressed," I said.

"Your point being?"

"Where's Mitch?"

"Working, why?"

"Wondering," I said. "I came by to…" I hunted through my brain for an excuse. "Return books. Leant me. Mitch." I stared at the bottle in Patch's hand, hoping he'd buy my lame lie. Patch put down the bottle.

"It's not what you think," he said. Think? Had I been thinking? "I'm not pilfering Mitch's wine. Well, I am pilfering Mitch's wine, but I plan to replace it tomorrow. First thing." Patch picked up the bottle again. "So I'm going to take the wine. Downstairs. To my apartment. Where I live."

"Patch?" A disembodied voice floated from somewhere down the stairs. Patch looked at me, smiled, didn't answer. "What's the matter? Can't find the corkscrew?"

"I'll be right there," Patch said, still looking at me.

The door to downstairs opened and there stood a very pretty raven-haired brown-eyed woman. A petite little woman in an itty bitty teddy.

"A nurse," I said, as sudden recognition switched on the fluorescent lamp in my brain. She worked in the ER. Though she was usually dressed when she did.

"Mom, Laura. Laura, Mom."

"Laura," I gushed. "I meant to say I recognized you. From the ER. From when I was there. With Patch. And without Patch."

"His hand," she said, being helpful, "and your arm."

I held up my wrist. "All better. We're accident prone, we Othmars."

We spent the next few minutes staring at my arm, the wine, and the door.

"Well then," I said, breaking the awkward silence. "I ought to be on my way. Patch. Laura. So nice to meet you. I mean you, Laura. I already know Patch." With that I tottered backwards out the kitchen door and shut it firmly in front of me.

Allie didn't get home until Sunday morning. Her love life was, apparently, in better shape than mine.

"How'd it go?" she asked. I told her it hadn't. She sighed and called Mitch. She got his voice mail. "Leave a message," she mouthed, holding out the phone. I held up my hands as though she held a live grenade. "I can't." I mouthed back.

"Oh, for God's sake." Allie put the phone to her ear. "Hey Mitch. It's Allie and my mother. Give us a call when you get the chance."

"Give us a call?" I asked when she'd hung up.

"It would be easier if you'd just do your own messages," she answered.

Chapter Twenty

The Teddy Bear's Picnic

Mitch didn't call. Patch didn't call. Eva didn't call. Even Marissa didn't call. In fact, the only call I got was from Mrs. Osterhousen, mother of kindergartner, Ophelia, who asked if cupcakes were allowed in my classroom or if she should arrange for something else, an assortment of hot and cold finger foods, perhaps, for Ophelia's birthday celebration on Monday. Cupcakes were fine, I assured her. My love life was not, though I did not mention this to Mrs. Osterhousen.

As Mrs. Osterhousen reminded me, this was a school night and by ten o'clock I was on the couch in my pink teddy bear flannel pajamas sipping Sleepytime tea and watching the news. I heard the front door open and shut and there stood Allie, also in pajamas, though hers were blue cotton, with Mitch, wearing scrubs (green) that could be used as pajamas in a pinch.

The word sleepover dangled in my head. Innocent, at first. A nostalgic recalling of Allie and her friends giggling into the wee hours. And then of Patch and company tenting in the backyard. Of Patch and Mitch sleeping in the tree house. Of Mitch, all grown up. Sleepover got steamier. I could, in fact, feel the steam. Another one of those red-alert hot flashes.

"Well," Allie said. "I'm going to turn in." She did a charade of "boy, am I tired" complete with a big yawn and super-sized stretch. "Don't stay up too late." The hot flash got flashier.

"Tea?" I said. "Would you like tea?" Mitch, distracted by Allie's award-winning performance, didn't answer.

"Sorry?" he said. "I got your message. Allie's message. I was working."

"Working," I said.

"I heard you came by last night," he said as we watched Allie trot up the stairs. "Laura told me."

"Laura, yes." I did my own charade: baffled woman talks in sleep.

"That explains why you weren't home."

"Home?"

"Last night. I came by. You weren't here."

"You came here?"

"I came here but you were there."

"So that's why you weren't there."

"Because I was here."

"Exactly," I said. And we both started to laugh. "I wanted to apologize," I said, "for the group dinner."

"It was a surprise."

"No kidding."

"This going out thing isn't working very well, is it?" he said.

"Do you think the universe is trying to tell us something?" I said. Mitch looked slightly mystified at my new age turn of thought. "You know, is it a sign?"

"A sign? You mean like Employees Only or One Way?"

I nodded. "Or Stop. Or Do Not Enter. Or Dead End."

"Or Yield. Or Turn on Green Arrow. Interesting thought," he said.

"What do we do? Can we ignore a sign?"

"Maybe the universe is testing us," said Mitch. "My grandmother always said that sweat comes before success." Mitch sat down next to me. "Granny Tinker swore there were leprechauns living in her rose bushes. Nonetheless, she was quite pithy when it came to old Irish sayings."

The hot flash had found its way into every corpuscle in my body. I wondered if Granny got the bit about sweat from a menopausal leprechaun.

"Are you okay?" Mitch put his hand to my forehead. "You feel feverish."

"It's the sweat before the success," I said. "Also, the sweat that comes before old age. Like gray hair and laugh lines."

Mitch looked slightly mystified again. Then he said, "oh," and then he said "oh," again.

"Another sign," I said.

"Maybe a sign from Granny Tinker, calling from the land

beyond."

"I think she might be saying that I need to be dunked in a tub of ice water. Maybe just a nice cold glass of water will do the trick. Or iced tea. Is it okay to drink iced tea in cool weather?"

"A walk outside," Mitch said. "It's nice and cool. Chilly, really."

"Outside?" I got my London Fog, put on a pair of flip flops, and followed him to the porch. "This is better," I said.

"We could go for a ride. Maybe that's why we're out here," Mitch said.

"A ride?" I looked back at the door. "I'd have to change."

"I wouldn't chance it. Your family might show up and hijack us again."

"We wouldn't want any more surprises, would we?"

We climbed into Mitch's Honda, taking the pajama party on the road.

"I know a place," Mitch said. "All-night diner. Perfect pancakes."

"I can't go to a diner," I said.

"Why not?"

"I'm in my pajamas," I whispered.

Mitch glanced over at me. "I go there in my scrubs all the time. They won't know the difference."

"I'll know the difference."

"Dare you."

"You can't dare me."

"I double dog dare you."

I'd raised two kids. I'd taught school for twenty years. Sometime in the middle of the last century, I had actually been a kid. If there was one thing I'd learned from all this experience, it was that nobody can ignore a double-dog dare. Not even if the darer is a medical school graduate and the daree is a middle aged teacher in pajamas and flip flops.

The diner was called Fat Boy's. It was a silver-sided double-wide without wheels nestled onto a parking lot somewhere on the outskirts of Lowell. There was a big neon sign tacked to the roof, with a picture of a cherubic boy, smiling with a hot dog raised triumphantly in his chubby hand. There were three empty picnic tables, painted bright yellow, in one cordoned off part of the lot. It was the kind of place that, if you happened to go there in your pajamas, no one might happen to notice.

As it turned out it was also, like *Cheers*, a place where everybody knows your name. At least, if you're a regular, which, it seemed, Mitch was. "Dr. Tinker," said a rotund, also middle-aged waitress as we trundled through the door. Which, incidentally, played "*Charge!*" every time it opened. "Just so happens your table's empty."

I raised an eyebrow and buttoned the top button of my raincoat. "Your table?" I questioned.

"Wait until you taste the pancakes," Mitch said. We squeezed into the last booth in the corner, under a needlepoint sampler that said *Best Coffee in Town* and were handed a pair of plastic menus. The waitress, whose nametag said Pearl, said she'd be back in a flash. Or a jiffy. I studied the menu carefully. Mostly, because I didn't want to notice the several people at the counter who had stared at us when we walked in.

Pearl, true to her word, was back in a flash. Or a jiffy. "Don't tell me," she said to Mitch. "Apple pancakes, syrup on the side."

"You know me too well," Mitch said.

Then it was my turn. For all the studying I'd done, I was going to flunk the menu test. "Have the apple pancakes," Mitch whispered. "Can't go wrong with those."

"Apple pancakes," I said. Actually, I said it twice while pointing to the sampler. I followed my pancake cheer with a question. "Is it true?"

"Is what true, honey?" She looked at me as though I were a mental patient out on a field trip.

"Best coffee in town," I said.

"Depends on who you ask," Pearl said.

"Coffee," I said. "I'll try it." Then I remembered the time. School tomorrow. Ophelia's cupcakes with stuffed mushrooms and carrot sticks. "Decaf. I'll try the decaf."

Pearl nodded, tapped her pencil to a check-out slip, but didn't write it down.

"I'll have the high octane. I like living dangerously," Mitch said.

The pancakes were, as Mitch had promised, the best I'd ever had. And the diner, despite the *No Shoes, No Shirt, No Service* sign at the register, wasn't the kind of place that judged you by the clothes you wore.

I decided that those folks at the counter didn't really care enough to stare at us. Just friendly curiosity as to who had made the door go *Charge*, that was all. They were busy with their own pancakes. We were old news by now. They'd gotten used to us. Or I'd gotten used to them. Midway through the pancakes, sated and a little warm, I'd gotten used to them enough to unbutton the top buttons of my coat.

"Go for it," Mitch said.

"Excuse me?"

"Take the coat off, India."

I glanced at the counter. They were used to me in the coat. Without the coat, they might be inclined towards friendly curiosity again. "I don't think so," I said.

Mitch leaned over the table. "I double-dog dare you," he said.

I've already explained about the double-dog dare. At this point, however, I was ready to break, as Allie had suggested, a few eggs. Especially if they were arbitrary kid eggs. Mitch, it should be noted, had his jacket off. But, although scrubs and pj's are cousins, they are not identical twins. Besides which, Mitch looked terrific in scrubs whereas my pajamas just made me look goofy. We were at an impasse.

"No. I'll take my chances with the double-dog," I said.

Mitch called Pearl over to the table and explained the situation. She gave me the poor-woman's-not-right look again. "Double-dog dare?" she said. She considered for a moment. "If you want the real truth, you look a little weird in the buttoned-up rain coat, like a female flasher. If it were me, I'd go with off."

Mitch nodded. "You see? Pearl agrees."

"I don't know," I said. "I've never done this before."

"I triple-dog dare you," Mitch said.

"The ante has been raised," Pearl said.

"You can't triple-dog dare me. There is no such thing as a triple-dog dare."

"There is now," Mitch said.

The warmth I'd been feeling was getting closer to hot. Maybe it was just embarrassment. Maybe it was another hot flash. Maybe it was enough. I glanced at the counter, backs turned away from us to a one. I unbuttoned the coat and peeled it off.

"Good God, teddy bears," Pearl said.

It wasn't so bad, really, eating pancakes at an all-night diner in

121

teddy bear pajamas. It was kind of freeing, actually. Kind of fun. Being with Mitch was fun, too. I've always been a sucker for a man who could make coffee come out of my nose. What he said, entirely out of context, may or may not be funny. But it makes me crack up, even now. What he said was "When the chips are down the buffalo is empty." As I've said, it's a matter of taste or context, but my teddy bears sported a large caramel-colored stain soon after he said it.

This should have, would have, made me want to crawl under the table, but it was 1:00 AM and the last of the counter people had made the door say *Charge* and Mitch and I were the only customers in the place.

When we'd finally stopped laughing, I said "Tomorrow is Ophelia Osterhousen's birthday."

"Happy birthday, Ophelia," Mitch raised his coffee cup. "Whoever you may be."

"A kindergartner," I explained. "Her mother's bringing cupcakes and possibly a buffet of assorted quiche. You have no idea what cupcakes and quiche do to kindergartners."

"I better get you home, then. I'd want you to be well rested for the festivities."

I didn't want to go home. But there were those cupcakes and my teddy bears were wet and, well, it was time.

"I've lived in Massachusetts all my life and I never knew that Fat Boy's existed," I said as we climbed back into Mitch's Honda.

"I found it by accident. After." He stopped talking. For the first time all night, there was a silence between us. Mitch looked out at the road. "My ex-wife, Amy, left me for a neurosurgical residency at Stanford. She loved brains more than me, I guess. We were living in this little apartment in Somerville. And, after she left, I hated being there. I worked most of the time and when I wasn't working, I drove around. One night, after a twelve-hour shift, I found myself in front of Fat Boy's. I mean, how can you resist a place called Fat Boy's? I went in, Pearl fed me pancakes, and I've been going back ever since." He smiled at me. "So that's the whole sad story."

"Do you still see her? Amy?"

"No. We e-mail once in a while. She's marrying a guy in her department. Next June."

"I'm sorry."

"No. I'm good with it. Truth is, I'm happier now. I've met this terrific woman. God, she's got the best sense of humor and she's so

122

warm that I just want to bask in the glow when I'm with her." He put his hand over mine. "I think you know her. She's a kindergarten teacher. Lives over on Easterly. Kind of woman you can bring to a diner like Fat Boy's in her pajamas."

"Fat Boy's is a terrific place for a first date," I said.

"This was a date?"

"I had a wonderful time," I said.

This time, when he walked me to the door, I did get a good night kiss. I got several, in fact. Enough of them that, since I'd already laughed at caution, I considered asking him in. Though that step, the one through the front door, seemed huge. Too big, really. Mitch saved me from myself.

"You better get some sleep. Ophelia and the cupcakes and the Mariachi band and all." He kissed me one more long lingering time. "I'll call you? Tomorrow?"

"Tomorrow," I said.

"Tomorrow," he said, backing down the porch steps. He stopped, turned, stopped, turned back. "No," he said. "Not tomorrow."

"Not tomorrow?"

"It is tomorrow."

"It is?"

"Yes."

"Call me today, then."

"I'll call you today," he said.

I watched the taillights of his Accord slip around the corner. My cell phone rang. "Hi," he said, "what are you doing?" We talked while I went upstairs, brushed my teeth, and climbed into bed. We talked for another half an hour before I turned out the light.

"Goodnight," he said for the fourth time.

"Goodnight," I said.

"I'll call back today," he said. I don't know what he said after that because I fell asleep with the cell phone on my pillow.

Chapter Twenty One

Gifts Of Granite

School days are always tougher when you're exhausted. Kindergartners have radar for these kinds of things. Adrienne Osterhousen came in dressed in the same birthday outfit as her daughter. The smock top with the crocheted daisies along a gathered waist looked darling on Ophelia. It made Adrienne look, well, like she was dressed like her daughter. I took pity on her though, because she looked nearly as tired as I felt. She handed me two cake carryalls.

"Petit Fours," she said. "I made them myself."

"Petit Fours?"

"Pastries," she said. "I got the recipe from *Gourmet* magazine. They are a little labor intensive, let me tell you. But I think they'll be worth it. A little bundle of heaven, the magazine said."

Johnny Ramon had stolen Phillip Neussman's baseball cap and was tossing it around the room. Rachel Darwin was sitting in the doll corner twirling her hair and singing "I'm a dog, I'm a little dog." In my humble opinion, they didn't seem a petit four kind of crowd.

Or in the opinions of the little connoisseurs themselves. Ophelia passed them out during snack time, wearing the special birthday crown with "Six" in sequins that I saved for just such momentous occasions.

"What is it?" Mikey Langdon asked, sticking his finger into the little bit of heaven.

"My mom says I can't," Philip said. "It could have nuts." No nuts, I assured him. He looked disappointed.

Johnny Ramon took a big bite and spit it back out. It was at that point that Ophelia, a frighteningly nervous child to begin with, began to sob.

I reprimanded Johnny and told Ophelia it was a wonderful snack. To prove the point, I bit into one. The petit fours that Mrs. Osterhousen favored did not, apparently, have any sugar in them. "Birthday crackers!" I said, pulling an emergency box of Animal Crackers from my desk. The kids, even Ophelia, looked relieved.

Somehow, I made it through the rest of the day. Mitch called as the last of the PM kindergartens were rolling away on the bus. "I've got to get you in earlier," he said when I told him about my day. That was right before he said that he missed me.

Patch was in the kitchen with a box of books when I got home. "I'm moving out," he said. "And in. Tim and I found a place."

"Personal or professional?" I teased.

"Alas, Tim's taken," Patch said. "He was swept off his loafers by the handsome and swashbuckling Renaldo."

"Renaldo?" The thought of smooth-talking Tim with a Latin lover made me laugh.

"Yes. Renaldo. He and Tim kind of look alike."

"Maybe I should have them over. Tim and Renaldo. You and Laura." I almost added me and Mitch, but I stopped short. I think I blushed a little. Luckily, Patch didn't notice. He thanked me for the use of Tom's office and asked if he could leave a few things down there. Of course, I told him, relieved to find myself on solid ground.

I helped Patch hump several tons of law books to his car .The phone rang not long after he drove off. "I was hoping you'd call," I said, daring myself to use a low and sultry voice, feeling silly and wonderful all at once.

"Well, well, well," said a gravelly voice. Vaguely familiar. Definitely not Mitch.

It took me a minute. "Red Lansing?"

"As if you didn't know," he growled. Before I could ask what he wanted, he said, "Sweetheart, do me a favor. Take a look out that parlor window of yours." There was a pause. A pregnant pause while I imagined six geese a laying on my front lawn.

"Front window?" Sexy went to croaky. I imagined seven hundred croaking frogs, a plague of biblical proportions.

"Don't be shy, little lady."

I didn't want to. I swear I didn't. But it was like passing an accident. You just have to look. I snuck up on the curtain, grabbed it as thought it might bite, and pulled it back a fraction of an inch.

There, on the street in front of my house, sat the biggest reddest dump truck I had ever seen. A horn blasted. The headlights blinked on and off.

"How'd you like that, little lady?" Red asked.

I didn't answer. I was too busy imagining what the truck would dump.

The headlights blinked again. "That's just me winking at you," Red said. I pulled the curtain back a little more. The man sitting in the cab waved.

"Is that your truck?" I asked.

"Hell, no. I borrowed it. Just dropped by to show it off. Got something you might like."

"I thought we were through giving each other presents," I said. There might have been a hint of panic in my voice.

"Request permission to come calling."

"Calling? You are calling."

"Up the front walk. To your door."

I was about to say no. I was about to say I'd had enough of surprises, thank you very much, and please take whatever it is back to the gravel pit, or the junkyard, or the zoo, when the doorbell rang. I looked out the window. The truck's cab was empty. Whatever was in back was still on board. I answered the door in hopes of keeping it that way. There stood Red, a Stetson in one hand, the other hand behind his back, smelling as though he'd bathed in Old Spice.

"Open your hand and close your eyes," he said.

"I don't think so. For all I know, you've got a rattlesnake back there."

Red raised an eyebrow. "You got to trust me a little here. This is just a little present says I'm sorry for behaving in a less than gentlemanly manner the last time I was here."

It was that accident thing again. That accident thing and an absolute need to find out what this was all about. I closed my eyes and held out my hand. Red put something cold and hard into it. I opened my eyes. "A rock?"

"That's no ordinary rock, darling. That's a grade-A slice of New Hampshire granite."

"Granite?"

"There's more where that came from," said Red, glancing back at the truck.

126

"Oh, no. Oh, no, no, no. You are not going to dump a truck load of granite on my lawn. I'll have you arrested. I'll have you put away. I swear it."

Red chuckled again. "That's what I like about you, little lady. You've got spunk. I like a woman with spunk."

I'd show him spunk, all right. If he dumped a load of rocks onto my lawn, I'd put the rock in my hand right through that nice borrowed windshield of his. I told him as much.

"Whoa, honey. No need to throw rocks. I brought it to show you. It's valuable, you know. I'm not fool enough to dump it."

"Why would you want to show me granite?" I asked. I still had my phone in hand, ready to call in the SWAT team.

"So you can do your sculpting," he said, looking downright proud of himself. He winked. "If you take requests, a little old Cessna'd be nice. We could set her up by my hangar."

"You want me to sculpt you a Cessna?"

"Only if you want to. Hell, you can sculpt any old thing you like. Your call."

"Red," I said. "I don't sculpt."

"You don't sculpt?" Red looked a little confused.

"No," I said. I handed him back his rock. "I've never sculpted. I wouldn't know how to sculpt."

Red put the Stetson back on his head. "Don't know how? Really? Damnation."

"Sorry." I very nearly was.

"Damnation," he said again. "And here I wanted to do something nice. A peace offering, as we got off on the wrong foot and all."

"Red? Where did you get the idea that I was a sculptor?"

"Those ladies called, said you do beautiful work. That Luce Morgan, she said you were an artist. I know you're a teacher, so I figured you for an art teacher. And shoe art is kind of sculpture, right?"

"I don't teach art. I teach kindergarten."

Red, the wind knocked out of his sails, or the earth moved from under his granite Cessna, smiled sadly. "Kindergarten."

"Yep. Kindergarten."

The smile brightened a notch. "I remember kindergarten. Finger paint and crayons and play dough."

"That's about it."

"Play dough," he said. "is like sculpture. Kind of. Isn't it?"

"Play dough is not granite," I said. "I don't think you'd want a Cessna sculpted of play dough."

"Suppose that wouldn't look too good, huh?"

"I suppose not."

"So, I suppose you won't be wanting two tons of granite."

"I don't think so."

"Damnation," he said. He looked at the rock in his hand and put it on the stairs as though it were made of bone china. "At least let me take you out for eats. There's this place called the Feed Bag over in Avon. They got steaks the size of those granite chunks."

"I'm not hungry, Red."

"You could have a salad or something."

The last thing I wanted was a salad or something with Red, even if it was in the interest of détente. The kitchen light went on at Eva's. Another light went on in my head. "Eva might be interested. In dinner. Not granite."

Red looked uncertainly in the direction of Eva's house. "Eva, huh? I don't know."

"What's not to know? Go over and ask her."

"I can't just show up on her doorstep and ask her to dinner."

"Why not? You showed up on my door step with a load of granite."

"That's different. You and me, we got a relationship."

I wanted to ask him exactly what sort of a relationship he thought we had, when he said, "Truth is, I'm not so good with this stuff."

"What stuff?"

"Relationships. I think you and me, well, I think we got something here. There, I've said it."

Red took off his Stetson again and held it against his heart as though we might start saying the Pledge of Allegiance.

"Red," I began as gently as I could. "I'm not sure that a relationship with me is something that you want." Meaning, of course, that a relationship with Red might not be something I wanted.

"Is it the granite? The truck? Both of them together? Guess it's too much, huh?"

"It's a little much."

Red sat down on the front porch step, his Stetson on his lap.

He looked so forlorn that I couldn't help myself, I sat down next to him.

"Guess I better come clean, then," he said.

"Come clean."

"That granite? It ain't mine. I mean, I could get you some if you wanted..."

"No. No. That's fine."

"That granite belongs to Albert Houlihan. He owns Memorial Markers? I got him a good deal and well, I figured I could get more if you really liked it."

"Why would you go to all the trouble?"

"Ain't that obvious?" he said. "I was hoping you'd go out with me."

"Red, you don't have to bring a truck load of granite to ask a woman out to dinner."

"I suppose not. It was just easier that way. I guess I thought you'd be flattered. Being a sculptor and all."

"It is a change from flowers and candy," I said.

"Exactly." Red shot up out of his seat. "Exactly. You see, you understand that. I knew when you dumped those shoes in my hangar that you and me, we think alike." He was almost cute, standing there with his Stetson in his hand, his hair shooting up every which way.

"You've got flash, I'll give you that," I said. "Explains how you got four women to marry you. It was four, right?"

Red chuckled. "Ah, hell. I wish I could take some credit. Truth is, all I did was get drunk." He sat down again. "I go to Vegas, next thing I know, I wake up with some strange woman got a smile on her face wide as the Rio Grande. That's how I'd know I'd gone and done it again. I'm a sucker for a pretty face. They ought to outlaw those drive by marriage places."

"That happened to you four times?"

"Nah. Just twice in Vegas. Once in Tijuana. I married number three before I divorced number two. Told number two I was a Mormon, but she wasn't buying it. Now Maggie, that was number one. Met her back in Texas. She was a waitress at the local airport bar. God, I loved that gal." Red put his Stetson back on his head. "I talk too much."

"What happened to her? To Maggie?"

"She run off with a two-bit wildcatter twice her age. Left me by my lonesome."

"I've been there," I said.

Red chuckled again. "It was a long time ago. And anyway, it's got nothing to do with nothing." He patted my knee.

"Tell me true, Red. I'm not really your kind of woman, am I?" Good God, half an hour with the man and I'd started talking like him.

"Well, hell. Sure you are. I mean, you're just as sweet as a litter of kittens. I've never had a sweet woman before." I swear, he was blushing. Before I could disavow him of his belief in my sweetness, Mitch's Accord pulled up behind the truck. Mitch got out and circled the dump truck, shrugged at me, and shook his head.

"I guess no apology was necessary," Red said, the old contentious gravel back in his voice.

"Excuse me?"

"I'm not so dumb as I look. Just friends with Billy the Kid? Fool me once, shame on you. Fool me twice, shame on me."

Before I could defend myself— and, really, what defense did I have? Mitch loped up the stairs, kissed me casually, and handed me a gift bag. "Exclusively for you from the hospital gift shop," he said. Inside was a tiny teddy bear. "I tried to match the pj's," Mitch said.

"It's terrific," I said. I grinned like an idiot.

Red, who hadn't said anything, began to mumble. "Teddy bear. What kind of a dumb gift is that? I brought a whole truck full of granite."

"Granite?" Mitch had begun grinning like an idiot, too.

"Two tons of prime New Hampshire grade-A granite," Red said.

"You're not going to dump it on India's lawn, are you?" Mitch asked.

Red turned to me. "Please say it ain't so. You and little Billy," he shook his head.

"It is so." Mitch put a proprietary arm around me. "And I'm not little Billy."

"She was dancing with guys like me whilst you were still a gleam in your daddy's eye."

"I doubt that India ever danced with guys like you. Not then. Not now."

"We'll just see about that," Red said. "Goodnight, little lady." He tipped his hat and sauntered off towards the truck. The engine started.

130

"What was that all about?" Mitch asked as the truck bed began to lift.

"Oh my," I said.

"My car," Mitch said as two tons of granite slid from the truck onto the hood of the Honda.

"My car," Mitch said again, making a break for the curb. "My new car that I haven't finished paying for yet." He began sputtering expletives and something about Red needing emergency treatment. I was on his heels, saying something totally ineffectual like "*calm down.*" The noise had been enough to bring out all the neighbors: the Clarks, the Delbugios, the Ellenburgs, who all stood around Mitch's flattened car saying things like "Holy Mackerel" and "Did you see that?" and "Loud enough to wake the dead."

Eva had come out too and added "What the hell?" to the mix. Red had locked himself into the cab. I knew this because Mitch had climbed onto the running board and was simultaneously pulling on the door as he pounded on the window.

My phone rang. "Little lady," Red said, "You need to get your boy off my vehicle." Red waved at me from the cab and stuck his tongue out at Mitch.

"What is wrong with you?" I asked. I hung up on him and dialed 911. "There's been an accident. An incident. A thing. On Easterly Street," I declared to dispatch.

"What kind of a thing?" asked the calm woman's voice at the other end.

"Assault with a dump truck," I said.

"Assault with a come again?"

"Deadly dump truck."

"Someone's dead? That's murder, not assault."

"Not someone. Just the car. The car is annihilated." It took a few minutes for the story to get sorted. And a few more minutes for the police to show up. And for the fire truck to show up. Which was followed by the ambulance, which was followed by a big black sedan. Maybe I hadn't been as clear as I'd hoped.

"Mike?" Eva asked. Officer Hanlon nodded to Eva and me and then turned his attention to Mitch, who was still on the running board pounding on the glass and threatening law suits and concrete boots.

A pair of EMTs emerged from the ambulance and a pair of fireman from the fire truck. "Hey, Dr. Tinker, that you?" said one of the EMT's

Mitch stopped pounding and swearing for a minute and blinked at the blue lights all around. "Kimball?"

"Yep. Me and Larry and Pete and Riley from the station. What are you doing up there?"

"Trying to kill somebody," Mitch said.

"This your car?" Officer Mike asked me, pointing to what was left of the Honda.

"That would be his car." I pointed to Mitch.

"That's a shame," said Officer Mike.

Mitch climbed down from the running board. "That crazy son of a bitch massacred it," he said.

"That why you want to kill him?" asked Officer Mike. Mitch stared at Officer Mike as though he'd just as soon add him to the hit list.

"Can't say as I blame you, Doc," said Larry, the EMT. "I got your back. We all got your back."

"You can't kill him," Officer Mike said. "It's against the law."

"We could work him over a little though, right?" Kimball asked.

"Nope." Officer Mike climbed up onto the running board and knocked on the window. My phone rang again.

"Tell the nice policeman I'm not getting out until he arrests your crazy boyfriend," Red said.

I repeated the message, substituting Mitch's name for "crazy boyfriend." Mitch, AKA the crazy boyfriend, grabbed the phone. "Listen, you shrivel dick-headed idiot," Mitch handed the phone back. "He hung up on me."

"Call him back," Officer Mike said. I hit call back and handed the phone to the policeman.

"You need to step out of the vehicle, sir," Officer Mike said. There was a long pause, followed by some yeses and I sees. Officer Mike eyed Mitch. "No sir, I don't believe that he'll attack you." There was another pause. "No sir, I am not going to arrest him." This was followed by another pause and another I see. Officer Mike put his hand over the phone. "He claims it was an accident," he said. "He apparently hit the wrong lever."

Mitch grabbed the phone again. "I knew you were senile, old man," he said. "But I didn't think you were that senile." He handed the phone back to Officer Mike and gave a single finger salute to the cab.

Officer Mike hit call back.

"Wrong lever?" Carole Ellenburg said. "Can you imagine?" This was followed by a general buzzing amongst the neighbors. Officer Mike climbed down off the running board.

"All right," he said to the general assembly. "Excitement's over. Everybody go home." The buzz turned to grumbling, but everyone did as they were told. Officer Mike pointed to me and Eva and Mitch. "You, you, and you, into the house, please."

"What did I do?" Eva asked.

Officer Mike rolled his eyes. "For the love of Pete, Eva. Just go and sit in Mrs. Othmar's living room. Maybe you could make some tea or something."

"I will not..." Eva began.

Officer Mike raised a contemplative finger to his lips. "I'm sure," he said, "you'd like the scoop on what's going on here."

"You know," Eva said. "It's a great night for tea. Why, I was just thinking. Eva, I thought, wouldn't a cup of tea be terrific right about now?"

Mitch was still staring at the cab, or more to the point, at Red, who seemed to be watching the neighbors as they all milled back to their houses. I put my hand on his arm and gave a little tug. "Tea time," I said.

"My car," he said. "My new car that I haven't finished paying for yet."

The three of us went inside and didn't have tea. We waited and after a few minutes, were rewarded with the slam of a car door. Then in came Officer Mike with Red standing behind him. This was enough to get Mitch started again. He jumped up and pointed, a forefinger this time. "You wrecked my car," he said.

Officer Mike pointed his own forefinger in Mitch's direction. "Do not make me call for backup," he said. "Sit down." Mitch, thinking better of assault, plopped back down on my couch. "And you." Officer Mike turned to Red. "Over there." He pointed to a chair in the far corner of the room. Red, also thinking better for the moment, sat. "Now, we will handle this like adults. Got it?"

"Yes, Officer." Eva sidled closer to Officer Mike.

"Mrs. Othmar." Officer Mike ignored Eva, who then sidled over towards Red. "Care to offer up an explanation?"

I told the story. The whole truth and nothing but the truth. About the granite. And the teddy bear. I even told about the flying lessons and Fat Boy's diner. It made a swell story. Could have been a book. Eva stared at me open-mouthed by the end of it.

"So," Officer Mike said, "what we got here is a love triangle."

"No," Red and Mitch and I said, in unison.

"No?" Officer Mike went over the story, summarizing the plot, but leaving out most of the subtleties and details. "Boyfriend," he said pointing at Mitch. "And scorned ex," he said pointing at Red. "I call them like I see them, and this is your typical love triangle."

"I call them like I see them," Mitch said "And this flea-bitten dick-for-brains wrecked my car." He was half-way off the couch again. I pulled on his arm.

"This dumb-assed-snot-nose had it coming," Red, too, would have risen had Eva not put a hand on his shoulder.

"So, let me get this straight," Officer Mike asked. "Was it or was it not an accident?"

"Providence," Red stared at Mitch. "Divine intervention. An act of God."

Mitch ignored my arm and rose to his feet. Red did the same. They each took a giant step towards the center of the room and began circling each other like wary boxers. I'm not sure who said what, or which insult caused what, but the next thing we knew, they were rolling on the floor. Red had his hands around Mitch's throat as Mitch tried to knee Red in the groin.

"Gentlemen!" Officer Mike said. I suppose it wasn't the right salutation, because neither of them paid heed. "Gentlemen." Officer Mike grabbed his service revolver and held it into the air.

This was too much. Frankly, I'd had enough of them acting like little boys on the playground. I grabbed the revolver from Officer Mike. "What are you doing?" I said. Actually, I might have shouted. I was a tad upset. "This is not the OK Corral."

Officer Mike put up his hands. I gave him what I hoped was a smoldering look. It seemed to work because he looked like a turtle who wanted to pull his head into his shell.

I turned my attention to Mitch and Red, who had stopped wrestling and were both staring at me with wide-eyed attention. "You ought to be ashamed of yourselves," I said.

"Ma'am? Mrs. Othmar?" Officer Mike asked from behind me. I ignored him and pointed the gun at Mitch. "Mitch, really." I shook my head. "Get up *off* the floor."

"Sorry." Mitch scrambled back to the couch.

134

"And you," I said, pointing the barrel at Red, who was on his knees in an effort to make his way back to standing. "*What* exactly are you trying to prove?"

Red raised his hands into the air in an imitation of Officer Mike. "Little lady, I…"

"Don't you little lady me. You can't go around dumping granite on people's cars."

"Little lady…"

"Ma'am? Mrs. Othmar?"

"I think you owe Mitch a new car, don't you? I think that's the *least* you can do considering the circumstances. I think you will buy him a…a…" I turned to Mitch. "What kind of car would you like?"

Mitch furrowed his eyebrows. "Car, Mitch. Come on. There must be something that you've always wanted," I said.

"I don't know. Land Rover?"

"You will buy Mitch a brand new Land Rover."

"Land Rover? You got any idea how much one of those…?"

"*Land Rover.* Unless, of course, you'd prefer doing some jail time. Because I'm pretty sure that dumping granite on someone's car is illegal in this state. Isn't that so, Officer Mike?"

"Yes, illegal. Mrs. Othmar?"

"Eva?" I said.

"Yes, honey?"

"You know how to close deals, right? Could you escort these two hot-headed boys over to your office and maybe work out a contract? Something that says Mitch gets a Land Rover and I get the mess cleaned off the curb and nobody gets hurt?"

"Sure, honey. No problem."

"Mrs. Othmar? India?" Officer Mike was beginning to get on my nerves.

"What *is* it, Mike?"

"The gun? It's um. Loaded." I looked down at the revolver. The barrel that I'd been aiming at Red's chest was now aimed at Officer Mike's crotch.

"Oh," I said. "Yes. Well. Here." I handed over the gun. Officer Mike holstered it. Everything went quiet. They were all still staring at me. "Well, go on," I said. "Things to do, contracts to sign, drug dealers to catch. Get going." And with that, they all scurried from my house.

Chapter Twenty Two

The Aftermath Of Accidents

After they left, I very nearly pulled the emergency Chunky Monkey from the freezer. I could draw a hot bath and climb in with a pint and a spoon. Maybe I'd lace the ice cream with Jack Daniels first. But the thought of walking all the way out to the kitchen was a little overwhelming, so I sat on the couch and buried my head in my hands. When Allie came in half an hour later, I was still contemplating. "There's a crushed car in front of the house," she said.

"I'm aware," I said. Then, of course, I had to tell the whole sordid tale one more time for Allie's edification.

"Wow," she said when I'd finished. "You sure don't lead a dull life."

No, I conceded. A little dull would have been nice right about then.

"You and Mitch Tinker," Eva said as we were walking down Queen's Boulevard the next morning.

"How did the negotiations go?" I asked, mostly to change the subject. This was the third time Eva had evoked Mitch's name and we were still on the first leg of our walk.

"Swimmingly. They are both quite reasonable once you get past the temper tantrums. That Red's a hoot. And Mitch? Mitch is quite smitten. You and Mitch. Good God, India. I'm going to have to start asking you for advice in the romance department."

"So Red agreed to my terms?"

"Hard to refuse a woman who holds you at gunpoint. You and Red and Mitch. Holy shit, India."

"So everything's all set?"

"Of course, signed and sealed. What do you take me for?"

"It's not you I worry about. It's Red Lansing."

"Red's not such a bad guy. When you tire of the young and the restless, you might give him a second chance. "

"Eva…" I grabbed her arm and clenched my teeth.

"Okay, fine. You and Mitch. I'm just saying.."

"If you think Red's so great why don't you date him?"

"Rule four," said Eva. "Never date a man your best friend is involved with." With that, Eva picked up the pace. Mostly, I think, so that I wouldn't grab her arm again.

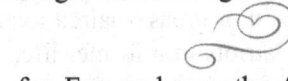

It was, for Eva and me, the first night of our community service. She came over to get me after school. "Ready to do penance?" she asked. She had dressed for penance, a black T-shirt and black jeans, the Eva-version of sack cloth.

The Darrow Street Mission's dining room had cinder block walls painted an alarming shade of tennis ball yellow. The room smelled of burnt coffee and something I would have identified, if pressed, as canned peas.

"Charming," said Eva, taking survey. "They certainly know how to enhance the whole dining experience."

We were met in the industrial strength kitchen by an industrial sized woman named Elba. "You the convicts?" Elba asked, her dark eyes dancing over us with something like amusement.

"No," Eva said and I said, "Yes."

"Uh huh," Elba folded her ebony arms. "What do you know about rice?"

"Rice?" I asked. "You mean, how to cook rice?"

"What do you think I mean?" Elba asked, sounding slightly annoyed.

"She's the one who cooks." Eva cocked a finger at me.

"I know how. To cook rice," I offered.

"Okay. You do the rice." Elba turned her stare on Eva. "And you clean out the storage room."

By 5:30 we were serving red beans and rice to what Elba called the guests. I was doing my level best to be polite and cheery. It was the least I could do for the dejected folks, mostly men, who slumped through the chow line.

"You know," Eva said, scrapping a scoop of beans onto a plate, "the whole Little Miss Sunshine act is getting on my nerves." I told her that she was just upset about the storage room. To which she shoved the plate at the waiting guest and glared at me.

"No meat?" asked the guest, a skeletal man dressed in a T-shirt with a Harley on the front and two holes gaping from the middle.

"Sorry," I said. "Come back tomorrow for smoked pork chops."

"Look, buddy." Eva pointed the serving spoon at the Harley. "Beggars can't be choosers." The guy slunk off with his food.

The next waiting guest, a greasy-haired man who might have been a linebacker for the Patriots in a former life, took his plate and said, "Honey, you ought to learn to treat us nice like your friend there." He pointed his fork at me and smiled a gap-toothed smile. "Now, she's what you call a lady."

"Acquaint yourself with a bar of soap and we'll talk about nice," Eva said.

The guest looked like he might slug her, then thought better of it. "You girls have a nice day," he said.

"The guy might have a point. About nice," I said.

Eva pointed the serving spoon at me. "You can get leered at by the guests all you want, darling. I have to be here, but I can act any damn way I please. And what are you staring at?"

She followed my stupefied gaze to the door, where Red and Mitch had just walked in. Together. Red tipped his Stetson at us.

I was stunned. Eva seemed amused. And Elba? Well, Elba seemed less than pleased. "You got a need?" she said, looking the two of them over.

"I thought you said anyone could eat here," Eva said. "Though God knows it would not be my first choice in fine dining."

Elba glared at her for a moment then turned back to Mitch and Red.

"We came to help," Mitch said, disarming Elba with a smile.

"That's right," Red said. "We owe some community service to Miss Othmar over there."

"We owe Ms. Othmar," Mitch said.

And before you could say red beans and rice, Elba handed them each an apron and a spoon.

As we served, Red kept nodding in my direction and Mitch

kept taking trays from me as though they might be too heavy. Afterwards, Red offered to do the pots and pans while Mitch loaded the dishwasher. Eva sat on a chair and messaged her feet. I grabbed the garbage. Or would have, if Mitch hadn't gotten there first. "I'll do it," he said. At which point Red came over and also grabbed the bag.

"No, no. I'll do it. I don't mind a little trash duty."

"That's okay," Mitch said. They tugged the bag between them and for a minute I thought all hell would break loose.

But then Red smiled at Mitch and said, "I'll just get back to these pots over there," and let go.

To which Mitch said, "I'll dry as soon as I finish garbage detail."

"That would be right nice of you, Dr. Tinker."

"Certainly, Mr. Lansing."

"What in God's name has gotten into you two?" I asked.

"Just trying to act civil, India," Red said.

"Yes. No reason we can't act like adults," Mitch said.

Red offered to drive Eva home and asked if I would be kind enough to give the good doctor a ride. "You rode in together?" I asked Mitch when he'd climbed into my car.

"No reason we can't act…"

"Like adults," I finished. "I know you're a grown-up, Mitch."

"Do you? I sometimes think that you think I'm still ten. My acting like I did yesterday doesn't help my case. I know that."

"You're making a case, are you?"

"Yes. I promise to act like an adult from now on. And I do apologize for my behavior yesterday."

"I apologize, too. I shouldn't have held you at gunpoint."

"Oh, I don't know. You looked kind of sexy holding a weapon."

I asked Mitch if he wanted to come over for a bit and he said, "Of course." Allie was home and the three of us made popcorn and cocoa. By nine o'clock Allie was doing an encore performance of "boy, am I tired," using the less obvious technique of stifling a yawn and saying she had to be at the zoo early.

"She's getting better at that," Mitch said as we watched her trundle up the stairs.

"She could win an Academy Award," I said. I snuggled down and leaned into Mitch's shoulder, taking in his smell, hand soap and shampoo. "I'm so relieved she's good with this."

"With us, you mean?"

"It's bound to be a little awkward. You're a whole lot closer to her age than to mine."

"I wish I were fifty," he said into my hair.

"Don't," I said. I turned and took hold of his face and made him look at me with those beautiful thirty-year-old eyes of his. "Don't wish twenty years of your life away."

"I just want this," he said. "I want us. I want you to know that what I feel about you has nothing to do with how old you are or how old I am."

"Age shouldn't play a part in matters of the heart."

Mitch laughed and kissed me lightly. "Nicely put. Poetic, too."

"I'm trying to let go of the age thing," I said. "Please know that."

"But?"

"But. But Sasha and Tom and Patch. But age has been a factor in that fiasco. A huge honking factor. I don't want to make those kind of mistakes. I don't want to hurt Patch."

"This is not the same thing. I'm not married and I didn't sleep with Patch's girlfriend."

"But you've taken up with his mother. And his mother is very taken with you."

Mitch stroked my hair. "I think we should talk to Patch. We should sit the boy down and talk to him. I'll tell him that I'm taken with his mother and that my intentions are entirely honorable."

"Are they?"

"Oh, yes. Absolutely." He kissed my cheek in illustration and I kissed him back. A little less honorably on the mouth. "Maybe not entirely honorable," he said.

And with that we decided that we'd meet at Mitch's when his shift ended at seven tomorrow. We'd have a heart to heart with Patch and tell him of our very honorable intentions. Ah, the best laid plans.

Chapter Twenty Three

Slander

The next morning, the weekly *Tamsett Tribune* hit doorsteps and mailboxes all over town. The *Tamsett Tribune* is a throw away, a free paper that everyone in Tamsett subscribes to whether they wish it or not. My copy was, as usual, waiting by the front door just under the mail slot. I didn't pay heed to it as I got dressed. I'd taken the day off to go to Boston and meet with Vaughn, the final prelude to my final divorce from Tom, which was a mere week away.

Allie picked up the mail and, with it, the paper, as I buttoned my blouse. I remember this because her "Oh, my God," came up the stairs with enough resonance to send me rushing down.

She handed me the eight-page paper. On the front, covering the top half of the page, was a photo of Mitch's wrecked car. The banner headline read: *Accident? Love triangle results in auto damage.*

Allie and I stood there, staring at the picture. Then Allie slowly, methodically, began to read: *Police were called to 142 Easterly Street last night when a dispute involving Red Lansing, 58, of 28 Merlin Drive and Mitchell Tinker, 30, of 64 Robinton Street resulted in damage of a vehicle. Luckily no one was harmed.*

According to eyewitness Eva DeSantis of 140 Easterly, Lansing was disgruntled that his ex-wife India Othmar of 142 Easterly was romantically involved with Tinker.

"Stop the presses." I grabbed the paper from Allie.

"Ex-wife?" Allie sounded mildly alarmed.

I marched across the drive to Eva's kitchen door and pounded hard enough to shake the glass. When Eva answered, I thrust the paper under her nose. "Care to explain?" I asked.

She looked confused. "Explain what?"

I rustled the paper, though it was too close to her face for her to read it. Eva, realizing this, took it from me. "Why are you reading this rag? The only thing it's good for is cleaning windows."

"Read," I said.

She took a look at the picture on the front. "Oh, my," she said.

"Oh my? You told," I grabbed the corner and glanced at the byline, "Harry Shapiro that Red Lansing was my ex-husband."

"I what? I never even spoke to..." I put my finger to the byline. "Oh, wait. Shapiro. He's Artie's son, isn't he? He does advertising or something."

"Ex-husband?" I said.

"I never said husband. Good Lord, India. Why would I do that? This gossip rag gets everything wrong. Everybody knows that. Remember the triplets story? It was Karen Sullivan, not Karen Dumaris, who had the triplets." She glanced at the headline. "They did get the address right. Have to give them that much."

I snatched the paper from her and tucked it under my arm and marched back to my own home at 142 Easterly Street. It was true, they had gotten the address right.

"Lila Stroud called from school," Allie said. "I told her that the story was not accurate."

I sat on the step and put my head in my hands. Maybe if I closed my eyes the *Tamsett Tribune* would cease to exist. The phone rang.

Allie picked up the receiver. "Hi, Mrs. Carlisle," she said. "No. It's not true." It seemed that the *Tamsett Tribune* wasn't going away any time soon.

By the time I ran, breathless, into Vaughn White's front office, I was half an hour late. I'd had to change my stockings because I'd torn the old ones to shreds in the driveway. By the time I'd found shoes, Allie had fielded six more calls. In my hurry, I'd left my purse and my cell phone behind. By the time I realized it, I was in Boston.

I ran past Vaughn's secretary and invaded his inner sanctum. "I am so sorry," I said. "Traffic."

Vaughn hung up the phone and folded his hand. "I've been trying to reach you all morning."

"Accident," I said. "There was an accident."

"You had an accident?"

142

"Not me. Not now. I was late. I forgot my cell. I'm so sorry."

Vaughn looked me over with something like concern. "Are you sure you didn't have an accident?"

"I'm fine. Honestly. Can we please just get on with this?"

Vaughn looked me over again. "Good God, India."

"What?"

"Your shoes don't match."

I looked down--sure enough I had a brown pump on my right foot and a navy pump on my left.

"If I were a psychologist," Vaughn said, "I might suggest that, subconsciously, you don't want to get a divorce."

"Don't be ridiculous," I snapped. "Watching Dr. Phil does not make you a psychologist."

"True enough. But as your attorney, may I suggest that you come to the proceedings next week looking a little less discombobulated? Unless, of course, you don't mean to go through with the divorce."

I spent the entire ride home thinking up clever comebacks to Vaughn's remark. I didn't come up with anything remotely clever. What I did come up with, what I knew, was that Vaughn's quip had a modicum of truth to it. I dreaded getting divorced. Not that I didn't want to get divorced, it was more that I found letting go to be hard. It's easy, to think when it's over, about how awful the whole ride has been. But the truth is more complicated than that.

The truth was that, once upon a time, Tom Othmar had loved me with the kind of fervor and fierceness that I only thought possible in fairy tales. He'd been the handsome prince and I'd been the princess enchanted. Enchanted I was. That was the real reason I dumped Vaughn. The real reason why I'd not hesitated to marry Tom when I was only twenty. It was the real reason I hung on when he worked late and stayed in the city, when a woman whom he said was "nobody" called him at home. Because I'd believed in that story, the story of us. It was still there, that antiquated fairy tale notion. I was older now, though, and it was time to let the fairy tale go.

And then there was Mitch, tall, handsome, and making me feel like a princess all over again. Only now, I knew what fairy tales could do to you. I wanted so much more of this new thing with Mitch. And the wanting scared the heck out of me.

When I got home, exhausted from the morning's events and my soon-to-be divorce, the thing I wanted most was to stick my head under the shower and forget that this day had ever happened. I knew that it might take more than that. Maybe a long hard sleep would do the trick. Maybe if I closed my eyes and slept until, say, next April, I'd wake up renewed and refreshed, to a brighter world.

I unlocked the kitchen door. A shower would be just the thing. A nice, long hot shower. I would have done just that, too, if Patch hadn't been sitting at the kitchen island next to the purse I'd forgotten and the newspaper I couldn't forget.

Patch pushed the paper in my direction using one finger. If he'd had a stick, he would have used it.

"It's not true. It's wrong. All of it. Most of it. I mean, me married to Red Lansing, how nuts is that?" I said. Patch looked up at me with a look of such devastation and anger and disappointment that it tore my heart in two. He was thirty, but he was still my kid. I'd been the one to bandage his scrapes and feed him soup when he caught a chill. I took his hand. "Patch?" I said.

He tugged the hand free. "What is it with you?" he said, his voice like a trap door shutting. "I trusted you, damn it. It would be nice to have one parent that you could trust."

"This has nothing to do with trust, Patch. This isn't about me being your mother."

"So it is true? You and Mitch?"

I was about to say how Mitch had become as good a friend to me as he'd been to Patch. How I'd come to count on him. How nothing had happened between us, but that wasn't the whole truth and it was abundantly clear that Patch wouldn't have believed me, anyway. "Yes," I said. "It's true."

"Jesus."

"I was going to tell you. Today. I was, but then this whole thing broke and it's been chaos. I'm sorry I didn't tell you."

"Maybe, Mother, you didn't tell me because you know damn well how wrong this is. You knew that I'd point that out to you."

"I knew you'd be upset, yes. But it's not wrong."

Patch looked at me in a way that made me want to climb under the table. He took the newspaper, crumpled it, and pitched it into the trash.

"You need to see this from my point of view," I said.

"No," he said, not turning around at the door, "I don't."

144

"We need to talk about this. Stay. We can talk about it."

He didn't stay. He got into his car and drove off without saying anything at all. I thought about following him, but what good would that do? I grabbed my cell phone and dialed Patch's number. He didn't answer. I left four messages on his voice mail, all of them some version of apology. I was sorry. I hadn't meant for this to happen. I never meant to hurt him. It occurred to me how much I sounded like Tom.

I was still on the step when Mitch drove up. "Little chilly out here," he said. "We should go in." I nodded, not moving and not answering.

"India?" he said, sitting next to me.

"Patch," I said, clutching the phone as though saying his name might make him call.

"Yeah, I know," said Mitch. "We had a little misunderstanding. Words were exchanged." He turned towards me and I saw it. The place where his lip was split.

"Oh, my God," I said, reaching out to touch it.

"It's fine. Nothing serious," he said, taking my hand and pulling it away.

Despite his protests, I filled a bag with ice and made him hold it to his lip. "What happened?" I asked.

"Nothing. Patch got a little upset with me. We had an argument."

"An argument that led to a split lip?" Mitch nodded. "Patch hit you?" I found this hard to believe. Patch wasn't the sort of person to go off and hit someone.

"Back," Mitch said into the ice pack.

"What?"

"Back. Patch hit me back." He looked at the floor.

"He what? You hit him? Hitting is not allowed. There is no hitting. No one hits anyone. Why would you do that?"

"I didn't hit him. Exactly."

"What, exactly, did you do?"

"He was waiting for me in the hospital parking lot. He told me he was moving out and then he said some things that don't bear repeating. I got mad and shoved him."

"You shoved him?"

"I shoved him and he lost his balance and hit his head on the hood of his car. Then he hit me." Mitch put the ice pack down. "He's

145

fine. After he hit me, I took him into the ER to have him checked out. Laura was giving him extra attention when I left."

"Well, this is just ducky," I said. I had begun pacing. "The two men I care about most in the world are slugging each other." Mitch began grinning, a big goofy grin made goofier by the fat lip. "This isn't funny," I said. "This is not the least bit funny."

"I swear that it will never ever happen again," Mitch put his arms around me.

"It better not ever happen again," I said, thumping him on the chest.

"Most in the world?" he said. He had me there. I had said it. I'd meant it, too.

"Most in the world," I said.

Chapter Twenty Four

Borrowed Pens And Bottom Lines

The following Friday I climbed back into my trial outfit, got back into my Camry, and drove into Boston to get divorced. It shouldn't have been nerve wracking. Sad, yes. The bitter ending that had begun to end six months ago. By now, I'd gotten used to the fact that Tom was not coming home. I'd like to say that I had forgiven him, but I wasn't that magnanimous. What I had done was to make an uneasy peace with him. What I had done was resign myself to fact.

Our divorce was touted, by Vaughn anyway, as amicable. Our children were grown and, in Patch's case, not speaking with either of us. Tom, looking what I'd like to think of as contrite, agreed that I should keep the house. I'd pay taxes and upkeep. He would keep the Boston condo. We split our assets with me retaining a forty percent share in Tom's business, and each of us keeping our own medical and retirement plans. It all looked very reasonable on paper. Rational. We were the model for how a thirty-two year marriage should end. The problem was that a thirty-two year marriage was ending. And, despite my best intentions, the ending churned in me like a runaway river in a flood.

The end, true to its amicable nature, was scheduled to occur in Vaughn's conference room. No judge, no banging gavel, no "hear ye, hear ye." Just a couple of lawyers, a couple of Bic pens, a whole lot of paper, and a few signatures.

I was the first to arrive. Vaughn's secretary showed me to the conference room, nodding to a box of donuts and a pot of coffee. The amicable ending was bad enough. I doubted that coffee and donuts would make it easier to swallow.

I wandered around the table after she left, picked up a napkin from a stack near the donuts, and began to knot it.

"Origami?" Tom's voice startled me. I'd been a million miles away, thinking about how Patch hadn't returned my calls all week, how Mitch had said "ouch" when I'd kissed his split lip.

I looked at the napkin in my hand. "You're early," I said. It came out like an accusation.

"So are you," he said, sticking his hands in his pockets and cocking his head sideways, an old habit that I'd always found endearing. Tom being charming. "How are you?" he asked.

"How am I?" I began shredding the napkin into strips. "Never better. You?"

"I've been better," he said. He took a chocolate donut with sprinkles and found a seat. He began picking off the sprinkles one by one. I knew this routine. He'd eat the sprinkles first, then the donut. I knew just as I knew he'd brushed his teeth in the shower earlier that morning and that he'd hunted for his keys until he'd found them in his pants pocket. That he'd hunted for his glasses, too. The ones he'd worn reluctantly to drive over. The ones he'd have to pull from his pocket in order to read through the documents that would put an end to all this familiarity.

I stared out the window. Outside, the sky was a perfect late-fall blue. It would be Halloween soon. At school, we'd made witches' hats and pumpkins and black cats with construction paper and crayons and paste. I used to do up the house. Long after the kids had grown, I still decorated for each holiday in its turn. In my attic, there are boxes upon labeled boxes: Halloween, Thanksgiving, Christmas, Valentine's Day, Easter, The Fourth of July. Each year for nearly thirty years I changed seasons with those boxes. Halloween meant a ghost wreath for the door, ceramic haunted houses for the mantle, pumpkin lights in the window. This year, I hadn't bothered with decorations. It was nearly too late now and I hadn't the heart for it anyway. What I would do was stop at CVS and buy eight bags of trick or treat candy. But first, I'd get a divorce.

Tom took a bite of his denuded donut, the sprinkles on his napkin like a cartoon snowfall. "Aren't you going to eat those?" I asked, pointing.

"What? Maybe later."

I was saved from having to say anything further by Vaughn, who made a grand entrance carrying a sheaf of papers under his arm like the morning news and holding the door for a regally thin

148

brunette. "After you," Vaughn said to the brunette in that way he had, a way that was both gracious and mocking.

We settled onto either side of the conference table, the brunette, Charlotte Slater, sitting next to Tom, and Vaughn next to me. Like a double date was how I would describe it to Eva later. Four adults gone out for donuts and divorce. The other thing I would tell her is how quickly it all went by. The lawyers hashing over the last of the legal jargon, the clients waiting to get it over with. The final signing, dating, and notarization. And it was done. No earthquakes. No Armageddon. Not even a casket. Just handshakes all around, a *well, that's settled* said by one or another of us, a gathering of jackets, and an awkwardly shared elevator to the lobby.

Tom held the lobby door for me and Ms. Slater, shaking her hand one last time as we all passed into the street. I walked off in one direction, she in another. "India?" Tom's voice came up behind me, he was sprint walking to catch me. "What are you going to do now?"

I wasn't sure how to take the question. Now, as in for the rest of today? Or now, as in for the rest of my life? I chose to answer the former. "Go home. Read a book," I said.

"Do you want to grab some lunch first?" I stared at him. Though I didn't say no. I didn't mention that it was only 10:30 in the morning. "I was hoping," he said, "that we could be friends."

"I have enough friends," I said.

"I just meant..."

"I know what you meant."

"So that's it then? I don't get to see you again? Ever?" Tom cocked his head as though he couldn't quite believe this. As though his charm ought to count for something.

"That about covers it."

"You don't do mad well, Indie. Have lunch with me."

I took my keys from my purse and turned them in my hand.

"Please don't let's leave it like this," he said.

I should have. I should have left it just like that. I should have left him standing on the street with his hands in his pockets. I should have shown him what I thought of amicable. But he was right, I didn't do mad well. And thirty-two years don't simply dissolve, they don't just disappear. I didn't get to just walk away. It would have been great, in theory, to just walk away. But in another six months, another year, I knew that I'd come to regret it.

"Coffee," I said. "It's too early for lunch."

"Coffee," he said, "and I'll throw in a bagel."

Regret is a funny thing. Six months or a year from now I might have regretted the lack of closure, the lack of ceremony that just walking away would have represented. For now, I regretted agreeing to coffee. I regretted the basement café, the wobbly table near the window that looked out onto a brick wall, and the feet of passing pedestrians. I regretted that Tom knew to order the dark roast for me, knew to fix it with a hint of milk and a scant teaspoon of sugar. He knew I would want a poppy bagel with raspberry cream cheese. I knew his coffee would be white with cream and his bagel would be garlic. Vampire bagels, I would have teased once upon a time.

"This is good," he said, setting down our order. "This is better."

"Better than what?"

He studied me for a minute. Tom being studious. "I'm sorry, but just walking away after that. It seemed wrong." He steepled his hands as though pleading for me to agree.

"You think coffee and bagels are going to heal all wounds? The new miracle food. You could make a fortune."

He looked at me as though I'd struck him. "No. Of course not. I was hoping that…that we could get to a new place. There are lots of divorced couples who manage to stay friends."

"To be amicable?" I said. I wasn't good at sarcasm and Tom was not good at listening for nuance.

"Exactly," he said. He went on to name three couples, old friends of ours, who had remained friendly after splitting. I could have named four couples, at least, who hadn't.

I spread the raspberry cream cheese on my bagel. It looked artificial. I was sure that it would taste that way, too. Like a false promise. I put the plastic knife down. "I can't do this," I said. I stood up.

"Please, don't go. I'm trying here. Can't you see that?"

"This is trying?" I took the bagel, cream cheese and all, and threw it into the trash. Someday, I might regret this. But for now, it felt pretty damn good.

Tom caught my arm on the outside stairs. "I'm sorry."

"I know. You never meant to hurt me. I've heard it."

"Please, just.." And his cell phone rang. I would have walked off if he hadn't been holding on to my arm.

"You better answer that," I said. "It's probably Sasha wondering if you are finally free of the wife who doesn't understand you."

"This hasn't been easy for me, either, you know," he said. The phone stopped ringing. Tom let go of my arm.

"Really?" I said. "Good." The phone started ringing again and I marched resolutely up the stairs. I got into my car and drove away from Boston. I waited until the rest stop on Route 128 to pull over and have myself a good long cry.

Chapter Twenty Five

Gauntlets

Eva was waiting at my house with a bottle of Stoli. "Drink this," she said, pouring it into an ice-filled glass.

I took a long swallow. It didn't burn away what I was feeling. "I didn't think it would be this hard," I said. We had, after all, spent months negotiating, splitting, rewording. We knew the end was coming, we had worked towards ending. So why was the end so hard?

"Allie called three times," Eva said. "And Mitch. The next time you get divorced, please take your cell phone so that you can talk down the Boy Wonder." I took another swallow of vodka and thought of Tom's cell phone ringing and ringing.

"Did Patch?" I asked.

Eva shook her head. "He will," she said.

He didn't. Not that day nor the next nor the one after that. I knew Allie had spoken with him, I overheard her hissing into the phone, the words "divorce" and "make Mom happy" coming out loud and clear.

"He's rented a condo at Wuthering Heights," she told me. It was Sunday and we were reading the paper and eating muffins. I had been divorced for three days.

Allie took a slip of paper, wrote on it, and slipped it next to my coffee mug.

I turned it around. It said 14 Heathcliffe Lane.

Patch's car wasn't in the driveway, but the door had been left ajar. I knocked twice and called his name. When no one answered, I stepped over the threshold, door still in hand, and called again. There were boxes blocking the entrance to the kitchen. I stepped around them and put the plate of macaroons I'd brought on the counter. The front door slammed shut and there stood Patch, arms folded, next to the pile of boxes.

"I brought macaroons," I said. I thought of the café, of Tom buying me a bagel. Stupid to think macaroons were miracle cures, either.

Patch went to the counter and sniffed the cookies as though they were suspect. "I made them myself," I said.

"Mom." He raised his hands as though I'd caught him at something illicit.

"This thing with Mitch," I said. Might as well cut to the chase. "I understand why you're upset, I do. But please know that it has nothing to do with you. I love you, Patch. I always have and I always will."

"You love me. Yet you think it's perfectly acceptable to sleep with one of my friends. Please understand that it doesn't sit well, Mother. You of all people should know that."

He fingered one of the cookies and bit his lip.

"I didn't," I said, feeling the blood seep up into my cheeks. "Sleep with him." I didn't add *yet*. Because if things kept going in the direction they were going, I would. Probably sooner than later.

"Then it shouldn't be hard to end it," Patch said.

"End it? That's..." How could I finish that sentence? That it wasn't fair? "I don't want to. End it," I said.

"Then we have nothing to discuss," Patch said.

"He's being an ass," Allie said. "He's totally unreasonable." She and Eva and I were drinking white wine and eating Cherry Garcia.

"He's clueless," Eva said.

"He's right," I said. Allie stopped mashing her ice cream. Eva put down her glass. "Mitch is way too young for me. I mean, it's flattering, all the attention he's given me. But really. You said so yourself, Eva."

"The evidence shows," Eva said, "that I was wrong." She took her wine glass and raised it in a toast. "Mitch is totally and heartily

153

crazy over you. That is abundantly clear in the way he acts around you. And judging from the way you look every time his name is mentioned, it is also abundantly clear you feel the same about him. You are happy with him and I am happy you are happy. I was blind not to notice it earlier. There, I've said it. I've overruled myself. I find for the Boy Wonder. He is perfect for you."

"Maybe I should give Red another chance," I said.

Allie put her spoon down. "Please tell me you're kidding," she said.

"Red's not so awful," Eva said. "But your mother can't have him. Because I'm having dinner with him on Friday."

"What happened to rules two and four?" I asked.

"They have also been overruled in light of new findings."

"What new findings?"

"I find that I am intrigued by a man who dares to use granite," Eva said.

"We need to talk," I told Mitch the next day. He was taking me for a ride in his brand new Land Rover, fully loaded with stereo speakers and a moonroof, courtesy of Red Lansing's bad temper.

"I should get my car compacted more often," he'd said as he pulled me from the house to the car. He went on for quite a while about four-wheel drive and how he couldn't wait to try it out on the mountain roads when he went ice climbing.

Mitch, it turned out, liked to ice climb. One of many things I hadn't known about him. I could not imagine Tom hanging off the face of an icy cliff. Tom was more of a bookstore and symphony guy. I never considered ice climbing, although the adventure might be fun. Mitch grinned when I confessed this. "Maybe we'll start with rock climbing. Next summer. If you dare."

Next summer! I was having trouble with next week, which would bring my fifty-second birthday. And in a few weeks after that, my first Thanksgiving as a divorcee. Between now and next summer was Christmas and New Year's and Valentine's Day and Groundhog Day and St. Patrick's Day and Easter. I hadn't known any of them single for a long, long time.

"I don't know," I said. Which was right before "we've got to talk" slipped out of my mouth. It got quite a reaction. Mitch pulled on to the shoulder of the country road we'd been bumping along. The

154

car came to a thudding stop.

I looked out at the tree branches scraping the passenger side window. "Patch," I said.

"Patch," he repeated.

"He's really unhappy."

"Patch is a big boy, India." Mitch didn't sound happy, either. "He's a grown up. I'm a grown up. You are a grown up. We should all just grow up."

I didn't mention the babbling over the new car. Do grown men open and shut the moonroof four times to show it off? Well, maybe they do. "But maybe he's right. Maybe…"

"Dear God, not the age thing again. I thought we were past that." I felt his hand on my shoulder. "What do I have to do to convince you I don't give a damn about that? " Mitch's hand brushed through my hair and caressed the back of my neck. "You're smart and funny and very beautiful. I like being with you. And Patch has nothing to say about it."

I turned to face him. "You like rock climbing. You like *ice* climbing. I like falling asleep in front of the ten o'clock news. Where do you see this going?"

"It doesn't matter where it goes." Mitch's hands cupped my face. "You know, when I took the job in Tamsett, I couldn't have said why. I had better offers. I was working in a first class trauma center at Brigham's and I could have stayed there. My friends thought I was kind of nuts. But Tamsett held some good memories for me and I was looking for something. I didn't know what. Then last spring you walked into the ER and I had this feeling. That I'd known all along why I had to come back." Mitch smoothed his hands over my cheeks. "Maybe that sounds crazy. Maybe it is crazy. The bottom line is that I want you in my life, India. And I don't give a good God damn what anybody else thinks about this. I don't care what Patch thinks."

For the last thirty-two years, I'd built a life with Tom, raising a family, paying off a mortgage. And what had that brought me? A cup of coffee and a bagel. Maybe Mitch was right. To hell with it. For once, I ought to allow myself to do what's right for me. I took Mitch's face into my hands and kissed him. "I want you in my life, too. You make me really happy."

"The timing may be all wrong for this," he said, pulling something out of the glove compartment. He handed me a long white envelope. "Happy Birthday," he said.

Inside was a brochure for the Mount Washington Hotel. "What is this?"

"A weekend," he said.

"A weekend?" I said this pretty calmly considering that, inside, I was saying, *"A weekend?"* And there it was again, that mix of oh, my God, help and oh, my God, yes.

"The Friday and Saturday after your birthday. We'd come back Sunday." Mitch pulled back out onto the road. "Unless you'd rather not go."

"I want to go," I said.

"But?" he said.

I looked at him, exasperated. "But nothing. I want to go. Thank you," I said. I kissed him again, trying to convince him even as I convinced myself.

Chapter Twenty Six

Interventions

My birthday fell on a Thursday that year and coincided, as it happened, with Eva's and my last day of community service. Eva thought a birthday at Darrow with the derelicts was about as appealing as a birthday spent having your tonsils removed without anesthesia. I thought otherwise. Between work and the Darrow Street Mission, I'd been busy. And busy was exactly how I'd wanted to be.

I felt about my birthday much as I felt about my divorce. Given a choice, I think I'd rather not. Given a choice, I would have skipped merrily ahead to Friday, when Mitch would come pick me up in his brand new SUV and we'd head out for what Eva called The Great Northern Adventure. To say that I was nervous about the adventure would have been stating the obvious. It was a good thing I had Allie and Eva cheering me on. Because I couldn't help wondering what Patch was thinking. I didn't know what Patch was thinking because he still wasn't talking to me. Or to Mitch, for that matter.

Linda Elsberg, the reading specialist at school, baked birthday brownies, which were shared with the entire faculty at lunch. The staff presented me with a card and a gift certificate to Elizabeth Arden. "So you can spiff up for your big date with the hot young doctor," Ann Mullin, fellow kindergarten teacher, quipped. Hot young doctor? When had my life become an episode of *All My Children*? All that was missing was a schizophrenic twin sister and a bad case of sudden-onset amnesia.

Allie left a bouquet of birthday daisies in the kitchen. She'd been giving me birthday daisies ever since she discovered they were my favorite flowers when she was still a little girl. It made me glad to find them after work. Glad that some things don't change.

I had the balance of the day planned out. I'd do my time at the Darrow. Mitch was working, but promised he'd drop in on dinner break to say hey. Then Eva, Allie, Liz, and I would come home to the cake Allie had no doubt ordered from the supermarket bakery. We'd have cake and decaf. Then we'd say goodnight and the whole birthday experience would be behind me. Maybe, somewhere along the way, Patch would call. It would be great if Patch would call.

I hadn't figured on walking into the Darrow and having Eva, Allie, and Liz, along with Mitch, Elba, and a host of regular guests yell, "Surprise!" The place still smelled of canned peas and the cinder block walls were still an alarming shade of yellow, but there were streamers curled around the florescent lights, balloons tied to all the tables, and a huge sheet cake that said, "Happy Don't Remind Me Day India" written in bright yellow icing. There was one candle, a big black one, stuck into the middle of the cake.

Everyone had ziti with meat sauce, the nightly offering, followed by cake and coffee. I sat next to Mitch like a nervous bride. I couldn't help thinking about the Great Northern Adventure.

Eva, sitting on my other side, gave me a little nudge and said it was going to be a banner year. It was Eva who'd kept me from calling the whole adventure to a halt. "You'd be a fool not to go," she'd said, when I spouted my misgivings.

"I might be a fool anyway," I'd said.

"Nonsense. There's nothing to worry about. It's not as though you're about to lose your virginity."

I've never considered myself a prude, but she had stepped dangerously close to a big slag pile with that comment. It made me blush. And sputter. "That's just dumb." Which was, really, a pretty dumb thing to say.

Eva's eyebrows went up a notch. "How long has it been?" she asked.

"Eva, really."

"At least six months. No, longer. A *lot* longer." And with that, she'd stepped right into it.

"However long," I said, "It's none of your business."

"That long? Just so you know, it hasn't changed much since you've been away."

"You haven't changed your mind, have you?" she asked after

158

we'd pulled back into our driveways. Mitch had gone back to work. Allie and Liz had mumbled something about a bottle of wine and had gone off saying they'd catch up.

"No. Of course not," I said, willing myself to sound the conviction I didn't feel.

The light flashed on my answering machine. "Ed McMahon calling about the millions," I joked to Eva. But, secretly, I hoped it was Patch. It wasn't Patch. It wasn't Ed, either. There on the machine was Tom's voice invading the room. "India! Many happy returns on the day. You see, I remembered."

"Good Lord, even his phone messages are self-serving," Eva said.

"He was just trying to be nice. He wants for us to be friends."

"Really? How quaint."

"I told him no."

"Good girl. Though 'go fuck yourself' might have been a more satisfying response."

"Not my style."

"And this from a woman who is boinking a man half her age." And there it was, the incessant blushing again.

"We should start without them," Eva said. We had been waiting half an hour for Allie and Liz to get home.

"They're the ones bringing the wine," I said.

"They probably absconded with the wine and drank it."

"Now, now. They are young and in love and you need to cut them some slack."

Eva opened her purse and pulled out a silver flask. "You ought to take your own advice where slack is concerned. Does Tom know? About Liz?"

"Allie plans on telling him at Thanksgiving. She's going to his place. She's asked if she can bring her friend."

"Ooh, can I come?"

"It gets better," I said. I couldn't help smirking. "Marissa's going to be there. Tom hasn't told her the divorce is final. Nor has he mentioned Sasha."

"Dear God, he must want to kill the old girl for her money."

I would love to be a fly on the wall of that festivity, I told Eva. My ex-mother-in-law loved her son to distraction. But she also loved

159

propriety. Marissa was the status quo. She'd taken such pride in my long marriage. And she had always thought me perfect for her only son.

Tom had grown up in Newport, Rhode Island, though his parents were far from being millionaires. Thomas Senior had owned a small string of dry cleaning shops, three of them to be exact, in Brooklyn. When Tom was ten, Tom Senior sold all three shops and opened a fourth in New England. They lived in a bungalow five blocks from the ocean, a far cry from the mini-mansions and true mansions that dotted the town. If anyone asked why they moved, Marissa would shrug and say, "For Tommy, of course." Because, in Newport, Tommy could be with the right sort of people.

Tommy ended up going to Boston University with Vaughn, a man who was blue- blooded down to his knickers. And then Tommy ended up with me, the daughter of a history professor. My father and grandmother had raised me. My father taught me how not to make a fool of myself at social events. My grandmother taught me to use my brain. Then I met Tom and forgot everything I'd been taught.

Marissa was thrilled with me. A professor's daughter was just the thing for her Tommy. She did everything to ensure that things worked out for us. For years, she aimed at charting the course for us. And for years, I'd let her.

"It's going to be quite the feast," I said to Eva, raising my glass.

"Here's to Marissa Othmar and the shockwaves that will ensue." Eva clinked her glass to mine.

"I hope Tom has earthquake insurance," I said just as Allie and Liz stormed my kitchen, Patch between them like one of those criminals on *Cops*.

I nearly dropped my glass. In fact, the whiskey I'd been toasting with sloshed out of the glass and onto my shirt, leaving a bullet of a stain in its wake.

Allie, a foot shorter than her brother, and Liz, the same size as Allie, had Patch's arms twisted behind his back as they hauled him in my direction. It was quite the sight, sort of like the Keebler Elves commandeering the Jolly Green Giant.

"Say it," Allie said. Patch winced as she twisted.

I stood up. "Allie, stop."

She ignored me. *"Say it,"* she said.

"Happy Birthday," Patch yelped. Allie twisted again.

"No," she said. "One more time. With feeling."

"Happy birthday, Mom." Patch glared at me.

"And?" Allie twisted again.

"No," he said.

"Allie, you're hurting him," I said.

"*And?*"

"And I am heartily sorry. Now let the fuck go."

Allie did. And all hell broke loose. The next thing I knew, Allie was prostrate on the kitchen floor and Patch was sitting on her. "Do not ever do that again," he said.

"Honestly," I said. "Patch, get off your sister. How old are you?" I used my best teacher/mother authority voice. It still worked like a charm. Patch looked at me as thought I'd slapped him and climbed off Allie.

"Talk to your daughter," he said. "She came over to my house and assaulted me. Her and that one." Patch pointed to Liz, who looked mildly embarrassed.

"Assault?" I asked. Allie and Liz together probably didn't outweigh Patch. I couldn't help smiling.

"*Not* funny," said Patch. "She's a ninja. And that one," he pointed to Liz again, "ought to work for the CIA in the Special Forces unit." Liz was still studying her shoes, but I detected the smallest of smirks.

"If you weren't such a dweezil," Allie said, "we wouldn't have to resort to extreme measures." Allie stood up and brushed off her pants. "We're doing an intervention here, Mom. You and Eva can join in any time. The basic idea is that we want to remind dweebo what a terrific mom you are and what an asshole he's being where your happiness is concerned."

"Gee thanks, honey," I said. "You really shouldn't have."

"It's your birthday." Allie put her arm around my shoulder. "And Patch was what you wanted, right? You put up a good front, but I know his being a no-show at your party upset you."

"Well, yes, it did. But you shouldn't have. Patch is entitled to his opinion. He's upset with me. I understand that."

"You," Allie said, "are the only one who does." She went over to Patch and gave him a shove to the chest. "You owe Mom a present. Plus you've got to fix the dent in my car door."

"Dent?"

"He kicked it," Liz said.

"You knee'd me," Patch said.

"You deserved it." Liz wasn't looking at her shoes anymore.

Patch wasn't contrite. Not at first, anyway. Eva poured from her flask and Allie poured from the bottle of red and together they made him toast, along with the rest of us, to my fifty-second year. This began a long series of toasts: to my new found freedom, to the budding relationship between Allie and Liz, to Patch's new practice. "To India and Mitch and the Great Northern Adventure." Eva raised her glass for the umpteenth time. Patch put his glass down.

"What's that?" he said. Not as in *what is that*. More as in, *did I hear you right*?

"Mitch is whisking your mother away for a weekend." Eva swayed with her glass. "A Happy Birthday Travel Trip!"

Patch stared at me, shook his head, and made way for the door. At this point, the whole Special Forces scene began again.

The alarm went off, alarmingly, at 7:00 AM. I jolted bolt upright in bed, my head caught in a vise. This was not an auspicious beginning for the Great Northern Adventure.

Patch was sacked out, still fully dressed, on my living room couch. Allie and Liz were making coffee in the kitchen. Liz poured something noxious into a glass and handed it to me. V8 juice mixed with a little cranberry juice, she explained. A cure. I wasn't at all sure it could do much besides make me feel worse, but I drank it down in one gulp. To my credit, I didn't spit it back up.

By the time Mitch arrived at 9:00, I'd showered and packed my bags, and Patch had stumbled his way to the kitchen. He looked at Mitch as though his friend had just run over his foot with the new SUV. "So you're going?" he said to me.

Mitch had my bag in one hand, the other hand on the door. "It's a weekend," I said.

"That's how it starts," Patch said. "A weekend. Next thing he's moving in. I am *not* calling him Dad."

We'd been all over this and back again last night. Allie had gone on about how it was my life and did Patch really want to ruin my chance, perhaps my last chance, at happiness. I had taken a deep gulp of wine. Eva said that I was already on edge and the last thing I needed was Patch on my case. I gulped more wine.

"Give us a minute?" I said to Mitch.

"I'll just put the suitcase…" I nodded and turned to my wonderful and somewhat stubborn son.

"Yes, Patch. I am going. I'm sorry that you don't like it, but I'm going. And when I come back, I am going to keep on seeing Mitch. And you are just going to have to learn to live with it."

I looked back towards the house as we pulled into the street, causing Mitch to pull back into the driveway.

"Drive," I said, taking Mitch's hand and squeezing.

"Ouch. You sure?"

"Drive," I said, not adding please. And he did.

Chapter Twenty Seven

The Great Northern Adventure

It had been years since I'd had anything remotely romantic in my life. I'd been married. Tom and I had been busy. We'd been mulching the lawn and baking brownies for bake sales and getting estimates for the roof. We'd been covering up affairs and pretending that affairs never happened. Oh, there had been a once upon a time. There had been dating and a honeymoon in Key West. There had been a tiny apartment with a single bed. Patch came along the year after the wedding. I was twenty-one, and romance became something I read about in novels.

Until now. Until Mitch. Mitch with his Teddy bears and his apple pancakes and kisses that stretched into infinity. Mitch holding my hand and walking with me into the lobby of a beautiful old hotel. The place was a romance-novel setting, huge bouquets of fresh flowers on glossy polished tables, an entire wall of fireplace with chairs so plush you could spend a week in them. Through the windows, the mountains gray and green, shadow and light, a snow white napkin covering each peak. My heart bounced and bounded in that lobby.

Then came the room. Another gorgeous view. A private balcony. More oversized chairs. An oversized bed front and center. A humungous king-sized bed serving to remind me of how long it really had been. Bringing on that little voice of doubt again. *I'm so much older. Can I do this?* Balanced against *I want this.*

Before getting back to the room, we'd walked down a wood trail, scuffling the leaves under our feet, trying to catch the ones still falling. We'd had a candlelit dinner, where Mitch's thigh bumped against mine under the table. We'd sat in those chairs. All of it a preamble to the room.

"Here we are," I said, as Mitch opened the door.

"Yes," he said. "here we are."

I thought of the satin nightgown I'd slipped into my bag. Eva had given it to me for my birthday. It was red. It had spaghetti straps. It had fringes. Thinking about it made my face hot. "I'm going to brush my teeth," I said. I went into the bathroom and shut the door. The three-way mirror and stadium lighting did nothing for my self-esteem.

"India?" Mitch called from outside the door. I'd been staring at my reflection, taking inventory of every wrinkle and mole, for quite some time. "Everything okay?"

"Yes. Fine. I'm flossing."

I came from the bathroom still fully dressed. My teeth looked as though I'd just come from the hygienist. I had breath to match. Mitch kissed me. "Nice job," he said before disappearing into the bathroom.

Which is when it hit me. The two of us were circling each other like virgins on our wedding night. I looked myself in the eye in the mirror above the dresser and told myself in no uncertain terms that I was being a ninny. I was fifty-two years old, for God sakes. I had children. I knew how to do this. Then I stripped off everything I had on and dove under the covers before I could change my mind. Having a few second thoughts, I turned off the light.

When Mitch came out of the bathroom in the pitch dark, he bumped into the dresser. I turned the light back on and hunkered down. Mitch rubbed his knee.

"Soft sheets," I said. "Must be Egyptian cotton. Very high thread-count."

Mitch sat on the bed. My heart rate went up. "You look a little warm," he said, tugging at the covers. I grabbed him before he could pull them off. He kissed my neck, his hands moving down my arms.

"I'm not wearing anything," I whispered, getting into the spirit.

"That's too bad," he whispered back.

I pushed him away and shoved the quilt back over my shoulders. "Too bad?"

"I was hoping to help you out of all those heavy clothes," he whispered into my ear before kissing me hard.

"Oh," I said. "Oh." I pulled off his shirt, conveniently unbuttoned. "Turn around," I said.

"Pardon?"

"You heard me." He turned his back and I put the shirt on and buttoned all the buttons. "Okay," I said.

Mitch grinned. "Nice," he said. We began again. He unbuttoned a button. Then another. I stopped him after three. "My turn," I said. "Fair is fair." I undid his jeans and helped him struggle free of them. I was feeling wanton.

"One minute," said Mitch. He hopped out of bed and came back with a box of condoms. "I got the twelve pack," he said. Then he began unbuttoning again. Button four, button five, button six. I stopped him at the last button.

"Mitch?'

"Uhm?"

"I'm not. Well. Things aren't as. Firm. Not saggy. Well, okay, a little. Saggy. A little soft and..."

"India?"

"Uhm?'

"Please shut up now." He undid the last button and put his hands to my somewhat less than firm hips. We fell back into the soft high thread-count cotton sheets. And my thought, as his lips worked their way south, was *I've missed romance. I've missed romance a whole lot.*

Afterwards, we lay nestled deep in each other's arms. If there was a heaven, I thought, it would be filled with moments like this one, my ear against Mitch's chest, taking in each breath he took. Feeling each of those breaths like my own.

"What are you thinking?" Mitch asked, running his hand along my shoulder.

"That this is my favorite part," I said. "Being sated, happy. Feeling as though everything you need in this world is right here. There's a name for it. Afterglow."

"Afterglow." Mitch smiled down at me. "What about during?"

I ran a finger over his lips. "Oh, during is great. During is terrific. There could be no after without during."

"How do you feel?" Mitch rolled on top of me, "about after afterglow?"

I'd missed romance and long lingering mornings spent together in bed and the thunderous sex that comes with those moments. I'd missed skin on skin and lips on skin.

It all went by so quickly, in a torrent of moments, each more pleasing than the next. "I'd like to stay forever," I said on Sunday morning, while we were still on the island of that big bed, snow falling in huge wet late autumn flakes just outside the window.

"Maybe we'll get lucky and the car won't start," Mitch said, running his fingers along the curve of my breast.

Alas, the Land Rover was brand new. The snow melted upon hitting the pavement. Maybe forever was too much to ask. Forever was an awfully long time. In forever, I might start to miss Allie and Patch and Eva. I might start to miss the tumbling kindergartners in my classes. This was all so new. So romantic. But forever was a long time.

Home waited for us as though we'd never left it. Allie met us at the door, her face flush and set in a smile. "Tell me everything," she said.

To which Mitch, his arm draped casually over my shoulder, pulled me in tighter and questioned, "Everything?"

"Okay not everything *everything*. Things were good, right? Really good."

"I'd say things were pretty terrific," I said. Mitch's eyes caught mine. God, I could live inside those perfect light brown eyes.

"Pretty darned terrific," Mitch agreed.

"I made dinner," Allie said. "Chili. Well, it's from a package, but still." She sped past us into the kitchen and turned the flame down under a pot, then pulled a loaf of bread from Sullivan's bakery out of its sleeve. "Liz is here, too. I thought we could have dinner, you know, the four of us."

Liz appeared at the kitchen door as though she'd been waiting for her cue. Allie went to her and draped an arm over her girlfriend's shoulder. There we were, the four of us. Mitch and me, Allie and Liz, arms draped. Allie with a smile that I'd called crazed if I didn't know her better. Liz looking like the proverbial deer caught in the headlights. We seemed to stand there for a very long time.

"So," Mitch said finally. "Chili."

"Yes," Allie said. "Chili. And those blue corn chips you like, Mom. She handed the bag to me as though I'd just won them as a door prize. I was about to say lovely or thank you or how wonderful

Afterglow

when Liz cleared her throat.

"Now?" Allie said. Liz shrugged and rolled her eyes. "Well, okay. No time like the present. Liz and I are moving in together. Don't worry, we're not going to move into my room. I'm moving in with Liz. In Boston."

I was a little surprised. Not entirely, I have to admit, unpleasantly. I loved having Allie around, but she was twenty-five and still looking for herself. Maybe she'd found herself with Liz. That was a good thing. "That's wonderful, honey," I said and I gave her a squeeze. Then I gave Liz a hug and told her it was wonderful, too.

So Allie moved out. And Mitch didn't move in. Though he did keep a toothbrush where Tom's used to be and several changes of clothes in the empty side of my bedroom closet.

168

Chapter Twenty Eight

Thanks

Tom called two days before Thanksgiving. "It's going to be strange," he said, "not doing the whole family turkey thing. I'm going to miss your turkey."

I reminded him that he *was* doing the whole turkey thing. Marissa was coming from Providence. Allie and Liz were coming. I was the one who wouldn't be doing the whole turkey thing.

Mitch would be working a double shift on Thanksgiving so that the other ER doctor could spend the day with his wife and three children. "It's just another day," was Mitch's take on it. I didn't agree with his no big deal attitude toward the holiday. It seemed a big deal, maybe because I'd never spent a major holiday alone before.

"I'm sure Sasha will do just fine," I said to Tom now. I didn't even choke on her name. I had Mitch, after all, who would come by after his shift ended. I had Mitch, and Tom could have turkey and Sasha and his mother. He could even have the company of Allie and Liz. It would all turn out for the best. I wished the best for Tom.

Well, okay, I didn't really wish the best for him. Though I might like to be, I'm not that magnanimous. It would probably be a disaster and that would serve him right. I imagined the still frozen turkey that Sasha had forgotten to thaw, and burnt potatoes and undercooked squash.

"We're having it catered," Tom said.

"How nice," I said. I changed the imaginary scenario to Sasha dropping the pre-cooked turkey on the floor and Marissa smiling tightly while sipping her third gin and tonic and Allie introducing all of them to her girlfriend Liz.

"Would you," Tom said as I pictured Marissa, three gin and

tonics to the wind, winding her grandmotherly pearls in her fist while a large gravy stain grew on the plush beige carpet.

"Would I?" I repeated.

"You would? Really?"

"Would what?"

There was a long pause followed by one of Tom's it's-all-useless sighs. "Weren't you listening at all?"

The reflex response would have been, *of course I was*, complete with my trying to piece the conversation together. It was what I would have done. "No, actually," I said. "I wasn't."

"You aren't ever going to make this any easier, are you?" Sweet annoyance in my ex-husband's voice.

Now I paused. To contemplate hanging up the phone. "I asked," said Tom, "if you would care to join us. I graciously asked, in the name of family, if you could join us."

"Why, for the love of God, would I want to do that, Tom?"

"For your daughter, India. For our daughter. For love and peace and harmony. I don't know. It would be a gesture." His voice rose at "gesture". I hadn't lived with Tom Othmar for thirty-two years without learning to recognize the tone. It was the voice of desperation.

"Sasha's not going to be there, is she?" I took a stab in the dark and hit a nerve.

"Do not bring Sasha into this. This is about civility. Mary and Fred have been divorced for ten years and they still have Thanksgiving together."

"Sasha is not coming because you haven't told Marissa about her."

"Will you come? For Allie's sake? For my mother's sake? My mother loves you, Indie. She adores you."

"Poor Tom." I almost meant it. Marissa had hated Sasha when she was Patch's girlfriend. *Gold-digger*, she'd called her. *A little opportunist. A social climber*. Though what kind of social Marissa imagined her climbing, one can only guess.

"Okay. For me. For what we once had," Tom said.

"Had being the operative word," I said. And then I hung up without saying goodbye.

"You should have said yes. It would be worth it to see Marissa

Othmar have apoplexy," Eva said as we were walking early the next morning. She had just invited me to come with her and Red to the Feed Bag for what Red called a turkey buffet that will nearly kill you. It was billed as the Feed Bag Feast.

I told her that, tempting as that sounded, I was going to have to pass. I had plans. I was going to spend my Thanksgiving with Elba and the good folks down at the Darrow Street Mission. Mitch and I had bought half a dozen turkeys to donate. I planned to help cook them. I had even marched myself over to Patch's condo and begged him to come help me. My son may not have been thrilled with my new found romance, but he was a sucker for good deeds. Which was, incidentally, exactly what Eva called me. A sucker for good deeds.

Patch and I had come to an uneasy alliance. He made it known that he didn't approve of my relationship with Mitch Tinker. But I was still his mother, and he, long-suffering son that he was, would put up with my foolishness so long as Mitch and I didn't ask him to double date.

When I rang the bell on Thanksgiving morning, Patch didn't answer. His car was in the driveway and I could hear parade commentary floating in from the living room. I rang again, then opened the unlocked door, then called Patch's name, and finally walked into the kitchen.

Patch was on his cell phone, his back to me. "Yes," and "I know," he said into the phone. "What do you want me to say?" I came around so he'd see me and gave him a finger wave. "I'll have to call you back," he said. There was a pause. "In a little while. I'll call you. Yes, I promise. No, that's not what I said." He hung up and stuck the phone in his pocket. "Mom!" he said, as though he was surprised to see me.

In my defense, I had called before coming over. He had agreed to Thanksgiving at the shelter and to my swinging by to pick him up so we could ride over together.

"You're early," he said.

I looked at my watch. "Nine-thirty. Isn't that what we said on the phone?"

"Nine-thirty. My God, is it nine-thirty already?" His cell phone rang. He checked the number and put it on the counter as though it were an explosive device. It kept ringing. Actually, it kept playing the theme for *Mission Impossible*. We both watched it. Maybe it would self-destruct.

"Aren't you going to answer that?" I asked.

"Don't we have to go?" Patch asked.

I'd mentioned my grandmother's sausage stuffing to Elba and she soon had me making a several hundred serving sized version of it for the guests. It was the same stuffing I'd made every year since Patch was born. It had always been the hit of the Thanksgiving feast. Everyone loved it, though they'd probably have an on-the-spot coronary if they knew the fat content of the recipe. "Fat content?" Elba said. "It's Thanksgiving!" Granny Smirtoff would have said the same thing. Like my granny, Elba looked like she wasn't given to worrying over calorie counts generally.

Patch helped to stuff the birds and we set them to roasting. We peeled potatoes and squash. We had a wonderful time, laughing and reminiscing about Thanksgivings gone by and discussing the federal budget and just about anything else that had nothing to do with the Thanksgiving we were missing at the condo and the fact that I was still dating Mitch Tinker. It would have been a perfect morning if Patch's phone hadn't kept on interrupting. Sometimes, Patch just went on talking, letting the theme from *Mission Impossible* play as background music. Sometimes, he answered and went off into the pantry for a while.

"Is Laura going to drop by after work?" I asked after he'd visited the pantry for the fourth time. Laura, I knew from Mitch, was working until 3:00. She and Patch had begun dating regularly and, as far as I could tell, exclusively.

"I believe so, why?" Patch asked.

"I just thought," I said, giving a nod to the momentarily quiet cell phone. This kind of nosiness could get me banished from Patch's temporary good graces.

"Oh, that," Patch said a smidge too casually. "That wasn't Laura." He would have left it at that had the phone not begun another rendition of the theme song. "Okay," he said, staring at it, "It's Sasha."

"Sasha?" Hadn't we banned her name from the list of acceptable topics at the Darrow Thanksgiving Feast? Patch's bringing her up did not put me in a thankful mood.

172

"The woman who left you and took up with your father? That Sasha?"

"Yes, Mother. That Sasha."

"So, she's calling for what, cranberry recipes?" Patch sighed an almost-Tom-like sigh. "Oh, wait. She doesn't cook. Your father's having Thanksgiving trucked in."

"Actually, she does cook. And my father didn't ask her to dinner."

"I was right," I said, dropping the spoon I was pulling stuffing out of a bird with. "I cannot believe I actually was right. Your father didn't ask her because of your grandmother."

"Right again," Patch said. "And she told him to go fuck himself or something like that."

"Okay, that part I get. What I don't get is why she's calling you."

"Because we lived together for three years? Because I nearly married her?"

"Stop me if I'm wrong, but didn't she say no when you proposed? Didn't she move out on you and move in with your father? And when she did, did you not say she had ruined your life?"

"She didn't ruin my life," Patch said. "And I figured that when you counted your blessings this Turkey Day, she'd be first on your thank you list."

"I'd *thank* her? For what, throwing a thirty-year marriage into the dumpster?"

Patch began pulling stuffing from the turkey in front of him as though it were a surgical procedure that required all of his concentration. I put my hand on his wrist. "What?" I asked.

"We need to get this stuff out there while it's hot," he said.

"It's not going to get cold that fast."

Patch put down the spoon. "Okay. You and I both know Dad was... a less-than-model husband."

"That's beside the point," I said.

"Let me finish. You asked, after all. You know I'm not crazy about this Mitch thing, but I have to say it. You're happier than I've ever seen you. You were never that happy with Dad. "

"Oh, come on. Your father and I were..., we weren't without trouble. We were married for a long time."

"But you weren't goofy happy. Admit it."

"You think I'm goofy happy?"

"I think you are moronically goofy happy."

Patch was right. I was happier than I'd been in a long time. For the last few weeks I'd been kind of floating along. I just hadn't been aware how much it showed. We'd gone far afield of the subject of Sasha, though. It took a while for Patch to confirm what I already suspected. That Sasha had come to realize what a great deal she'd thrown away. And that Patch, poor fool that he was, actually considered taking her back.

Mitch was waiting for me when I got home. "You're early," I said.

"Slow night," he said as I handed him the foil packages I carried. "For me?"

"I figured hospital Thanksgiving fare is no treat."

"Are you kidding? They had cranberry Jell-o. It was a culinary delight."

"So we should put this stuff in the fridge."

"Hell, no. I've already preheated the oven."

We put the foil trays into the oven and retired to the living room. One thing led to another. Mitch complimented my blouse and began unbuttoning. I pulled off his shirt and began working on his belt. "Should we go upstairs?" I managed to eke out between kisses.

"Too far," Mitch said. Next thing, I was on the Persian rug gazing up into Mitch's face and the mantel just beyond. And the next thing after that, the fire alarm went off. The kitchen door banged shut and we heard Eva yell, "Holy shit." And the two of us went scurrying for our clothes like Adam and Eve after the Fall.

By the time we made it to the kitchen, Eva had the windows and door open. The oven door was open, too. Three black bricks smoldered inside. "What *is* that?" Eva asked.

"Dinner," I said, as Mitch exhumed the charred remains.

"That does not look tasty," Eva said.

"It's a good thing I filled up on cranberry Jell-o and turkey surprise," Mitch said.

"Turkey surprise?" Eva and I asked in unison.

"The surprise was that it wasn't turkey," Mitch said. "It was bean curd."

"A bean curd bird," I said.

"Now that's tasty," Eva said. "It's a good thing I happened by when I did. You two would have burned the house down." She raised her eyebrows and my face preheated much like the oven. By the look of it, so did Mitch's.

"It's a good thing I came by," Eva said again. "Which reminds me. Could you water my plants and feed Julius and Irving while I'm gone?" Julius and Irving were Eva's fish, two koi she kept in a large tank in her office.

"Sure," I said. "You going somewhere?"

"I'm flying to Las Vegas with Red. We leave tonight. Romantic, no?"

"You're flying? With Red? In that can opener he calls a plane? Three thousand miles across the heartland?" I was, of course, remembering my own flight with Red. "Are you nuts?"

"I'm crazy, all right. Love's grand, ain't it?" Eva smirked at us. "By the by, Mitch? Your shirt's on inside out." Mitch blushed to his auburn roots. "My work here is done," Eva said, waltzing from the kitchen.

I shut the door behind her. By now, most of the smoke had wafted out and the air was nearly breathable. "Why don't I fix you something else," I said, throwing the charred dinner into the trash.

"That's okay. What I'd really like is a shower." Mitch came up behind me and scooped the hair from my neck. "How about it?"

"A shower?" He kissed the nape of my neck in a way that gave me chills.

"We'll make an environmental statement. Saving water and all that."

"Seems the least we can do after smoking out the neighborhood," I said.

After making sure that the door was locked and the oven off, we headed upstairs and took up where we'd left off. Mitch washed my back and then let his hands slip down over my belly and further south. Then there I was, India Othmar, fifty-two year old kindergarten teacher from Tamsett, Massachusetts making like a porn star. And loving every minute of it. Mitch wasn't complaining, either. We got out nearly as steamed as when we'd gone in, toweled each other off, and tangoed to the bed. And there I was again.

"Happy?" I asked afterwards, trailing a hand over his breastbone.

"You have to ask?" he said, taking the hand and kissing it.

"Just checking in."

"For the record, I'm very happy."

"Patch said I've been acting moronically goofy happy," I said.

"I think we're both pretty goofy happy."

I slapped him lightly on the chest. "You think I'm goofy?"

"I think," Mitch said, rolling back on top of me, "That you are sensational. Exponentially sensational." And so began round three. Which ended, shall we say, with a bang. Which was followed by a ringing phone.

"Must be the vice squad," I said.

"In that case, let it ring," Mitch said. Which in my new India goofy happy way was exactly what I did.

My cell phone rang a few minutes later, just as I was nestling into Mitch's arms and falling asleep. It was Allie calling. I picked up the line.

Chapter Twenty Nine

And No Thanks

You know how they say that you ought to be careful what you wish for? Well, you ought to be careful what you wish for. It had, it turned out, been a banner Thanksgiving for Tom. His girlfriend had left him, his daughter had introduced him to her gay lover, and his mother had collapsed as they were dishing out the pie.

"Heart attack," Allie said on the other end of the line. "We're at Mass General."

"Is she okay?"

"No, Mom. She had a heart attack."

The new India, the one who'd shamelessly soaped the parts of her young stud of a boyfriend the bathing suit usually covered and then proceeded to go forth doing things in the shower you can't do on television, gave way to the old India. I jumped up and hustled into my clothes for the second time in an evening as I explained to Mitch what had happened.

Mitch lay back, still naked, on my bed. "So you plan on going down there right now?" he asked.

"I have to," I said, sitting down on the bed to put on socks. Mitch took my arm and pulled me to him. He smelled of the soap we'd showered with, and of us. "You don't *have* to," he said. He started kissing me again.

Four would have been a record, even for those heady early days of romance. Four would have been the India all-time high. But, much as I wanted to, I couldn't get out of my clothes and start again. I kept hearing the panic in Allie's voice. "She could die, Mom." Allie had sounded so close to tears that I wanted to climb through the phone line and hold her.

"I do have to go," I said, kissing Mitch and pulling gently

from his arms. "It's an emergency. Allie's grandmother is gasping what could be her last breath."

"There's nothing you can do right now," Mitch said.

"Doesn't matter, I still have to go."

Mitch sighed, then got up and began scrambling for his clothes. He pulled on his boxers, the erection he'd had not two minutes ago, another record for India Othmar nee Smirtoff, had deflated rather drastically. "What are you doing?" I asked.

"Coming with you," he said.

"Don't be silly. You don't have to. They're not your family."

Mitch stared at me a moment, his eyes squinted. Then he began putting his clothes on again. "I can drive."

"Mitch, honey. It might not be the best idea, your showing up."

"What, with your ex-husband and ex-mother-in-law?"

I didn't say anything to that, but it was true. I wasn't ready to share Mitch with the rest of the world, AKA Tom and Marissa. I was worried about what would happen if I did.

"Fine, then," he said, once he was dressed. "Then I might as well go on home and get some sleep."

"You could just stay here," I said.

"That might not be the best idea, India, honey," he said. Mitch had a bit of a temper and he tended towards sarcasm when peeved. His voice was sopping with it now. You could have mopped it off the floor. I suppose I shouldn't have, but I asked what his problem was. And none too kindly, either.

"My problem?" he said, grabbing the car keys that had skittered to the floor.

"Your problem. Everything is smashingly terrific and then the phone rings and you're all bent out of shape."

"You're the one who jumped out of bed, India."

"I think you could be just a tad more understanding, Mitchell."

He pointed the car keys at me. "And I think you could stop jumping every time Tom calls you."

"Excuse me?"

"You are all warmth and light until Tom Othmar has an emergency. And then suddenly I'm just the guy you fuck."

I stared at him. "That is totally ridiculous."

"Is it?"

"And uncalled for," I said, throwing my cell phone into my

purse. "You know what? You should go home."

"Fine."

"Fine."

We stood staring at each other again, like two boxers separated in a prize fight. "You know where to find me," Mitch said.

I heard the front door slam. I thought about throwing myself in front of his Land Rover and insisting that he come back inside. But I was too miffed for that. Marissa Othmar might not be my favorite person, but she was the closest thing I had to a mother. How could I just leave her in her hour of need? How could I leave Allie? If Mitch couldn't understand why I didn't want to bring my affairs and his into the middle of a crises, if Mitch wanted to act like a spoiled brat, then let him walk out. A spoiled brat was the last thing I needed right now.

Chapter Thirty

Waiting

The ICU waiting room could have passed for the fourth ring of hell. Chairs lined one stark white wall, vending machines the other. Fluorescent lights buzzed and flickered overhead. The place smelled of sweat and tears and fear, as if all those who had waited here for someone they loved had left an imprint. You could feel it, an oppressiveness like ripe heat on a saturated summer day, the minute you entered the room.

Tom and Allie and Liz were huddled together in one corner of the room, its only occupants. Tom got up as soon as he saw me. The lines around his eyes and mouth were furrowed deeper than I remembered. If I hadn't known better, I'd have thought he was the one who was ill. He put his arms around me and hugged me as though I were the last lifeboat on the *Titanic*. "You came," he said. "Thank God you're here." I'd be lying if I said that I didn't hug back. I held him as tightly as he held me, the two of us like slow-dancing teenagers in the middle of that awful room.

The news wasn't good. Marissa needed a quadruple bypass. The medical center's cardiac surgeons were apparently morning people and they had scheduled the surgery for 6:00 a.m. Marissa was sleeping, sedated, in the ICU.

"Anyone call Patch?" I asked. Tom's arm draped over my shoulder. Not in a proprietary way, more as though he was using me as a crutch.

"I did," Liz said. Liz, it occurred to me, was a lot sturdier than she looked at first glance. Allie was lucky to have such a sturdy person in her life. "There won't be much change until morning, they said. I told him he should come then."

"You should go home, too," Tom said to our daughter. "Get a

good night's sleep."

"You should take your own advice, Daddy."

"Yes, Tom. You look exhausted," I added.

"I don't want to go all the way out to Brookline," he said. "What if something…"

I grabbed the hand he had wrapped over my shoulder and squeezed it hard. "You listen to me. Nothing is going to happen. They said she's stable. Stable means stable."

"Allie's right." Liz took our daughter's hand. "We're all of us tired. Our apartment's not five minutes from here. There's an extra bedroom." She looked at us and then at Allie. "And a couch," she added. "Why don't you camp out with us until morning?"

Which is what we did. Tom, fully clothed, took the couch. I took the futon in the spare bedroom. As I pulled off my slacks and shirt and slipped under the bedclothes, it occurred to me that I hadn't showered. Did I smell of sex? Had Tom noticed? That I'd been with another man? If he had, would he have said anything? He was probably too tired and too worried to notice much of anything. And why, I asked myself, would it matter in the least? Still, I got up, begged a towel from Allie, and hit the shower.

Five a.m. was before the birds early. Before the worms early. Five a.m. could be described as an ungodly hour, especially after you've spent a restless night tossing on an unfamiliar futon, a night that hadn't begun until nearly morning to begin with.

We stumbled off to the hospital together. Tom met briefly with the surgeon and then we were all of us herded back into that awful waiting room. Which, if possible, was even more awful at such an ungodly hour.

And we waited. None of us had wanted breakfast. Even if we'd been hungry, the stuff in the vending machines looked as though it had been there since before the Korean War.

We waited. I thought about calling Mitch. He was, in truth, one of the reasons my night on the futon had been so restless. Cell phones weren't allowed in this part of the hospital. I was a little reluctant, just now, to slither off and call my lover. This is what I told myself. I said to myself, very firmly, "This is not the time to call your lover, India." The whole truth was that I was still a little miffed at him. He had walked out on me, after all. Let him be the one to call.

Patch showed up at 8:30 and, slinking in behind him, was Sasha Peterson. Tom stiffened visibly when he saw her. I'm not talking about the part of his anatomy that usually stiffened whenever a gorgeous young thing like Sasha sashayed into a room. I'm talking about his shoulders and the back of his legs. Even his eyes seemed to stiffen as they stared at the door. Sasha, oblivious, squeezed Patch's arm, marched across the room, and seized Tom's hand.

"I came as soon as I heard," she said. "I'm so sorry."

Tom nodded stiffly and said nothing. Allie, however, found the voice and the gumption to ask, "How did you hear?"

To which Sasha, brazen hussy that she was, batted her thicker-than-life eyelashes at my son. Who stood, also somewhat stiffly, by the door.

Patch, at least, had the decency to turn several shades of crimson. "I, umh, told her," he said. He shifted from one foot to the other and bit his lip. Mitch was right, he was a terrible liar. Allie noticed, too. I knew by the way she narrowed her eyes. She, too, bit her lip, though I'm pretty sure that she did it because she didn't want to blurt out anything she might regret later.

Tom, well, Tom wasn't noticing much of anything. "Thank you," he said. "Thank you for coming."

The waiting had been awful to begin with. Now it became both awful and awkward. I glanced around the awful room. Yup. It was definitely the seventh ring of hell.

Hell is for all of eternity. Luckily, waiting at Mass General is not. Though for a time, it surely did feel that way. I sat next to Tom. Patch sat next to Sasha, the four of us lined up against one wall like a sitting version of a police line-up. Liz and Allie walked down the hall, came back, walked back down to the cafeteria for coffee and brought back sandwiches that, even if they had been created by Boston's finest chef (which they most assuredly were not) no one would have wanted to eat. Conversations sputtered, revved, and died. All of it as mundane as the sandwiches: "Is there mustard?" Think it will rain later?" "It's been pretty dry." "A few degrees, and it will snow." "What color would you say that chair is? Mauve?"

A herd of elephants sat in the middle of the room. No one dared mention them. But, as I said, waiting is not for all eternity and after a good long time had passed, enough time for the elephants to all settle to grazing, the surgeon walked in. With good news. Marissa

182

had come through surgery and her heart, though a little ragged, would probably keep on beating for quite some time.

Relief hit Tom like a physical thing. Maybe it was the same for all of us, but with Tom I could see it, the way the tight-strung muscles in his shoulders and his hips and the back of his neck elongated. "Can we see her?" he asked the surgeon.

She was still coming out of anesthesia and on a respirator, the surgeon told us. But yes, we could see her. Two at a time. Briefly.

I stayed in my seat. Allie and Liz were by the windows. Patch stood near the vending machines, leaning in with his hands in his pockets and looking so much like a younger version of his father that I looked away. Sasha had drifted over to Tom. Her hand feathered his elbow. Feathering lightly, I suppose, because Tom brushed it away as though it were a mosquito. He turned to me. "Indie? Would you?"

He was so un-Tom-like in his unsure-ness. What could I do? I got up and made a show of straightening my blouse so that I wouldn't make a show of taking his arm.

Marissa looked terrible. The surgeon had warned us that there would be tubes and monitors. He'd mentioned the respirator, assuring us it was temporary. What he'd failed to mention was that her skin, the soft ivory complexion of which she was downright vain, would be gray. She looked like a lump of clay, hooked to machines.

"Dear God," Tom said, his knees buckling the slightest bit. I clasped his arm and reminded him of what the surgeon had said. "Right," he said, regaining himself. "Give her a few days, and she'll be telling us all what to do." He smiled a little. This, I thought, would be exactly what Marissa would say we should be doing. Standing arm in arm at her bedside, admiring her endurance.

Chapter Thirty One

Memory Lane

"I think I'm going to go for a walk," I said. We had left Marissa's bedside, still side by side but not touching now. I couldn't face the prospect of another minute in the waiting room. I wanted to talk to Mitch. I needed to talk to Mitch. During all the long wait, while wondering about Tom and Sasha and Patch and Sasha and worrying over Marissa, I had told myself to go to a happier place. And every time I went to the happy place, there was Mitch: Mitch with his head back, laughing. Mitch holding my hand. Mitch making love to me. I didn't get to the Mitch being mad part. To Mitch storming out. He would understand. He wouldn't stay angry forever, would he?

"I'll come with," Tom said. "If that's okay?" It wasn't okay. Not really. But there we were, back in the awful room.

"Sure," I said.

We walked along the Charles River. It was a breezy day, mild for late November. A few brave souls had spread out on blankets on the esplanade and lay soaking up the last of the late afternoon sun. We walked without talking. There was too much for us to discuss and neither of us wanted to discuss anything. We walked into the city, along the streets of Beacon Hill down one hill and up the next. I fell into a sort of trance, measured by the rhythm of footfall. My thoughts scattered and flew about: Mitch, Tom, Eva, Marissa, Allie, Patch, Mitch again. I wandered over the hills and valleys of the past months, the past years.

Tom stopped. I walked on, still entranced, and didn't notice for a number of paces. I turned, finally. He was looking up. I knew exactly where we were. Upstairs, on the left hand side of the building at the end of the street, was the apartment. The one with the bow window. In another lifetime, Tom and I, still in college, had lived in that place. We'd moved a single bed, the only size that would fit, into the alcove of that bowed window. We'd lain on that bed skin to skin under the quilt my grandmother had sewn, and tried to separate the streetlights from the stars.

Tom held out his hand. I walked back to him and took it. We looked to that window together.

"We should go," he said. I thought he meant to the hospital. It was late afternoon. Late fall. It would be dark soon. I took a step back in the direction we'd come. Tom pulled my hand.

"Up there," he said. "We should go up there."

"Up there?"

"Why not?"

"Because. Somebody lives there." Somebody who is not us, is what I didn't say.

Tom was already walking towards the house, towing me half-heartedly behind him. He rang the bell for the upstairs apartment. I counted to three. "No one's home," I said.

He rang again. We heard someone walk down the stairs. The door opened, halfway, and behind it stood a thin young woman with stringy blonde hair. "Not interested in being saved," she said, holding the door frame.

"Saved?" I asked.

She blinked at me, then at Tom, and opened the door a crack wider. "You're not Christers?"

"Christers?" Tom asked.

"You know; Watch Tower, Seventh Day, Mormon. Whatever."

"We wanted to look at your apartment," said Tom.

She nearly shut the door, then opened it again. "Who told you it was for rent?"

"We used to live here," Tom said.

The girl's eyes narrowed like the door. "Right. I may not be born again, but I wasn't born yesterday."

"We just wanted to see it," Tom said. "For old time's sake."

"Right. Then you stick a gun in my ribs and she takes all my stuff." The girl, in jeans worn through at the knee and barefoot, didn't look like she had a lot of stuff worth taking, but she did look ready to slam the door if we tried to force our way in.

Before Tom opened his PR firm, he'd been a salesman, a very

185

good one. I'd forgotten how good a salesman until we stood on that stoop in a place we no longer belonged with a girl who'd rather not. He convinced her and, I regret to say, me, that not only did we have no intention of doing her any harm, but that it was in her best interest to let us in. Because these were memories, darling. The precious memories of a couple of ordinary middle-aged people. And would it not be perfect, would it not be a story to tell all your friends about: how these harmless middle-aged people had shown up on the doorstep and been mistaken for Christers and then for thieves? Was that not worth a laugh and a free drink? Tom folded a twenty dollar bill and pressed into the girl's palm. He had me at twenty, but the girl reminded him that she hadn't been born yesterday. Another twenty did the trick.

The apartment was pretty much the same as we'd left it. A single room, with a stove and a refrigerator separated out by a counter. The single bed had been replaced by a futon, still in the bow window. On the far wall was a bookcase made of fruit crates, which reminded me of the book case Tom and I had fashioned out of plywood and concrete blocks. Ours had listed sideways. One night, after we'd set the bed to thumping hard against the sill, the bookcase had collapsed and all of our books and record albums had avalanched to the floor.

Tom must have had similar thoughts. He walked to the case and dusted it with his fingers.

"No touching." The girl stood at the open door of the apartment, ready to strike.

"Give us a few minutes," Tom said. The girl gaped at him. "Please. It's our anniversary." I should have stopped him. I didn't.

"You are *not* going to do it in my bed," the girl said. The futon had no sheet. The blanket looked as though we might have left it behind thirty years ago and no one had bothered to wash it since.

"You are kidding, right?" I said.

She pointed a finger at me. "*No* messing around."

Tom raised his right hand. "No messing. My solemn promise."

"Ten bucks," the girl said.

"You're kidding, right?" Tom said.

"Ten bucks. I wasn't born yesterday."

Tom sighed and reached for his wallet. "And you were afraid that we'd mug you."

She grabbed the money and stuffed it into her shirt. "You've got five minutes. And do not lock me out. You lock me out, I will call the cops."

"What are you doing?" I asked Tom, after she'd left us alone.

"Remember that turntable we had? We played that Randy Newman record and it would skip? We had that bottle of Mateus with the candle stuck in it. God, when I lit that candle I thought I was the king of romance." He kneeled on the futon, leaned over the back, and looked out the window. "You can still see the river."

"If you tilt your head sideways," I said, leaning against the counter.

Tom got off his knees. "The night we moved in, I bought you daisies and you braided them into your hair. Daisies were the only thing you were wearing." Tom took my hand and squeezed it. "We were happy then, weren't we?" He bit his lip. That's where Patch got it, along with those blue eyes I'd loved so long.

"It was a long time ago."

"What I'd give to have it back. Just for a day. For a night." He brushed his hand over my cheek, then took my face in his hands and kissed me. The fairytale prince kissing the princess. Only we weren't royalty and this wasn't a castle.

"We can't do this." My hands were betraying my words by caressing Tom's face.

"Why not? We were married. For a long, long time."

"We were married. Were."

"I didn't want to end it." Tom put his arms around me and kissed me again. He kissed me like the boy I'd shared this apartment with all those years ago.

I wish that I could say that I pushed him away. I wish I could say I thought of Mitch and said no and marched down the stairs, but I was caught up in that dream of long ago nights. Like a princess enchanted, I fell under a spell. I put my arms around my ex-husband's waist and hung on for all I was worth, not wanting to let go of memory.

Chapter Thirty Two

Don't Answer That

Tom nuzzled into my neck and I felt a pulse, a vibration. Somewhere near my hip. On the left side. My cell phone. Tom felt it too.

"Wow," he said. "The earth moved." I took the phone from my pocket, was about to answer, when the door burst open. The skinny girl reappeared with an equally skinny boy on her heels.

"Time is so up," she said.

The boy looked us over. "You said," he said to the girl.

"Shut up, Fred." The girl pointed a finger at us. "Out now. Or I'll..."

"Call the cops," Tom and I finished for her.

"Operatives, my ass," the boy mumbled. "CIA, yeah, right."

Tom put his arm around the kid. "Son, you have no idea. My wife over there..." He pointed at me and shook his head. "The stories I could tell if I had clearance." He glanced around the room, then whispered. "You're not worth frying, but I'd flush the stash." He winked at the kid. "A favor. Consider us even."

I could hear Fred as we headed down the stairs. "Shit, do you think they're for real?" To which the girl answered, "Don't be an idiot, Fred." When I glanced back at the window from the street, two faces glanced back down.

"I cannot believe you," I said.

Tom was grinning. "What? Come on, that was fun. About time we had some fun." He put an arm around me and drew me in. "We haven't had fun in a long time, Indie." We walked along the Charles River, towards the hospital, towards Marissa, towards the awful waiting room with its terrible vending machine coffee. It was dusk and the streetlights were winking on. There, out of the shadows,

Mass General loomed like a modern version of the dark castle.

Tom stopped when he caught sight of it. This time, in step, I stopped with him. "Let's not go back," he said.

"What? Tommy, we've got to." The name, *Tommy,* flew out of my mouth unbidden. I hadn't called him Tommy in thirty years. The name didn't go unnoticed. He turned so we were face to face.

"I just can't right now. Mom's in good hands. She won't know if we're there or not. Not until tomorrow, anyway. So let's not go back until tomorrow." He smoothed back my windblown hair with one hand. "Come on, Indie. What do you say?"

I didn't say anything. I didn't move away, either. My phone vibrated again. Tom pulled the phone from my pocket and pitched it into the river. I stared at him. "What did you do that for?"

"Isn't it obvious?" He put his arms around me again. "I love you. I've loved you for thirty-five years and I doubt I will ever stop loving you. And you love me. I know you do."

"So you throw my phone in the river? Are you insane?"

"Say it, Indie. Say I love you, Thomas Othmar."

I couldn't, wouldn't, look at him. I pulled away. "I can't. We can't go back."

Tom took my hand and walked me to a nearby bench. "Look, I made a mistake. A huge, ugly mistake. I won't excuse it, but it was a mistake. I know I can't change it. But I would like to try to fix it."

I knew, had known all along, about Tom's infidelities. Faced with any sort of evidence, I'd told myself I was paranoid. I'd deluded myself by saying it didn't matter. It was me he came home to. Me he was married to. Even Sasha. God, I would even have blotted Sasha out as a gloppy mistake, would have gone on with my fuzzy little life if it hadn't been for Patch. Tom had hurt Patch and I couldn't forgive him that. In the months since Tom had been gone I'd grown selfish. I wanted something more than a sometimes husband. I wanted all or nothing. My fuzzy little life wasn't so fuzzy anymore.

"Sasha wasn't the first," I said. It wasn't an accusation. Just a statement of fact. Tom looked as though I'd slapped him. "I'm not stupid, Tom. I'm not even as naïve as you seem to think I am."

Tom dropped my hand. "I never thought you stupid. Or naïve."

"Then tell me the truth. Danielle White. That secretary, what was her name? Rochelle? Roberta? When I was pregnant with Allie. That weather girl on channel 56. She was gorgeous." I was crying now.

Tom took me by the shoulders. "Stop it, India." Tom nodded towards the river. "You're seeing someone."

"Yes. Not that it's any of your business. But I am seeing someone."

"I want you back, Indie. You are the one I married. You are the one I want to be with." Tom put his arms around me. I'm not proud to say I didn't stop him. I wanted his "I'm sorry." I wanted his assurances. Even now. Even after everything. "I am so sorry to have hurt you," he said, his mouth close to my ear. "You were, are, the best thing that's ever happened to me. I'd do anything for your forgiveness. I can't stand the idea of you being with someone else. My God, just the thought of it."

I didn't answer him, couldn't, because I was crying too hard. Tom put his hand to the back of my head and stroked my hair in a way so familiar and comforting that it made me cry all the harder. "Tell me that we've still got a chance. That's all I ask," he said.

I dried my eyes on my sleeve. "Some things are so broken that there isn't a glue in the world that can mend them."

"Pieces. We can start with pieces."

We got up and headed towards the hospital, walking back over the shards.

Tom and I, Mitch and I. I needed to go and see Mitch. I needed to find out where we stood. I needed to find out how strong this thing with Mitch was, this new thing in my life. In truth, I knew the answer. I was head-over-heels crazy about Mitch. But it was more complicated than that. Maybe the other truth is that I was responsible for the complication.

Later that evening, I drove over to Mitch's without stopping at home. He was packing up the back of the Land Rover with camping and climbing gear.

"Going somewhere?" I asked, leaning back against my car, trying hard to act casual.

He gave me a look that said he wasn't about to kiss me any time soon. "I'm going ice climbing with some friends. If you'd answered your phone, you would have known that."

"I'm sorry. Things have been a little crazy."

"Ah, yes. Family emergency. Guess that's why you can't pick

190

up the phone."

"I lost my phone. The hospital—"

"India."

"Okay. You're right. I should have called. I should have. Again, I'm sorry."

"Fine. You're sorry. I'm meeting Rob Fallon in five minutes so I've really got to go. And, by the by, my cell phone doesn't have network up north, so I won't be phoning. Oh, wait. That's right. You lost your phone."

"Stop it, Mitch. Stop acting like a two-year- old."

Mitch climbed into the Land Rover. "Then stop treating me like your boy toy."

"You are not a boy toy. You know that. You know how I feel about you. Please, let's talk this out."

"Nothing to talk about. I'm too young for you. And you're still hung up on your ex-husband."

"I am not."

"You are too."

"I am not."

"Are too." Mitch slammed the door shut.

I jumped onto the running board and knocked on the window. Mitch frowned at me, but he rolled the window down. "I am not," I said.

"And I'm childish?"

"I am sorry I didn't call. I am heartily and awfully sorry. Please, please don't drive off like this."

"India. You've got to figure this out. Maybe I do, too. We need some time. Some space."

"Are you dumping me?"

"No. I can't—I won't play backup for Tom Othmar. It's first-string or nothing."

"It's not that simple."

"It *is* that simple." He reached out and stroked my cheek. "I've got to go now."

I got off the running board and watched his tail lights fade.

Chapter Thirty Three

True Confessions

I was fifty-two years old. Old enough to make decisions for myself. And so I decided to keep Tom in my life. Not as a husband. I couldn't go back to that. But we had too much history between us for me not to keep him, somehow. As for Mitch, well, when it came to Mitch my head and my heart were in complete disagreement. My head said that Mitch had no right to demand anything of me. After all, he was the one who said we'd take it day to day, see what comes next, not worry about the future. Ah, but my heart, that big bleeding contrary organ, said otherwise. For the first time in a very long time I'd been deliriously goofy happy. Who would want to let go of that? To which my head said happiness is fleeting and reminded me that I'd been happy with Tom once upon a time. And my heart, always with the final word, said that I loved Mitch. I loved him. And that, said my heart, was the cause of and the answer to all my troubles.

Marissa was fully conscious by the following afternoon, and Tom and I went to see her together. "You're looking well," I told her as we came through the door. It sounded like a dumb thing to say, given the circumstances, but Marissa looked well despite the tubes and sprockets. She was sitting up as far as the bed would allow, her hair pulled back into a neat bun, wearing lipstick in a shade of pink that matched the quilted bed jacket she wore.

"Pretty," I said of the jacket.

"This old thing? I've had it for ages. Thomas bought it for me when Tommy was born. I haven't had much occasion to wear it." Marissa held my hand with firm conviction. With the other she motioned to Tom, who hung back at the door. When he'd taken his place on the other side of the bed, Marissa took his hand and joined our two hands together like a priestess conducting a ritual. "Everything is going to be fine," she said.

I pulled my hand back, but Marissa would not let it go. Tom, perhaps remembering better than I how willful his mother could be, did not try to move his hand. "You look wonderful," Tom said. "You gave us quite a scare."

"My dear Tommy. I am heartily sorry about this whole affair. But I will be fine. I'm not finished here just yet."

"That's a good thing," I said, "because we'd like to keep you around a little longer."

"My dear India. My dear children. If I were to die today," Marissa squeezed our hands between hers, "which I will not, I would die a happy woman. I have been blessed with a wonderful family.

"Tommy, my sweet, would you get me some ginger ale? A bottle from the cafeteria would be just the thing." Marissa let go of Tom's hand.

Tom bit his lip "Sure." He turned to me. "I'll see if the kids are here yet."

When he had gone, Marissa motioned to the chair near the head of the bed. When I sat, she took up my hand again. "I knew you would come."

"Of course. I care about you."

"That's not the point, though, is it? The point is that you and I are family."

"Yes. You'll always be family," I said.

"It's not me that I worry over, dear. I can care for myself. Despite all this. I'm a tough old broad." Marissa stroked my hand. "And I do know that you care for me. That's your nature, India. You're a caring person. It has made you a wonderful mother to Allie and little Tommy." It always took me by surprise when Marissa called Patch little Tommy. He wasn't little anymore and, though Thomas was his given name, Marissa was the only one who used it. Probably because she'd insisted on it in the first place. "Tommy with a law practice, he makes me so proud. And Allie, well, Allie will get past this identity crisis, won't she? She may be a little flighty, but she's a good girl."

"I don't think that Allie's relationship with Liz is going away anytime soon," I said. I'd forgotten how aggravating my mother-in-law could be. If she hadn't been lying in a hospital bed, I would have walked out on her.

"Please, India. Allow me to finish." She stroked my hand again and squeezed it. "I see you've taken off your ring."

"Tom and I are divorced. He did tell you that?"

"Yes, my darling girl. Tommy told me about his...dalliance. He told me how very sorry he was." She let go of the hand. "I've created a crisis, I'm afraid, with this little illness of mine. But a crisis is a fine time to come to terms, to be honest about things. Don't you agree?"

This time I got out of the chair. "I have nothing to confess," I said. My thoughts flashed to Mitch, arms reaching to me on my bed, naked and erect and perfect. I was not about to go there with my ex-mother-in-law. And what I said was true, I had nothing to confess, because I was not in the least sorry.

"Sit down, India. I'm talking about my confession. Not yours." The stern tone, the hard line of Marissa's mouth, had the desired effect on me. I sat despite myself. Marissa looked to the door. "Thomas senior had his share of...indiscretions."

I barely remembered Thomas. He'd been twenty years older than his wife, a man in his mid-sixties when I'd met him. I'd been eighteen then and he had seemed ancient. More a grandfather than a father. He died not long after Patch was born.

"I was not his first wife," Marissa said. "He was a married man when we met. I was eighteen, much the same as you were when you met Tommy. I was very young. And very innocent." She smiled at me. "His was a loveless marriage. There were no children. His wife could not abide children. It took four years for us to marry."

"You've never told Tom?"

"That I was the other woman? Heavens no! That is not the end of the story. When I was pregnant with Tommy, I found out Thomas was having an affair with his bookkeeper. It had taken five years to get with child, you understand. It could not have been easy on my husband."

"So you forgave him?"

"Eventually, yes. First I ran off to my mother in Connecticut. I packed every stitch of clothing I owned and went to her in the middle of the night. Of course, she took me in. I cried myself to sleep in my girlhood bedroom. The next morning, my mother had taken my suitcase, still packed, and put it back into my car. She told me that I had made a covenant with Thomas and that I was about to have his

194

child and that I needed to go back to him. My mother was not the sort of woman one argued with, you understand. I got back into the car and drove back to Thomas."

"And that was the right decision?" I asked. Marissa didn't catch the bitterness in my voice. Or if she did, she didn't let on.

"Yes. Of course. It is never easy in a marriage. I am certain you've learned that by now. But you make your bed. You weather the storm. There were other dalliances. Quite a few. I weathered them."

"I'm sorry, Marissa," I said. "I am so sorry for all the pain you must have endured. I know it. I've lived with it myself. For thirty-one years, I lived with it. And I've had enough of it." I said my piece as gently as I could. Then I stood and kissed her on the forehead. "I'll be back to visit, I promise." Before she could say anymore, or notice the tears that had come unbidden, I was out the door.

Chapter Thirty Four

A Litany Of Extremely Stupid Decisions

By Tuesday, Marissa had taken up residence in a regular room at Mass General, with assurances from the cardiologist that she'd be playing Canasta with her friends at Paradise Point before Santa came. Heck, she'd even have time to finish her Christmas shopping. Eva was still in Vegas, gambling with, or on, Red. And Mitch hadn't returned from scaling ice cliffs in the White Mountains.

As had become the story of our mistimed romance, I wasn't home when Mitch called on Wednesday. His message said something to the effect of *we need to talk*, which seemed to me like the prelude to an honest and for real dumping. Since the idea of that seemed too much for the heart-end of me to bear, I didn't call back. This was a move that I would, in retrospect, refer to as extremely stupid decision number one.

On Thursday, I followed ESD Number One with yet another extremely stupid decision. In light of trying to find the something, someplace, where Tom and I had a relationship, I cooked up a casserole of pasta with sausage and goat cheese, one of Tom's favorites, and packed it and a salad into Tupperware bowls. I intended to drive down to Brookline and surprise him with it. He'd suffered a lot of stress with his mother's hospitalization, and I figured a nice meal would cheer him. It would also allow us, in a friendly give-and-take way, to reassess our relationship and decide where or where not to go with it. I actually prided myself on my maturity.

I was putting the containers into a Macy's shopping bag when Mitch pulled into my driveway. My heart wanted to race out the door and into Mitch's arms, gambling wildly that he'd take me into them. My head, on the other hand, wanted to lock the door and pretend I wasn't home. My head was already making up excuses for why my car was in the driveway. My indecision was laced with the pitter patter of panic, which paralyzed me into doing nothing at all, which is how Mitch found me, standing statue-like in the kitchen using the Macy's bag as a shield.

He looked a little paralyzed himself. "Hey," he said, standing statue-like at the kitchen threshold.

"Hey," I said. It might have been better if we'd stopped with that enlightened bit of exchange. But, of course, we didn't stop there.

"I called," he said.

"I know. I got the message."

"Going somewhere?" Mitch nodded to the shopping bag. And again, if only we'd stopped there. If only we'd kept up the stilted pace of that conversation. If only I'd said yes instead of making extremely stupid decision number three. It seemed like the right decision at the time. At the time, I felt it was the mature thing to do. What I should have done is made some excuse, put the food into the fridge, and thrown myself into Mitch's arms. But I was set on putting my whole world together. On having Tom and Mitch in it. I wanted to be honest with Mitch. I should have known better. I should have known that I had the power to hurt Mitch. Badly.

"I'm going to Tom's," I said.

Mitch's hand clenched around his car keys. "Oh," he said. "Well, that's just fucking lovely." He turned and marched back towards his car.

I did, at least, have the smarts to try to stop him. "Mitch. It's not what you think." The shopping bag thwacked my thigh. I put it down in the driveway.

Mitch, to his credit, did not drive off in a huff. He stopped, turned back to me, with his hand on the door handle. His shoulders were hunched in a posture of misery. I could see his rib cage moving, deep breaths in and out, under his shirt. I put my hands to his shoulders. "Please. Don't," he said.

"It's not what you think," I repeated.

"You haven't a clue what I'm thinking," he said.

"I'm not... We're not... Look, you're the one who said we needed to talk. That's why I didn't call you. I may be a little rusty on relationships, but I know what *need to talk* means."

"It means I need to talk to you, India. That's all it means." He turned around, eyed the bag, looked back at the house. "I wanted to tell you..." He shook his head. "It doesn't matter, does it?" He opened the car door and climbed in. "I really thought. Damn it. I can't keep doing this. I can't keep being a fool for you." His voice shattered like glass. "Goodbye, India."

"No, Mitch. Not goodbye." But Mitch had already closed the door and started the engine. For the second time in a week, I watched his tail lights as he drove away. Only this time, I knew he wouldn't be driving back.

I sat on the kitchen steps with the bag at my feet and my head in my hands. I'd lost Mitch. How could I have been so stupid? How could I have lost Mitch?

A car pulled up and for one hopeful second my heart leapt. I picked up my head. It was Eva, climbing from the cab of Red's truck. She ran over, fists raised in the air, and did a little dance in the driveway. Red was a few steps behind her, his hands in his pockets, looking like he'd just eaten the world's best steak and washed it down with a brew.

"Why so glum, chum?" Eva stopped her dance and put her hands to her hips.

I felt my bottom lip revolt. "Mitch...left...me..." I managed to get out despite the trembling.

"No," said Eva. "I bet it's just a lover's spat. Everybody has those. Right, honey?" The honey she was referring to was Red.

She sat down next to me and curled her arm around my shoulder. Red stood watch over us, the two of them like an odd pair of guardian angels. "I guess this may not be the best time to tell you," Eva said. She held up her hand, which sported the biggest, gaudiest diamond I'd ever laid eyes on.

"You're engaged?" I sniffed out the words.

"You are looking at the new Mrs. Red Lansing."

"That's wonderful," I said. I put my head into my hands and sobbed until my shoulders shook.

"There, there." Eva patted my back as though she were burping me. "Honey," she said to Red, "that bottle of Stoli we brought back?"

"Want me to go fetch it, sweetums?"

"Yes, sugar. I think it might be just what the doctor ordered." The word doctor reminded me of Mitch, which made me sob all the harder. "Let's get you inside." Eva picked up the Macy's bag. "What's this?"

198

"Dinner."

"Dinner?" She peeked into the bag.

"For Tom."

Eva dropped the bag. "Have you lost your mind? I can't leave you alone for a few days without all hell breaking loose."

"I know," I said.

The three of us settled into my kitchen with tumblers of Stoli on the rocks. "Drink," Eva said. I drank. The burn felt like a punishment and I pushed the glass aside. I started to talk. I talked and talked. About Marissa's heart attack. About Tom, and walking back to that old apartment. About Mitch. And Mitch. And Mitch. And more Mitch.

"What am I going to do?" I asked in conclusion.

"Sorry?" Eva asked. I'd forgotten. Eva, my dear friend Eva, was a terrific doer. But a listener? Not so much. And Red. Red had left the building.

"Never mind," I said, patting her arm. I thanked her for the drink, which I hadn't drunk, congratulated her on her marriage to Red, which I hadn't given her a chance to talk about, took up my bag, and walked out the door.

"Where do you think you're going?" Eva asked, following me out. Red stood on her kitchen stairs, wearing a robe open to boxers with cartoon hearts. More of Red than I needed to see. Eva waved to him. He waved back.

"You two kids have fun," I said.

Eva pursed her lips and glanced at her steps, empty because Red had gone back inside. "Where do you think you are going?" she asked again.

"To finish what I started." I put the bag down on the passenger seat of my car.

"I can't let you do that."

"Sure you can."

The light went on in Eva's bedroom. She stood, mesmerized. "There's a reason that man attracts women, India. God knows it's not his looks. I mean, holy shit, he knows his way around a girl." She shivered visibly. I got into the car. "You should not do this," she said, still looking to the bedroom window.

"I know," I said.

I drove off, making extremely stupid decision number four. I was hurting. I needed someone to prop me up. It wasn't about to be

Eva, preoccupied as she was with Red and his cartoon hearts. I was not ready to drown my sorrows in Stoli. And my kids, well, they were my kids, which should be enough said.

I drove to Brookline remembering that old apartment. How we'd laughed at Fred and the skinny girl. How Tom had been so much like the Tom I remembered. How Tom had all but asked me to bed. I'd show up and see what happened. Maybe Marissa was right. Maybe, in the hard road of long relationships, anything can be forgiven. Of course, I knew that what I really wanted was to be with Mitch. But I couldn't be with Mitch. So, I told myself, love the one you're with. Which, incidentally, was the song playing on the classic rock station I'd snapped on driving into Boston.

Tom answered the door in sweats and a T-shirt, barefoot and wet-headed. "India," he said. There was a little stop-step in his voice. I chalked it up to surprise.

"I brought dinner," I said, holding up the bag.

"Great," he said, taking it.

"Aren't you going to ask me in?" It had started to drizzle. My hair and jacket were damp.

"Of course. Sure. Come in." Tom's condo, like Tom himself, was neat. So neat, in fact, that it looked like no one lived there. The foyer's walls were bare white. The kitchen didn't even have a clock. Tom set the bag on the counter and I turned the knob to pre-heat the oven.

"I'm not that hungry," he said.

I felt chagrined. Here I'd just barged in and started cooking. Doing for Tom as I had always done. Old habits die hard. I turned the knob back to off. "Fridge?" I asked.

Tom opened the refrigerator door and I put the dishes inside. "I can't believe that you're here," Tom said.

"Yeah. Me neither." I took a deep breath. "I thought about what we talked about. Walking. How you and I still love each other. How we've lost sight of that."

Tom circled his arms around me and sighed. "India."

I began to unbutton my jacket. "We should talk. Decide where we go from here."

"India. Honey. I was kind of planning to go to the hospital. I was practically out the door when you showed up."

I stepped back and looked him over. "Were you planning to go in your sweats?"

200

"No. No. I just threw these on. I was in the shower. Coming out of the shower. Look, why don't you come with me to the hospital. Then afterwards..." Tom pulled me into him and kissed me hard.

"Afterwards what?" The voice came up from behind me. Still dazed by the kiss, I turned around. Sasha stood in the doorway. Stark naked.

The sole of my shoe tapped on the tiles. I blinked like a crazy person. Blinka-blinka-blink. I couldn't stop myself.

"I'll be upstairs," Sasha said. "Your call, Tommy."

"India. It's not as bad as it looks." I shook my head. At him. At myself. At my stupidity. I grabbed the Macy's bag, stuffed the Tupperware back in, and headed out the door. Tom loped into the driveway after me, still barefoot. "Indie, I can explain."

I dropped the bag and rounded on him. "Really? This I'd like to hear. I'd *love* to hear how you weasel out of this one, *Tommy*."

"She just came over. Uninvited. I swear, nothing happened."

"You know what? I don't give a good God damn if you fucked her or not." I wasn't given to using the f word. I was, at the core, still a kindergarten teacher and a mommy. But it felt good, really good, to see Tom blanch at his little ex-wife. So good, in fact, that I said it again. "You can fuck the whole condo complex, for all I care. I'm sure the neighbor women would just love a fuck from a stud like Tommy Othmar. Maybe you could open a business. Fuck is us." I was loud enough to advertise the new business to the entire condo complex.

"Jesus, India. Calm down." Tom was delightfully unnerved. "Let's go inside and talk about this."

"*Talk* about it? You have got to be kidding me. Mr. We-fuck-em-all wants to *talk* about it?" I took the casserole from the bag and ripped off the Tupperware lid. I opened the waistband of Tom's sweats and dumped the pasta on his crotch. A waste of good pasta, but well worth it.

"My God, India. Are you insane?"

"Go upstairs and have Sasha lick it off," I said, getting into the car. "And by the by, if you ever come on to me again I will rip out your tongue and stick it up your ass." I drove off. Actually, I peeled out of the driveway.

Chapter Thirty Five

Rocky Road Part Two

The adrenaline rush was fabulous. It got me home in half an hour. It was an absolute miracle I wasn't stopped for speeding, because I was very close to breaking the space-time continuum. What goes up must come down, and when I pulled into the driveway of my dark house next to Eva's dark house, I marched into my kitchen, slammed the door shut, and slid down to the floor.

My second affair with Ben and Jerry lasted nearly forty-eight hours. It ended when I threw a pint of Whirled Peace at Eva's head. A half-empty pint, to be exact. I was sampling new flavors.

"Go away," I said. "I'm busy."

Eva picked up the carton and trundled over to my bed. "You are watching *Scooby Doo*," she said.

"I am wallowing. I am allowed to wallow."

Eva put down the carton and folded her arms. "How long do you intend to keep this up?'

"Until tomorrow," I said. It was true. I needed some time to lick my wounds. Or my spoon, as the case might be. Tomorrow, I planned on picking my sorry little carcass out of bed and heading down to Boston to shop with Liz and Allie. Shopping with the girls, I hoped, would provide a welcome diversion. Then, if I still felt like my heart had been ripped out of my throat, I'd drown myself in a tub of Chunky Monkey.

Eva was not on board with wallow time. She began rummaging through my closet.

"What do you think you are doing?" I asked.

"I am finding something for you to wear. I am taking you out."

"Out where?"

"It's a surprise."

"I hate your surprises."

Eva ignored my comment and laid a pair of jeans and a pink angora sweater at the foot of the bed. "Pink is definitely your color," she said. " I'd go with the pink."

I scooped up the clothes and threw them in the direction of the closet door. "What part of 'go away' did you not understand?"

Eva scooped the clothes up again. "I went to a lot of trouble for this surprise. You need to humor me."

"No."

"Please?"

"No."

"I'm not leaving until you are showered, dressed, and making your way towards the door," Eva said, switching off *Scooby*. Eva being Eva, I was pretty sure she would stand there until tomorrow morning to get her way.

"You are stubborn," I said.

"I know."

"You are a pain in the butt."

"I know."

I got out of bed.

Eva pointed to the spot I'd vacated. "What is that?"

"Mitch's toothbrush," I said. I'd been sleeping with Mitch's toothbrush. I was not proud of this fact. But it was the only thing he'd left behind and it felt right as part of the whole wallow experience.

"That is pathetic, "Eva said.

"I know," I said.

I made a grab for the toothbrush, but Eva beat me to it. "I'll just hang on to this until we get back," she said, stashing it in her pocket. "Now get dressed."

"If I go with you, will you give me the toothbrush back and leave me in peace?" I asked.

"Maybe," she said.

"You are relentless," I said.

"I know."

"Relentless and hopeless." I went off to take a shower.

We drove in her car down the street, past the turn for the hospital, where Mitch was probably saving someone's life. Someone who wasn't me. Past the turn for Mitch's house and down County Route One. We turned in at the Tamsett Municipal Airport.

"Oh, no," I said. I went to open the door on the passenger side of the car. Eva was one step ahead of me. She'd put on the child safety locks. She drove up to Red's hangar and parked the car. A plane waited on the tarmac. Not Red's little Cessna. This was a bigger plane. A cargo plane.

"I am not flying," I said when she told me get out of the car. "Last time you said go flying, I broke my wrist and vomited all over myself."

"And Mitch had to take care of you," Eva said. The mention of Mitch's name, coupled with the proximity of Red and a flying machine, nearly brought on a bout of hysteria.

"Come on," Eva said as though I was a fractious horse, "you'll like this. I promise."

"Hello, gorgeous," Red climbed from the cockpit.

"Everything all set, sweet yuckums?"

Red saluted. "Yes, my lady." Then he grabbed Eva's behind and the two of them started making out on the tarmac. I turned to make a break for it, but Eva, still kissing Red, grabbed my arm.

"Where do think you're going?" she said, disentangling herself from her new husband.

"Home," I said.

"Oh,, no. We went to a lot of trouble for this little field trip. A *lot* of trouble. Your hiney is getting on the plane."

"My hiney is staying grounded," I said. I began marching back to the car. I got halfway there when Red grabbed me, slung me over his shoulder like a bag of soybeans, and deposited me in the cargo section of the plane. There were two seats alongside the cargo door. He strapped me into one of them. Eva strapped herself into the other.

Red strapped himself into the pilot's seat. "Ready, sweet thang?" he said, looking over his shoulder.

"Ready, sugar lips."

I unstrapped and got up. "Wouldn't do that if I were you," said Eva. The cargo door was open. The ground was becoming a distant memory.

"How we doing back there, oh love of my life?" Red asked.

"Perfection just like you, lover."

"Oh puh-leese," I said. I strapped myself back into the seat.

"Ready, baby cakes?" Eva put on some sort of holster, like a leash attached by hook to the plane. She harnessed me in as well and handed me a helmet and told me to put it on.

I got it. I finally got it. In an effort to traumatize me out of melancholy, they were going to make me jump. Sky diving. Give India a thrill and make her pee her panties all at the same time. "I am not jumping," I said. Actually, I shouted, partly to be heard over the din and partly because I was growing a might tense. "I am *not* jumping from this plane," I repeated, to be sure that I was heard.

"Of course you're not jumping," Eva shouted back. "Why would you do that?" She had climbed into the back of the plane. She came back with something in her hand. A brown leather pump with a two-inch heel. She handed it to me.

"A shoe?" I shouted. "Aren't we done with the whole shoe thing?"

"Take a good look," Eva shouted. I looked. It was a nice brown leather pump. Expensive looking. New looking.

"Not Klein's?" I ventured.

"Prada," shouted Eva. "About one hundred and fifty dollars a pair. But we've only got the one, so seventy-five-dollars-worth of shoe." Eva pointed to the open cargo door. "Throw it out."

I eyed the pointy heel. "What if it hits somebody? It could poke an eye out."

Eva leaned out of the opening. "Nice going, sweet buns." She turned to me. " I've had Red fly us over the river. Worst you can do is spear a fish."

"Expensive way to catch a fish," I said.

"She hurled yet?" Red asked.

"Not yet." Eva turned to me again. "What are you waiting for?"

"Remind me again why I want to hurl a seventy-five dollar shoe into the Tamsett River."

Eva grinned. "Because it's Sasha's shoe."

I threw the shoe out the opened door. Eva handed me a New Balance Sneaker, then an espadrille. She followed with a lovely open-toed gold sandal with a five-inch heel. And so it went. She handed. I hurled. The more I hurled, the giddier I got. We handed and hurled for quite some time. Finally, Eva held up a sling back with fur trim. "The Grand Finale," she announced, " a Manolo." I hurled. She clapped.

"How many was that?" I asked, as Red winged us back to the

airport.

"Sixty-eight. The woman has a shoe fetish."

"That," I said, "was amazing. That was about as much fun as I've ever had."

"Revenge is sweet," Eva said. "I told you you'd like my surprise."

"Thank you. Thank you. Thank you." I said. I nestled back into the seat. I felt as though I might be able to put the Half Baked back into the freezer when a dark thought crowded past the euphoria.

"How did you get those shoes?" I asked.

"Sasha's apartment. How else?"

"You broke into her apartment? That's breaking and entering. I'm pretty sure you can go to jail for that. Why is it that all your surprises carry the threat of prison?"

"There was no breaking. Only entering. Patch had a key."

"Patch is involved?"

"Patch would have pitched them himself. He generously ceded the shoes to you because we all felt the honor should be yours."

"Great, we can all go to prison together. Maybe we can give each other tats."

We bumped back onto the landing strip. "My dear India, you are far too prone to worry," Eva put her arm around me. "Imagine for a moment that you are Sasha." Eva picked up an imaginary phone and batted her eyelashes. "No, Officer. Just the one shoe. No Officer, no one broke in." Eva hung up the imaginary phone.

"Poor little Sasha," I said. "She's going to have to hop around on one Jimmy Choo."

Chapter Thirty Six

Intervention, Insurrection, And I Love You.

We drove back home in Eva's car, Eva and Red cuddled in the front, me huddled in the back. As we tracked back, the giddiness I'd felt was replaced with remorse. I endured quietly, so as not to disturb the kissing noises Eva and Red were making at each other. Revenge was sweet, but it hadn't brought Mitch back. And Mitch was the real reason I'd been holed up with Ben and Jerry. Mitch, and my inexcusable stupidity. I'd hurled the best thing that had ever happened to me into the river as surely as I had those shoes.

Eva caught my eye in the rear-view. "You're crying," she said. "She's crying," she said to Red.

"Damnation," Red said, checking the rear view.

"It's not that I'm not grateful. You've been terrific," I said.

Red winked. "Don't you fret, little lady. Life has a way of coming back around."

I didn't believe him. I wasn't Pollyanna, at least not anymore. For years, I'd told myself that things would work out with my marriage despite evidence to the contrary. The thing is, the shit always hits the fan. And Mitch deserved better than someone who was willing to keep letting the shit hit. Someone who, even a few days ago, was still willing to forgive an ex-husband who did not warrant forgiveness. I told Red and Eva as much.

"You should think about what you deserve," said Eva. "You love Mitch and you deserve to be happy."

I smiled at the two of them. There they were trying so hard to cheer my sad little heart. "Thank you. Both of you. But Mitch... I hurt him. I messed up big time. I treated him badly and I should have known better."

"So tell him that," said Eva.

"Honey," I said, taking her arm, "some things aren't meant for happy endings."

We were pulling into the driveway by then. Red and Eva looked at one another and then Red said. "Give us a minute, will you, sweet thang?"

Eva gave her husband one last peck and walked off towards her house. "I'm going to get that champagne," she said. She turned to me. "Shoe celebration."

Red took my arm and steered me towards my own door. We sat opposite each other at the kitchen island, Red's Stetson propped between us like a centerpiece.

"Little lady," Red said, "you need to fight for your man."

He looked so sincere, sweet really, that I took his hand. "I appreciate what you're saying, Red. But I did him wrong and now I have to live with the consequences."

"You didn't do anything so gosh darn ornery that it can't be fixed. I've seen the way that boy looks at you. Good Lord, little lady, that kind of love's hard to find at any age."

"I love him, too." I was going to say, "but…"

But Red wouldn't let me finish. "He is head over heels crazy about you. That's what you got to keep in mind. Why do you think I accidentally dumped granite on his car?" I smiled and squeezed his hand. "If it were me, and a girl looked my way like that, I'd chase her to Toledo and back again, and that's a fact."

The thing is, Red was right. And I had forgiven Tom a lot worse than what I'd done. Maybe I needed to give Mitch the chance to forgive. If by the slightest chance he forgave me, I would never hurt him like that again. I could and would promise him that with all my heart. Red was right. I needed, at the very least, to try. I needed to talk to Mitch, no matter how it turned out.

"You're right," I said as Eva walked in with a bottle of champagne tucked under her arm.

"Right about what?" she asked.

"I need to tell Mitch how I feel about him."

"That's my girl," Eva said. I went to the key rack and grabbed my car keys. "Where are you going?" she asked.

Wasn't it obvious? "To see Mitch."

"What? Now?" Eva looked a little nervous. Not Eva-like at all.

"No time like the present."

"Have some champagne first."

Red glanced at Eva who glanced out the window. "Sure, little lady. A little pre-talk fortification do you some good."

"Thanks, but no. I've already been delayed by Ben and Jerry. Champagne can wait. Mitch cannot."

"Few minutes aren't going to hurt, little lady."

"That's right. What difference will a few minutes make?"

"What in God's name is wrong with the two of you?"

"Nothing," they said in unison. Eva stood in front of the kitchen door. Almost as though she were blocking it.

"I am going," I said. "I am going right now." I pushed past Eva just as Allie's car squealed into the driveway and stopped behind Eva's.

Allie and Liz got out. "Hey, Mom! How was the shoe drop?"

"Excellent," I said. "Terrific. I'll tell you all about it later." I had taken a few more steps towards the Camry when Mitch's Land Rover pulled up behind me. Mitch and Patch barreled out of the car.

Mitch stopped when he saw me and gave me a once over. "You're fine," he said. He turned to Patch. "She's fine." He turned to get back into the SUV. Liz pulled a gun from under her jacket and stuck the barrel into his ribs.

"Not so fast," she said.

"What are you *doing*?" I said. I was just a mite upset. Allie pulled a second gun from under her jacket and trained it on me. I went from a mite upset to slight hysteria.

"*Guns*? Are you *insane*? You would *shoot* your own mother?"

"This," said Patch, "is an intervention."

"*What*?"

Patch explained patiently that since Mitch and I were being stubborn and pathetic, it was decided that we needed a little help in getting back together.

"At *gunpoint*?" I said as Mitch growled, "Pathetic?"

Eva fished Mitch's toothbrush from her pocket and handed it to Mitch. "Exhibit A," she said.

"My toothbrush?"

"She's been sleeping with it."

"Really?"

"Don't you *really*," said Patch. He turned to me. "When I went over to get him, he was sitting on the couch fondling your scarf."

"I was not fondling…"

"*Fondling*. I know a fondle when I see it, man."

"Why were you at Mitch's?" I ventured to ask.

Mitch sighed. "He told me that you'd fallen down the stairs."

"*You what?*"

"It got him here, didn't it? In a hurry, too."

"Let me get this straight," I said,. "You lied to Mitch so he'd come over, and then you planned to hold us both at gunpoint until we kissed and made up?"

"Basically," said Patch.

"Actually, we thought we'd lock you in the dining room until you kissed and made up," said Allie.

"By holding us hostage at *gunpoint*?"

Allie shrugged and looked a little sheepish. "They're not real guns."

"They're tranquilizer guns," said Liz. "We borrowed them from the zoo."

"Tranquilizer guns?" I asked.

"We put in enough for rabbits," Allie said.

The slightest hint of a smile flirted with Mitch's lips. "Rabbits."

Liz poked him with the barrel. "Big friggin' rabbits."

"All of you are big friggin' insane," I said. "Whose idea was this little intervention?" I put imaginary quotes around intervention.

The guilty parties, all five of them, looked at each other, guilty as charged. Apparently, they were taking the Fifth. "Never mind," I said. I held out my hand. "Give me the gun," I said to Allie.

"Mom.."

"*Now*, Allison Paige Othmar."

She handed me her gun. "Liz?" I said, holding out my other hand.

Liz looked to Allie. "I'd do as she says," said Allie. "When she starts using full names, she means business." Liz sighed and handed over her weapon.

"Are we done here?" asked Mitch. He turned and reached for the door of the SUV.

I poked the barrel of the gun into his ribs. "Not so fast," I said. He turned around, I kept the gun trained on him. I threw the second gun to Patch and held out my hand. "Keys," I said.

"*What?*"

"Give me your car keys."

Mitch looked at me as though I were ready for consignment to

210

a locked attic. Then he fished into his pocket and handed me the keys.

"Get in," I said, pointing the gun at the passenger door.

"Big friggin' insane," he muttered.

"Get. In."

He did as he was told. I got into the driver's seat and tossed the gun back to Allie. "Go find some rabbits," I said.

I knew I was taking a risk. But I had nothing to lose. No, not true. I had Mitch Tinker to lose and I was not about to lose him without a fight. It was not going to be easy. Mitch sat with his arms folded and his face turned to the passenger side window as we powered through Tamsett. He didn't talk to me or look at me until I turned onto Lookout Road.

"The point?" he said. "You shanghaied me so you could bring me to make-out point?"

"It's private," I said. "And we need to talk."

There was a reason kids liked the point. It was out of the way, a mile up a lumpy and cratered road. It was very, very dark. And, because there were no streetlights, you could see the moon and the stars, which made it kind of romantic in a cheap-romance-novel kind of way.

It was private. It was also deserted. "How do you even know about the point?" Mitch asked.

I ignored his question and he turned back towards the window. "Look," I said. "I'm sorry. I am really, really sorry. I know that's not enough, but here's the thing. I feel downright giddy every time I'm with you. That first time, when I saw you in the ER, my heart did this little tap dance and it's been dancing ever since. It turns flips every time you kiss me, it sighs every time you look at me. I love you. I'm crazy in love with you and there is absolutely no excuse for what I did. Tom is a bad habit. Like nicotine. I thought maybe we could all live in this big happy world and be friends. But I was wrong. And I swear to you, with all my heart and soul and ten fingers and ten toes that it will never happen again. And that if you give me another chance, just one more chance, I would be the happiest woman on the whole damned planet."

I stopped. Mitch was still looking out the window. There was an awful, uncomfortable silence. Well, I thought. At least I tried. Please, I thought. Don't let this be the end.

"I knew you weren't hurt," Mitch said. He turned to me.

"When Patch came over. I wasn't positive, but he kept biting his lip, and I figured something was up."

I reached for Mitch's hand and held it in both of my own. Please, I thought. One little miracle isn't a lot to ask for, is it? It wasn't a miracle, exactly. But in that starry lot it sure did feel like one.

Mitch took his other hand and caressed my face. "I love you," he said. "I'm crazy about you. God, just thinking about you." The darkness etched into his face and I couldn't read his eyes. I waited for the but. And it came. But it was not what I expected.

"If this is going to work, and God knows I want it to work about as much as I want to breathe, then you have to trust me. You have to let me have all of you, not just the good and nice parts. You have to let me be there for you. Your problems are mine. My problems are yours. Can you promise me that?"

"Oh, I promise. I won't leave you out ever again. You can have all my troubles, Dr. Tinker. You can share the good, the bad, and the ugly. I could use the help."

Mitch smiled and cupped his hand around my hands. "One more thing. You need to tell Tom Othmar to fuck off."

"Already did," I said.

Mitch leaned back, assessing. "Really?"

"Yup. Fuck off. I might also have threatened to rip out his tongue and stick it where the sun don't shine. Or something like that."

"Excellent," Mitch said. Then he kissed me. A long, thoughtful, lingering kiss that lead to more heated kissing, which lead to some nibbling followed by more kissing. We were at make-out point, after all.

There we were, Mitch's hands under my shirt, mine under his. "I am sorry," I whispered into his ear.

"Apology accepted," he breathed into my neck.

After which I changed the subject. "I want you," I said. "Now. Right now."

"What, here?"

"We are at make-out point," I pointed out.

"There's an air mattress and a sleeping bag in the back," he said.

"Excellent." I broke off from making out just long enough to climb over the seat and pull Mitch over with me.

212

There we were, just like any other pair of starry-eyed teeny boppers at the point. He got me out of my clothes. I got him out of his. We climbed under the sleeping bag. And yes, a few stars exploded. We reinvented the big bang. Then, just as the big bang expanded into planets and suns and whatnot there was another bang. This one at the window.

"Open up, please."

Mitch, gentleman that he was, tucked the sleeping bag back around me before rolling down the window. A blinding light shown in.

"Dr. Tinker? Mrs. Othmar?" The light moved down and our pupils readjusted to the darkness.

"Officer Mike?" I pulled the sleeping bag up so far that my bare feet showed through the bottom.

"It's exactly what you think," Mitch said.

"I thought so," Officer Mike said. "Guess I don't have to call your parents."

"Guess not," I said.

"Okay," Officer Mike said, "here's what I'm going to do. I'm going to get back into the cruiser and I'm going to drive down to the Dunkin Donuts on Elm Street. I'm going to get myself an extra large coffee with extra cream and sugar, and I'm going to chat up Ellie who works behind the counter, while I drink the coffee. Then I'm going to mosey on back up here."

"We'll be long gone," Mitch said.

"That's what I wanted to hear," Officer Mike said, saluting us.

"Think we've got a few more minutes?" I asked, snuggling onto Mitch's chest after the cruiser drove off.

Mitch kissed my forehead. We lay there for a little while longer. Just enough to soak in the ambiance of the night and the sleeping bag and the skin.

"Hungry? "Mitch asked.

"Famished," I said.

"I know this place that serves a mean apple pancake."

That's how we ended up at Fat Boy's, sitting side by side at the last booth under the *Best Coffee in Town* sign.

Pearl brought us apple pancakes and decaf. Then she stood back with her hands on her hips and looked us over.

"He triple-dog dare you again?" she asked.

"No. Why?"

"You got your shirt on inside out."

Mitch laughed so hard that coffee came out of his nose.

"I wouldn't laugh if I were you," Pearl said. "Your shirt's on backwards."

I took a gander at Mitch. Sure enough, the tag off his long-sleeve T-shirt was sticking out of his neck.

"Should we change?" Mitch asked.

"Not on your life," I said.

I imagine that, back on Easterly Street, Allie and Liz are getting into their car, tranquilizer guns tossed into the back, and riding home to the apartment they share. Across the way, Eva is getting an eyeful of Red's boxers and all that's in them. Patch, I hope, is calling Laura and telling her she's terrific.

At the bottom of the Tamsett River, sixty-eight singleton shoes are becoming a housing development for fish.

And, here at Fat Boy's Diner, Mitch's kisses taste like apples and maple syrup, with just a hint of cinnamon.

About Annie Hoff

Annie Hoff writes comedy and romance. When she's not huddled over a laptop with her 15th cup of coffee, you're likely to find her off watching a play with her hubby, relaxing while listening to music, or out in the woods taking lots of pictures to support her photography habit.